Death and Blintzes

DEATH AND BLINTZES

A Belle Appleman Mystery

Dorothy and Sidney Rosen

Academy Chicago Publishers

Published in 1998 by
Academy Chicago Publishers
363 West Erie Street
Chicago, Illinois 60610

The lines of poetry quoted on pages 107 and 131 are from
"The Garden of Proserpine" by Algernon Swinburne.

First published in 1985 by the Walker Publishing Company, Inc.

Library of Congress Cataloging-in-Publication Data

Rosen, Dorothy.
    Death and blintzes : a Belle Appleman mystery / Dorothy and Sidney
Rosen.
          p.   cm.
    ISBN 0-89733-450-7 (paper)
    I. Rosen, Sidney. II. Title.
[PS3568.07648D4   1998]
813'.54—DC21   98-2815
                                                  CIP

To David,

this chronicle of the world of his grandparents.

ONE

It didn't take long to figure out everything wasn't exactly hunky dory in the pants shop of the Classic Clothing Company.

Friday was payday. I sat tacking belt loops on men's pants. My sewing machine already had a temper as bad as mine. Sure enough, for the tenth time that afternoon I tried to yank out the material but the needle wouldn't budge. *Nu*, again?

Enough with the sob stuff, pooh-poohed the machine. The Depression's still shlepping along. Better you should sell apples on street corners?

Okay, you win. I sighed, wiggling at the needle real careful. Eating is one pleasure I wouldn't exactly want to give up.

Right away the needle got unstuck and the pair of pants came loose. Hurray. Besides, my two weeks training was over and the job was mine, thank God. What a break for me that Mary Castaldi was the one who took me in hand, showed me how to keep my stitches straight, and gave me the whole *megillah* on what was what. Older than me—I'm thirty-six— and skinny, not a pick on her bones. With a big gap between her front teeth. But a regular angel.

"Listen, Belle Appleman," she told me right off, "you got nothin' to be scared of here. We got a union now takes care of us. Nobody can give us the evil eye, honest." She shook her head. "You're awful young to be a widow."

She was telling me about keeping part of the tag off each bundle of belt loops to show what got done. You were supposed to do so many bundles an hour from the mountain of pants and loops shlepped in by the stock boys.

"You got trouble with the machine, you call Sam," Mary let me know. "But other troubles, like wrong pay in your envelope or somethin' like that, you go to the shop steward, Jeanette Laval. Over at Inspection, other end of the building."

Sam was Sam Rothberg, the foreman. He yelled at us girls a lot, but Mary said not to mind. "That one's got the heebiejeebies lately."

Someone was standing by my machine. I looked up—it was a long way to look. Nate Becker, a regular stringbean, through him I got the job. A fortyish bachelor type.

"So, how are you making out, Belle?" Brown eyes glinted behind steel-rimmed glasses.

"Remember what you told me? Any idiot could do it?" I laughed. "You said a mouthful!"

"Better than the WPA, no? This is steady." He bent his lean frame down to talk confidential. "Walk you home tonight?"

A surprise. After all this time, he maybe noticed I'm a woman? I gave him my Mae West eyelash flutter. "Why not?"

He grinned and went back to the cutting room. Cutters are the cream of the workers around here. On account of so much depends on them with the price of cloth today.

Where I was sitting, I faced the long end of the room, and down in back I saw Sam. He was busy talking to a slim blonde with one hand on her hip. The shop steward, Jeanette Laval. You didn't have to be a genius to see even so far away what was on the man's mind.

Gertrude Scharf, with the Dutch bangs, who sits at the machine on my left, also noticed what was going on. "Can you beat it?" she exploded. "That one's at it again. Anything in pants, married or not. Makes you sick!" She popped her gum in disgust.

While Gertrude was talking, Jeanette turned her back on Sam and walked off. He stood there a minute, hands in his pockets, staring after her.

"Maybe they were talking union business," put in chubby Tillie Doyle, on my other side.

But Gertrude was on her high horse. "Union business! Tillie, are you nuts?" She snorted. "Monkey business, that's her specialty!"

"Yeah," Tillie agreed. "I heard she went dancing with Sam at Revere Beach, couple Saturday nights ago. Maybe the whole weekend—"

"Shhh," Gertrude whispered, "here he comes—"

"Get a wiggle on, ladies! Let's buckle down!" Sam had a kind of high-pitched voice for a man. "We're here to make pants, remember?"

I looked at Sam. What would a beauty like the Laval girl be doing going out with a married man? In the looks department he was nothing special, believe me, short and heavyset and already going bald.

"Talk about Mussolini," hissed Tillie. Somebody giggled, then all of a sudden it got real quiet. I saw all the heads swivel toward the doorway. A man was standing there, getting the once-over from every girl in the place.

One look and I could understand why. He was handsome, I mean Hollywood-movie-star handsome, tall and broad-shouldered, wavy blond hair with one lock that fell over his forehead in just the right spot. A regular Nelson Eddy. Hard to tell his age, maybe mid-thirties. I gave Tillie a little poke. "Who is that?"

"One of the cutters," she whispered. "Big shot in the union. Isn't he the cat's pajamas? Single, yet."

He began to move through the room from one girl to another, speaking just a moment or two with each one. A wave of excitement passed through the air as he came, all the girls sitting up straighter and smoothing their hair.

Then he was standing in front of me, holding out his hand. "I'm Paul Warshafsky, Secretary of the Joint Board."

I held out my hand and he pressed it. Some grip. "And you're—?"

"Belle Appleman."

"Belle Appleman." He rolled my name around in his mouth like he was tasting something new to eat. "How come we haven't met before?"

I shrugged. "I've been right here. Where were you?"

He laughed. "Off in the cutting room, unfortunately." His eyes were green like the ocean. "You're a union member, aren't you, Belle?" I nodded. "Well, I'm reminding everyone that there's a meeting at headquarters Monday night. The hall's on Kneeland Street. I hope you can make it." He smiled again.

In such a smile a woman could drown herself. I gave my voice a Bette Davis husky ring and told him, "I'll try."

"Good. I'll see you there," he said, and moved on to talk to Tillie. After he passed, the girls started working again. But there was no talking. Maybe each one of us was enjoying a little daydream about Nelson Eddy's double.

It was Mary, sitting opposite, who spoke up all of a sudden. "Don't get me wrong, but everybody makes too much bad talk about Jeanette. It's not nice." Mary was so good, she hated to hurt anybody.

"Gee whiz, Mary," answered Gertrude. "Someone in such an important union job shouldn't be on the bosses' side. A shop steward's supposed to look out for us, the workers, right? Well, last week, Selma Weiss"—she turned to me—"she sews on pockets. Anyway, Selma had a two-dollar mistake in her pay envelope, and Jeanette didn't do nothing about it for three whole days, imagine! Too busy running around nights and yawning days. Acts like the Queen of Rumania, if you ask me!" She gave the pants a mad yank from her machine.

How come she kept picking on the Laval girl? Gertrude was no fool, a snappy up-to-date type with a nice shape. Was she just plain jealous? Or really worried about the union? About unions I didn't know from nothing, except that Classic Clothing was a closed shop. When I started, I had to join the United Clothing Workers of America. Jeanette Laval gave me my union card and told me to come see her if I had a complaint. I thought she acted real nice.

All the time, tacking, I was making a Victrola record in my head of what people said. Probably I learned to do that at my last job, at the Myrtle Street Drug. It was nifty, I was in charge of the cosmetic counter. But tough luck, the store went out of business.

What a pleasure lunch hour was in those days, reading my favorite magazine, *True Detective.* A good detective always remembers little things, itsy-bitsy stuff other people never notice. So I began keeping my eyes open. And I got a kick out of shmoozing over homicide cases with Jim Connors, a detective from the Joy Street station. He used to drop in to play cribbage in the back of the store with my boss.

Funny how Belle Appleman got to be chums with a big Irish detective. A married man yet. Was his marriage not so lovey-dovey he worked so much on the night shift? He never said and I never asked. Belle Appleman minds her own business.

That first night, eleven o'clock when the drugstore closed, he offered me a ride home. "Thanks, I can walk," I said. "It's not so far where I live, Allen Street." To tell the truth, I was a little scared to go with a *goy* from Codman Square.

Jim just smiled and said, "Look, Mrs. Appleman, your boss trusts me, the city of Boston trusts me, so why don't you trust me? It's late, and you have to walk past the Charles Street jail. And it would be my pleasure to drive you home." Like a gentleman, not fancy-shmancy like Adolph Menjou in the movies, but polite. It was a real surprise to hear such soft talk from an Irish cop, you know how it is. You grow up being a little afraid of them, thinking they're kind of tough. So I said okay, and he opened the door of the police car for me, and he just took me home and said goodnight.

"One of these days I'll solve a murder the police couldn't," I told him once. "Then you'll have to make me a regular detective."

"Belle, darlin'," he answered, with that Irish brogue he could start and stop any old time. "If a criminal knew you were on the force, he'd never be committing the crime in the first place."

Jim was kidding but I wasn't. After that he drove me home lots of nights What my nosey upstairs neighbor Mrs. Wallenstein thought, I couldn't care less.

My hand reached for another bundle. "Listen, Gertrude," I said, "what did you mean about Jeanette being on the bosses' side?"

"It's the bosses—" began Gertrude, but Tillie overrode her.

"See, Belle, it's no news the bosses hate the union. My first year here, when it came in, Victor Gordon tried every trick in the book to keep it out. You can't imagine what went on! But we raised the roof, didn't let them pull anything. We had to go on strike to do it, but we won! Got a forty-hour week and fringes. And a raise, too. And that other pip, Karsh, he hates the union even worse—"

"Who's Karsh?" I interrupted.

"You don't know? Marvin Karsh, Gordon's partner. He'd be tickled pink to change this place back to a sweatshop again. Give him a gun, he'd shoot Roosevelt!"

Mary Castaldi spoke up suddenly. "Somebody spilled the beans. That Karsh, he hadda fight with Gordon over the union. Gordon, he say okay, we lost, we give the workers the union. Karsh, he say no soap. That one, he's *malvagio*!"

Some place you picked to work, Appleman, I said to myself. Everybody fights with everybody.

"Never mind that," said Gertrude. "Listen to this. Straight from the horse's mouth!" She tossed us an all-knowing look. "You know how lousy the clothing business is these days— who's buying new suits? This place is practically in the red, for God's sake! But any day now, we're going to get a big government contract. Army uniforms, I heard."

"Gee, I hope so," Tillie muttered. "That's all I need now, to lose my job; I'm gonna stop off on my way home and light a candle, I'm tellin' ya."

"Keep your shirt on," said Gertrude, "I heard it's in the bag."

"I don't care," said Mary. "I'm gonna light one, too."

Quitting time came, and I got my pay envelope and punched out at the time clock. Al Pallotti, one of the two factory guards, was sitting at the desk. A retired cop, must have been a heller with the girls when he was young. Don't stop too near Pallotti, the girls warned me the first day, he's got terrible wandering hands. Before you know it, Tillie said, he'll have you backed into a corner, taking your measurements.

"Hiya, carrot-top," Pallotti called. "Got any free time this weekend? Plenty of jack in my pocket—"

"Tough luck, Al," I told him. "Melvyn Douglas just called and invited me on his yacht."

"Ya gotta watch them Hollywood wolves," Al kidded back.

"Trouble enough watching you," I said under my breath and dashed past him down the stairs to the door.

Nate was waiting on the sidewalk. I waved at some of the girls who were going the other way, and we walked down Nashua Street. We could hear a train puffing its way into North Station.

It was nice to be walking along with a man again, even if it was just Nate Becker. I knew him since only the past winter and spring from Evening English. He sat next to me and my best friend, Sarah Siegel. Nate always acted like I was one of the guys. Was it because there was usually a bunch of us?

No, I figured out he was born a bachelor. I used to wonder how many women tried to get their hooks in him. Only he was a tough bird, a bird that didn't want no female in his nest.

"Say, Belle," he said, "you got anything special on tomorrow?" He grinned down at me. "Weather report says fair and warm. How's about a Saturday walk on the Esplanade?"

"Swell!" I tried not to look dumbfounded.

"Meet you at Barney's delicatessen around noon, okay? Lunch is on me."

Lunch, even? This was a new one. I gave him my Loretta Young dreamy smile. "It's a date."

A few minutes later, I said, "Nate, tell me something."

"Sure, what?"

"I'm getting the feeling in the factory, things don't seem exactly kosher. I mean, when the girls gab, it's like everybody's kind of jittery."

Nate shrugged. "What's to tell? We got a labor-against-capital situation here, that's all. The bosses want to get rid of the union, they keep trying like crazy. But it's a different world today than fifteen, twenty years ago, Belle. No chance they'll pull it off. Positively not!"

"Oh," I said, "you're talking about the one named Karsh?"

Nate's voice became bitter. "Marvin Karsh? There's a name for a man like that I wouldn't say in front of a lady."

"What about the head boss, Gordon?"

"A different type altogether. At least, he's more open, more honest. Believe me, there's no love lost between those two. Maybe it's a law of nature, partners shouldn't trust each other."

We were walking up Allen Street toward my apartment. "You wouldn't believe the talk that goes on about that shop steward, Jeanette Laval," I said. "She was nice to me."

"Too much yackety-yack in that place." Nate made a sour face. "Everybody has to stick their noses in everybody else's business."

We stopped, we were at my front door. "But the things they say about her, Nate—what do you think?"

"What's to think?" He shrugged. "Don't forget, tomorrow, Barney's, see you at noon." He turned and started to walk away.

"Wait a minute, what's your rush?" I asked. I heard a window squeak open and I looked up. My nosey upstairs neighbor, Mrs. Wallenstein, stuck her head out and made believe she was looking at the sky for rain. "How come all of a sudden you don't know from nothing? What's the big mystery about that girl?"

He came back but he wasn't smiling.

"What mystery? She's a regular Jean Harlow." He rubbed his chin. "There isn't enough gossip about her, I should add my two cents' worth?"

"Terrific," I said. "And you told me the union meant I couldn't get fired, like in the sweatshops. But already the union's got troubles here. So I shouldn't be interested? If something happens to my job, they're waiting in line to hire me?"

"Have a heart, Belle—" Nate put out his hand. "That's not what I meant. But you don't realize, you got a bad habit mixing in, especially where it's not your business. Even in Evening English—"

That got me. "Hold your horses, Mr. Becker. All this time you're giving me marks on behavior?"

He got red. "Belle, it's just—"

"It's just dandy!" I told him. "Thanks a million for the report card!" I stormed through the front door, letting it slam behind me.

I hoped Mrs. Wallenstein got an earful.

TWO

Everybody knows Barney's delicatessen is the best place to eat in the whole West End of Boston.

Just walking by and sniffing the air, you can go *meshugah* from hunger. Hot pastrami piling up from the slicing machine, smoked whitefish with golden skins, shining layers of pink lox, juicy half-sour pickles. Whenever Appleman feels low in spirits, one whiff of Barney's special perfume lifts her right back up.

So when Nate called in the morning to apologize, I decided to keep the date. Why did I have to get so mad at him yesterday, anyway? *Gottenyu,* that red hair of mine makes me flare right up.

We sat at a corner table. I had my favorite, lean corned beef on rye, and Nate chewed on hot pastrami on a roll. We both sipped hot tea from glasses, Russian style. People in the old country weren't so dumb. They knew if you wanted to be cool on a hot day, you sipped hot tea. Today's kids drinking all that ice-cold tonic, what do they know?

All around us was a *tarrarom* of customers. An old man with a white beard and a black felt hat sipped his tea through a piece of sugar in his mouth and read a Yiddish newspaper. At the next table two young men were talking real loud.

"Look what's happening with the Reds in New York! They're taking over the whole Socialist Party!"

"Why not? Those Communists are organized, they got discipline. Socialists just sit on their behinds talking and get no place!"

"So pretty soon we'll have Stalin in the White House?"

"Fat chance! Roosevelt won't ever move out!"

I looked at Nate. "What's all this fighting between Socialists and Communists?"

He shook his head. "A stupid business. They want the same thing to happen—that people should be equal and everybody have enough to eat. All the benefits of society ought to be shared—there shouldn't be a few people who got everything and a lot of people who got nothing."

"So why don't they get together?"

"Good question! We—I'm a Socialist, Belle—feel it will happen by itself. Look how many socialist ideas Roosevelt's got going already, like the NRA. So, you'll see, pretty soon capitalism will turn into socialism. But the Reds are in a big hurry, they don't want to wait. They want things to change by revolution, like in Russia. That's the difference."

I nodded. Bosses and workers I could understand, but this business seemed silly to me, people who wanted the same thing fighting with each other. I decided to change the subject.

"Nate, I never really thanked you for getting me the job."

He smiled. "Maybe not the greatest, but it's a job."

"Who can be fussy today? For a woman alone, it's not easy." I hoped he didn't think I was hinting at anything.

Nate finished his sandwich and wiped his mouth with a napkin. "Belle, about you I wouldn't worry. You got the right kind of *chutzpah,* you'll make out."

"If that's a compliment, I'll take it." I gave him my Joan Crawford look and put down my empty glass.

"So, ready for that walk on the Esplanade?"

It was only a few blocks to the river. On the Esplanade by the Charles the whole world was soaking up the June sunshine. Parents were wheeling baby carriages, giggling young girls were showing off their summer dresses, and men in seersucker jackets were giving them the eye. The water was sparkling like the rhinestone counter in Woolworth's. I fished in my bag for my sunglasses and put them on. They were a loose fit and always slipped down my nose, but at least I could see without squinting. Nate wore the clip-on kind over his glasses.

Kids were flying kites and rollerskating on the cement walks. I never had rollerskates, I was already too big for them when I came to this country. And I never had a child of my own to buy them for.

Nate was humming the Eddie Cantor song about tomatoes being cheaper, it was time to fall in love. I looked up at him. Such a thin stringbean. A man alone, what did he eat? But it felt nice to be walking and holding on to a man's arm.

So what if I lost a job I liked and had to become a tacker in a factory? Listen, Appleman, what did you expect to be, a member of President Roosevelt's cabinet like Frances Perkins? A Harvard graduate you're not. Job-shmob, tomatoes are cheaper, like the song says, and you can afford to buy them. I began to hum along with Nate.

He smiled down at me. "Do grown-up ladies in big hats eat ice cream cones?"

I touched the rim of my leghorn straw with the velvet streamers. "Sure, why not?"

We strolled up to the Teahouse, a long building with a Japanese type roof, where they sold all kinds *nosherai.* Nate ordered maple walnut for me and strawberry for himself. Then we wandered down to the boat landing and leaned against the iron railing. The Round-the-Basin boat was way out near the Cambridge side. Little puffs of smoke floated in the sky from the smokestack. For ten cents you could have a ride.

From the ice cream I was getting a moustache, so I fished in my bag for a handkerchief. The motion made my sunglasses slide down my nose, so I bent my head to push them up with my hand, they shouldn't fall off.

That's when I saw it at the shallow edge of the river right below. I took off the sunglasses and looked again.

What I saw made the ice-cream cone slip out of my hand and fall in the water.

THREE

"Nate," I said.

But my voice came out like a little croak, and he didn't hear. I cleared my throat. "Nate, look!"

He looked at me. "Where?"

I pointed a shaky finger. "Right under us, in the water!"

Nate swallowed the last of his cone and leaned over. Then he sucked in his breath and said, "*Gottenyu!*" We stood there, hanging onto the railing, looking down. Goosebumps popped out all over my skin.

Water's kind of funny in bright sunlight. You see things in it all wobbly and stretched out, like in one of those funhouse mirrors at Revere Beach. So at first what I saw didn't look real. But it was there all right, like a big doll, long hair streaming.

It was the body of a woman, face down.

"What should we do?" I asked.

Like usual, Nate was practical, no matter what. "Call the police, naturally. Come on, there's a phone in the Teahouse." He hesitated a second. "You're okay? Maybe you want to stay here?"

Who wanted to stay there, looking? I told him I was okay and we should head for the telephone. Lucky no one was using the pay phone in the Teahouse. Nate fished out a nickel and dialed the operator. "It's an emergency," he told her. "Get me the Joy Street station. Hello, police? I'm calling to report a dead body. Where? In the Charles River. Yeah. The Esplanade, near the boat landing. I'm calling from the Teahouse. What? Oh, Becker, B-e-c-k-e-r. Yes. Okay, I'll wait there."

He hung up the receiver. "Let's go back. They're sending the police boat, it won't take long."

If Nate hadn't invited me for an ice-cream cone, we would've been far along the Esplanade and maybe never would've seen the thing in the water. Sometimes, you make one little decision, it changes your whole life.

By the time we got back, a little group of people was there, everyone pointing and talking. A man in a plaid sport shirt was saying, "We'd better report this to the police."

Nate spoke up. "I already did. They're on the way."

People moved aside to let us through like we were important. Nate went over to the railing and looked again. "Didn't drift far yet," he said. I just kept my eyes on the white dome of M.I.T. across the water.

"Prob'ly jumped off the bridge last night," said the plaid shirt. "Ever since twenty-nine, suicide rate's kept up with the Depression."

Just then we heard a siren screaming, and a police car zoomed up right along the cement walk, where cars aren't supposed to go. It drew up at the landing and two men got out. One was a young cop in uniform, and the other was a big man wearing a brown suit and snap brim fedora. My old friend, Jim Connors.

The crowd fell back, except Nate and me. Jim stared. "Belle, what're you doing here?"

"Eating an ice-cream cone, till I spotted the body," I said.

He took off his fedora and scratched his thin, sandy hair. "They said a man called in."

"Oh, it was Nate Becker here. Nate, meet Detective Jim Connors."

The two shook hands, then Jim became all business. "We'd better have a look, Rafferty," he said to the young cop. "The boat'll be coming any minute now."

They walked to the railing and bent over. "There it is, sir," said Rafferty.

A Metropolitan Police motorboat came churning up. Two men in light blue uniforms stepped out on the landing. One of them tied the boat to the dock. The other took out two long poles with hooks on the ends.

Jim knew their names. "How are you, Reilly, Farrell?"

"Great day for a suicide," remarked Reilly. They put the long poles into the water and began poking around, Farrell whistling like he was just fishing for cod. The crowd was bigger now, and I was wishing we could get away from there. But I could see Nate wanted to stay for the whole business.

"Got it, here it comes," said Reilly.

Held by the hook caught in the dress, the body rose slowly out of the water. Moving their poles carefully, the policemen got it up over the side of the landing and onto the wooden planks. The body made a soft plop when it hit, and little streams of water began to run away from it on all sides, a regular pool dripping back into the river.

I could see the head now, face up. It was a young woman, the hair plastered, long and limp. Her dress was stuck tight. High-heeled sandals were still strapped to her feet.

Her face, that was the bad part. The skin was pasty, the eyes open and staring at the sky. A small nose smashed in. So many bruises and scratches, you could hardly tell what she must've looked like. Right away I stopped looking.

Nate went closer and peered down. All of a sudden he sucked in his breath and put his hand over his mouth.

"Nate—?" I began.

But Rafferty's voice called, "Here comes the meat wagon!" An ambulance came screaming to a stop. Two men in white uniforms got out with a stretcher and blanket. People moved aside to let them through. They lifted the dripping body from the landing and placed it on the stretcher.

"This one hasn't been in the drink long," one of them said. "Otherwise she'd be floating."

"Yeah," said the other. "But she never would've made the diving team. Looks like she hit part of the bridge on the way down."

"Maybe the current smacked her up against the bridge pilings."

Thank God, they stopped talking and put the blanket over the body, face and all.

"The M.E.'ll meet us at the icebox," said one of the white uniforms to Jim. They picked up the wet mound, carried it over and pushed it into the ambulance, slamming the doors shut. Then they got in front and screeched away like they were going to a fire.

Nate grabbed my hand and pulled me over to where Jim Connors was standing. "Sergeant Connors, that girl? I know her!"

I stared at Nate. I didn't recognize the body. Of course, I didn't look too long, who wanted to?

Jim's eyebrows went up. He took out a little black notebook and a pencil. "Who is she?"

"She's from the same factory where we work. Jeanette Laval!"

Jeanette Laval? That blond beauty, what woman didn't envy her? I gave a shiver.

Nate was still talking. "—in the pants shop."

"And what factory might that be?" Jim asked.

"Classic Clothing," I answered. "Nate got me a job there, too. On Nashua Street."

"That's near North Station," put in the young cop.

"Thanks, Rafferty," said Jim, fixing his gray eyes on him. "It's a mine of information you are today." Rafferty's face got red.

"D'you remember what time you saw the body, Belle?" asked Jim. He was writing in his notebook.

"Yes," I said. "I looked at the Teahouse clock when we went to make the call. A little after two."

"Thanks to you both for helping out," said Jim. "Not the nicest thing on a day like this." He put away his notebook. "Seems like the wrong time of year for suicide, with everything so green and the sun shining. Yet they say spring's the touchiest period of all."

Before I could stop myself, the question popped out. "Jim, you know already it's suicide?"

Jim pushed his fedora back and gave me that blank detective look. "This one'll be easy enough to check. When they do the autopsy, they'll examine the lungs. If there's no water in them, it means she was dead before she hit the water."

"That means," Nate asked, "you got no chance for a mistake with the drowning?"

Jim nodded.

"But what about her face," I said, "so banged up?"

"That's anybody's guess," said Jim. "Maybe she has a fight with the boyfriend and he beats her up. Girl gets despondent and decides to end it all. Or maybe the medic was right, the river just swept her into the bridge structure. The current's pretty strong in the middle."

"So could your doctor tell if the face banging happened before or after she died?"

"I think so." Jim grinned at me. "Belle, you've been at those *True Detective* magazines again."

"But it could be murder, no?"

Jim gave me that why-are-you-complicating-my-life look. In my drugstore days, we used to argue all the time about the cases in those magazines and the local murders in the headlines. He taught me the difference between real evidence and what they call circumstantial. So I learned plenty. But this was no time to tell Jim how to run his business.

So I just gave him my Myrna Loy look.

He adjusted his fedora. "Your new job must be agreeing with you, Belle. You're looking mighty shipshape."

My eyebrows did a Mae West uplift.

Jim smiled. "Well, time to get going. Nice seeing you." He touched his finger to his hat and said "Let's go" to the waiting Rafferty.

I stood there remembering Jeanette Laval handing me my union card, Jeanette Laval listening to Sam Rothberg, and Jeanette Laval being run down by Gertrude and Tillie.

Why did they dish out so much dirt about her? Was it because they were jealous of those Jean Harlow looks?

They didn't have to be jealous now.

FOUR

All of a sudden I realized Nate was speaking to me. "So what do you want to do, Belle?"

What did I want? I wanted not to find a girl's body in the Charles River. "It's a spoiled day, let's go back." But on the way I had an idea. "Listen, Nate, it shouldn't be a total loss. How about you come back to my place later for supper? Sarah, too. Nothing fancy. Okay?"

His face brightened. "It'll be a pleasure." At the front door of my apartment house he gave a gallant Leslie Howard bow. "See you later, madame."

I gave him my Norma Shearer smile. "Six o'clock." He went away on those long legs, whistling the Eddie Cantor tune. As I climbed the stairs to my second-floor apartment, the image of Jeanette's dripping figure came into my mind. *Nu*, supper with friends would cheer me up.

First I gave Sarah a ring. She's alone like me, a couple years older. We met when we both were new widows and needed each other. Her apartment's right near mine, on Blossom Street.

"Sarah, got anything special on tonight?"

"Sure, Clark Gable just called. Why?"

"So stand him up and come here instead. Nate's coming, too."

"Nate's coming?" Sarah was a natural matchmaker. "That's nice. You think he's interested in—"

"He's interested in eating," I interrupted. "Maybe I'll make blintzes. So about six o'clock, okay?"

"Wonderful!" Sarah said. "A real party. Could I bring something?"

"Yourself," I told her.

I got busy in the kitchen. Cooking, like eating, always makes me feel good. Of course blintz-making goes better with two people, but what doesn't? My Daniel, may he rest in peace, always helped me. His job was to check if the frying pan was hot enough, while I mixed the batter. He would flick a drop of water in the pan. If it sizzled, he'd shake his head. But if the drop began to hop around, he'd toss in a lump of butter and yell, "Now!"

Then I would scoop out a just-right spoonful of batter, plop it in the pan, and watch Daniel turn and twist the pan to run the batter evenly around the edge. Out would flop a thin disc of blintz skin. And pretty soon we'd have a big stack. Daniel would put a spoonful of the cheese filling in the middle of each blintz, while I would fold the edges and roll the whole thing up. It was always a game to make things come out even. Daniel used to wipe away a smudge of flour on my nose, and I'd tell him the batter on his hands only made things worse, and he'd say, "Love me, love my sticky fingers." And that would lead to kissing and other things I wouldn't mention.

Remembering, I reached up a hand and wiped off the end of my nose. My blintzes were all filled, rolled, and folded. I covered them with a clean dish towel and put them in the icebox. For dessert, I mixed up some *mandelbrot* and put it into the oven to bake. When it was done I sliced it and set the slices back in the oven to crisp up.

A quarter to five. Was it only this afternoon that we saw a dead person from our factory lying at the bottom of the river? Before I knew what I was doing, my fingers were dialing the number of the Joy Street station. "Is Detective Connors there?"

"He just left. Wait a minute—" I heard a yell, "Hey, Jim, it's for you!"

A minute later, "Connors here."

"Jim, it's Belle. That girl we found this afternoon, you know, in the river—"

"Jeanette Laval? What about her?"

"Jim, I know it's early to ask, but maybe they did an autopsy already?"

He gave a little chirp. "Belle darlin', you think the M.E. drops everything to fool with a suicide stiff? With murdered bodies lying around in the cooler? And today's Saturday, remember, he works bankers' hours."

"So? What's so funny? You're holding out on me—"

"As if I could." His voice turned dry. "Well, on our way to the morgue, that notion of yours that maybe the girl was murdered got to me. Couldn't get it out of my head. And the M.E. just happened to be finishing with another stiff brought in from the Dover Street section, some poor guy knifed by his wife in an argument. So I got him to do a fast autopsy then and there."

"And he found water in the lungs?"

"Yup."

I took a deep breath. "Jim, maybe it's a foolish question. But is there a way to tell if the water they found was Charles River water or not?"

Jim gave a chuckle. "I guess our drug-store sessions paid off. Seems the water in her lungs was ordinary tap water from the city of Boston. What do you make of that?"

"So I was right, it could be murder?"

"Right. She was drowned somewhere else."

"And the scratches?"

"Made after death. Except the nose—that was broken before."

"Imagine, she worked in the same factory as me and Nate!"

Jim's voice got sharp. "Don't be getting any ideas, now. Like working on the case on your own—just because you found the body—"

"Shame on you, Jim Connors!" I said. "You know Belle Appleman always minds her own business."

"Yeah," he answered, "and it's snowing in Miami."

"Thanks a million," I told him, and hung up.

Just time to fix up before my company came. Lucky for me, my red hair is naturally curly, so a quick shampoo in the shower did the trick. Then I sizzled the blintzes till they were brown and put them in the oven to keep warm.

When the bell rang it was Sarah, in a nifty outfit, like usual. "Sarah, that brown linen! Just like the cover of *Vogue*!"

Sarah smiled and patted her marcelled blond hair. "Here, Belle." She handed me a paper bag.

"Sarah, I told you not to! But thanks." I peeked inside. A jar of her gefilte fish. "All this you brought?"

"A little extra while you're cooking, what's so hard? You like my new suit?" She pulled the jacket down. "My boss gave me twenty-five percent off."

"I should be so lucky to work in a dress shop with such a boss!"

Sarah peeked in the kitchen. "Belle, we're eating in there? With Nate coming?"

"Why not, it's a big kitchen and it's breezy. And by me, you and Nate are family, not company."

The doorbell rang again. It was Nate, holding out a paper bag, also. "Better put it in the icebox right away, Belle, it's ice cream."

"Maple walnut?"

"What else?" He took off his glasses and wiped them. "Hi, Sarah, how are you?" Before she could answer, he turned to me. "Don't tell me I smell blintzes—"

"Okay," I said, "I won't tell you."

"Blintzes!" he said in the same voice like someone who found a diamond. And in no time we were sitting at the kitchen table telling Sarah how good her fish was.

"Wait!" I jumped up. "I forgot something." I ran to the bathroom and got the bottle of grape wine and put it in the middle of the table with three wine glasses.

"Belle," asked Sarah, "who keeps wine in the bathroom?"

"Me," I said, "for when I wake up in the middle of the night. A little drink puts me to sleep." I turned to Nate. "So pour some, Nate, and we'll each make a toast. Sarah, you first."

"Here's to good friends and blintzes," said Sarah. We all laughed and sipped. "Now you, Nate."

"To a new member of the United Clothing Workers, Belle Appleman!" He lifted his glass toward me and we drank.

"My turn," I said. "Let's drink to the memory of a poor girl drowned in the Charles River. To Jeanette Laval."

Both Sarah and Nate held on to their glasses and looked at me. "Who's that?" Sarah asked.

"Drink the toast and let's get to the blintzes," I told her. "We'll talk about her after."

Nate drank, ate a blintz, and gave a sigh. "President Roosevelt in the White House couldn't eat better tonight!" He put down his fork. "By the way, Belle, don't forget. Monday night there's a union meeting. Seven-thirty at the head-quarters on Kneeland Street. You want to go? I'll pick you up."

"The meetings, they're important?"

"A new member should come."

"Okay, I'll go."

"Never mind the union," put in Sarah, "what's with this drowned girl?"

I told her the whole story. Sarah shook her head and clucked and made sad noises. Nate didn't talk, he just kept eating blintzes.

"Nate," I said, "guess what, there's a new development."

He stopped in the middle of a blintz. "What could be new? She jumped off the Harvard Bridge and killed herself, that's all."

"No, she didn't." I told them what Jim Connors said. Most of it, anyway. Sarah choked on a piece of blintz and coughed. "So you see, Nate," I went on, "the poor girl was murdered. Maybe by somebody in the factory?"

Nate laid down his fork and spoke kind of slow. "Look, Belle, this girl—you never had time to know her. Don't start mixing in. In the factory, some people didn't care for her. It's not a secret I wasn't crazy about her myself, for example. That means I killed her?"

"Of course not," I said. "But I got the idea there was some kind of funny business going on—"

"Listen to me, Belle." Nate's voice got louder. "I'll say it again. Don't start mixing in. Nobody likes a buttinsky—"

"Buttinsky? Thanks a million!" I got up.

He took out a handkerchief and wiped his forehead. "I didn't mean it that way. But it's a matter for the police. Let them handle it."

Sarah was getting nervous. "Belle, you baked something for dessert? Something smells wonderful. What about tea?"

We paid no attention to her. "Listen," I said to Nate, "what's so awful about helping to catch a murderer? Jeanette Laval was a human being. And she worked in the same place we do. A member of the same union, also. We're right there in the factory, the police are outsiders. They'll have to guess what's going on. We can find out easy."

"Take my advice and stay away from it!"

"That kind advice I don't need." I was walking up and down the kitchen. "The police can't all be geniuses. We're on an inside track. What's so terrible, trying to figure things out?"

"You're talking about fooling around with murder like it's tacking on a loop," said Nate. "For someone so smart, you can be awful dumb!"

I stopped walking. "It's nice to know what you really think of me!"

"Just because you know a cop, all of a sudden you're a regular investigator." Nate stood up. "All right, go ahead. Forget the job, get all excited, start snooping. But I don't want no part of this *mishegoss*`! Count me out!"

"So who needs you!" I burst out.

Sarah gave a gasp. "Belle, what are you saying?"

Nate moved toward the door and turned around. "You're some cook, Belle," he said real quiet, "those blintzes I won't forget."

"But Nate, you didn't have dessert yet," Sarah said in a little voice. It was too late, the door closed. Nate was gone. Sarah and I stared at each other.

"Some combination," I said. "Death and blintzes!"

FIVE

Half in a dream, floating on that wave someplace in between waking and sleeping, I stretched out my arm to feel the familiar warm figure that cuddled next to me most of my grown-up years. Empty. My hand found nothing except the flat, cool sheet. The emptiness jolted me right out of never-never land into the real world, and I woke up soaked in the sweat of remembering.

Daniel, may he rest in peace, was gone such a long time already. But some things you never get used to. Waking up alone was one of them, and it was worst in the middle of the night.

My pillow felt hot, I turned it over and thumped it. No use. What was keeping me awake? Maybe it was the change, getting used to a new job. Or was it a dream about the girl with water dripping out of her clothes? Who sends you a telegram in the middle of the night: WAKE UP! I remembered something Daniel once told me about a famous man named Freud. He figured out that we have two layers of thoughts in our heads. Under the top layer is one called—what was it? The unconscious, that's it. If the top layer isn't really satisfied, you can't hide it from the bottom layer.

Nu, Appleman, don't just lie there feeling sorry for yourself. You want to sleep, you know where to go. I got up and padded to the bathroom in my bare feet. There was still some wine left in the bottle. Wine always made me sleepy, I noticed it as a girl when we drank it at Passover. I poured half a glass, sat down on the wicker hamper, and began to sip. It was warm and sweet, and I could feel my legs getting heavy as it went down. Half a glass was enough, my head started to get light. I went back and climbed into bed, the sheets felt cooler. I gave a stretch and began to remember some of the good days with Daniel.

On our wedding night I was kind of nervous, what girl isn't? I hardly ever knew any boys before him, I was still so young. Gossip about wedding nights from the girls in the shirtwaist factory where I worked made it all sound scary. But this was my Daniel, how could I be scared? He talked to me about all this before, always so easy, so comforting, explaining all about making love. So why was I shaking? Excitement, naturally.

Anyway, I remembered how he was lying next to me on one elbow, just when he'd joined me in bed. He was talking real soft, and he put his arm around to gather me to him. But in my excited state, I rolled over, threw out my arm—and that was it. Daniel fell out of bed with a thump. Tears came in my eyes, maybe I'd hurt him. But he popped back up over the side, grinning. Then we both sat on the edge of the bed and laughed till our stomachs hurt. After that everything was fine. But all our years together, Daniel would remind me with a grin how I threw him out of bed on our wedding night. Remembering, I fell asleep.

When I woke up, the sun was shining into my bedroom. It was Sunday, no factory to rush off to. I jumped out of bed, put on my long flowered housecoat, and went in the kitchen to start the coffee and cut up an orange. A *klop* at the front door reminded me the Sunday paper arrived. The *Boston*

Globe, fat with advertising. I brought it over to the table to read with my toasted bagel, cream cheese, and lox.

The front page didn't make me happy. HITLER STRESSES PEACE. How could people pay attention to such a crazy man? What I was looking for I found on page five. A few lines only.

"Drowning Victim in Charles River," said the headline. The article only told that twenty-three-year-old Jeanette Laval worked at the Classic Clothing Company and lived with her mother, Mrs. George Laval, at 359 Eggleston Street, Jamaica Plain. The police were investigating. No mention who found the body.

For the hundredth time I found myself wondering how a beautiful young girl living in America could wind up dead in a river. Did she know she was going to be killed? Was she afraid? My mother, may she rest in peace, always gave thanks we got to this country. Maybe we lived in two dark little tenement rooms. But we didn't have to be scared about a knock on the door in the night, from pogroms with drunken Cossacks smashing and shooting. In America you don't have to be afraid.

I swallowed the last bit of bagel, finished the coffee, and shuffled through the rest of the paper. Usually I don't bother with the Society pages, but a small notice caught my eye:

NADLER—GORDON

Mr. and Mrs. Morris Nadler of West Newton announce the engagement of their daughter, Felice Leah, to Joseph Gordon, son of Mr. & Mrs. Victor Gordon of Brookline. Mr. Nadler is president of the High Fashion Clothing Company. Mr. Gordon is president of the Classic Clothing Company.

Hoo-ha, the big boss of my factory. Congratulations, Felice Leah Nadler, whoever you are. You're a boss's daughter, you caught a boss's son.

Washing up the breakfast dishes, I decided the whole business was like a typical *True Detective* story. A beautiful young girl is murdered and tossed in the river to make it look like a suicide. She's been fooling around with lots of men, single and married. Some of the girls she works with are terrible jealous of her fast promotion. The bad part is she also had a responsible union job. There's a kind of war between the workers and the bosses, and the talk is she's maybe on the bosses' side.

So, Appleman, are you going to pay attention to Nate? Or start making out a plan like a good detective? First you pick the best suspects. Then you begin checking them out.

I got a pencil and some paper and wrote down names. Sam Rothberg, he sure went for that girl. Gertrude Scharf, she sure hated her. The detective magazines taught me that women can murder just as easy as men, sometimes easier.

Wait a minute. What did that mean, Jeanette being on the bosses' side? Was she fooling around with them also? But they were much older men. So that left Joey Gordon, a good-looking guy in his twenties. And the son of a boss is a boss also, no?

I remembered my first day in the factory, when I was sitting in the office waiting, and this slim young man stops and smiles at me. "Anything I can do for you?" he asks.

Dressed like a boss, but not stuck-up at all. "Thanks, I just got a job here," I told him. "I'm Belle Appleman."

"Oh, you're a new one." He said it kind of sad, but I couldn't figure why. He held out his hand and I shook it. "I'm Joey Gordon. Don't worry, it's not so bad."

It felt funny getting sympathy even before you started. I never dreamed he was a boss's son. Later on Gertrude and Tillie told me about him. He was supposed to be taking business courses at B.U. When Victor Gordon found out he was taking up art instead, he yanked him out of college to work in the factory. But Joey didn't live with his folks.

So I wrote Joey's name on the list also. First, he was the only young boss around for Jeanette to make a play for. Second, don't artists believe in free love and all that stuff? I chewed on my pencil for a minute, and then wrote down Felice Nadler. Why not? If there was really some funny business going on between her fiancé and Jeanette, wouldn't she have it in for her?

Another name came to me, for answers. Jeanette's mother, her address was in the paper. But how many places could I be at the same time? Appleman, you need help. Nate Becker? Out of the question after yesterday. Jim Connors? For him, people who mix in official business are just pests. So that left Sarah. I gave her a dial right away.

"'Morning, Sarah, how are you?"

"Good morning." She was quiet a minute. "Only maybe you should be calling Nate Becker?"

"Hmmph!" I snorted. "Why should I call someone who tells me I'm a buttinsky?"

Sarah changed to her confidential matchmaker tone. "Listen, Belle, why do you fight with him? He's a good man. To everyone else you're nice, with him you got to start arguments."

"Who started? You heard what he said. For that I should give him a big hug?"

"A big hug couldn't hurt, believe me!"

"Sarah! Anyhow, women are smarter than men in lots of ways."

"It's a man's world, no matter what." She gave a sigh.

"My Daniel always claimed women got a special kind of *sachel*. A sixth sense, he called it."

"Could be."

"The police department is all men, no? But who's better at getting in with people and finding things out?"

"No question." Now she sounded positive.

"You're such a good saleslady, Sarah." I could almost see her face starting to beam.

"Mr. Klein says I'm the best in the store."

"You know how to size up people, that's why. Right away they trust you. That's why you can help me find out who killed that girl."

"What? Remember what Nate said about mixing in?"

"Mix-shmix! That's what men are always telling women—keep out of things! Well, there's something you could do. Better than the police, even."

"Me? What do you mean?"

"In today's paper there's the address of the girl's mother. Of course, the police'll go there to ask questions. But the poor woman must be a wreck. So we'll wait till after the funeral. Then you can go pay a visit and ask a few questions. With you she'll talk."

"Questions? What kind questions?"

"Don't worry. When it's time, I'll tell you. You got today's *Globe*? It's on page five, the article with the address. The girl's name is Jeanette Laval. So cut it out and keep it, okay?"

"Okay," echoed Sarah. She didn't sound thrilled.

"Thanks, Sarah, you're a good sport. You won't be sorry, honest. It'll be a cinch."

So now what? Joey Gordon, the boss's son? I found in the phone book where he lived. On Pinckney Street, right around the corner from the old Myrtle Drug.

So after lunch I put on lipstick and got into my striped blouse and skirt. I did a quick check in the hall mirror to see if my stocking seams were straight. Then I remembered what my detective chum said over the phone.

Jim Connors, I said to the mirror, it's snowing in Miami.

Number 76 Pinckney Street was a little more fancy-shmancy than my tenement house on Allen Street. It was one of those old, rich family townhouses made into apartments. There were four bells. Over the last one, a card said: J. Gordon, Apt. 4.

I rang. No answering buzz. Two more rings. Joey wasn't in his studio. Funny, it was such a beautiful afternoon, with plenty of sunlight. Didn't artists like to paint on days like this? I tried the door. No use, it was the kind you couldn't open unless someone inside buzzed.

I looked at the bells again. The first one said: Sandowski, Supt. That gave me an idea and I rang. A minute later the door opened. A stocky man who needed a shave poked his head out.

"Mr. Sandowski?" I asked. He nodded. "I'm trying to ring Mr. Gordon's apartment. He's not in?"

"Haven't seen him since yesterday morning."

"A fine howd'ya do!" I made a Fay Bainter face. "I'm his Aunt Belle. He promised if I came, he'd take me out to dinner."

Sandowski didn't open the door any wider. "You're his aunt?" He gave me a fishy look.

"I came all the way from Newton," I said. "And I already sent my taxi away."

"Gee, that's tough—"

"Listen, Mr. Sandowski," I said, "you got a master key for the apartments, right? So how about you let me in and I'll wait upstairs for Joey."

His lower lip pushed out. "Jeez, I dunno—"

"I look like a crook? You're afraid I'll steal one of his pictures? I'm his Aunt Belle, for heaven's sake!"

Sandowski shrugged and opened the door. "I guess it's okay, sister." I followed him up to the top floor.

Joey Gordon's place was big and airy, one giant room. Like the artist's studio I saw once in a movie. One wall all window from ceiling to floor. In the corner a bed covered with an India print and heaped with a rainbow of pillows. Wicker furniture like you see on verandas, backed by bookshelves stuffed with books. A Persian rug, old, but you could tell it was the real thing. And everywhere you looked, paintings. Hanging on the walls. Stacked in piles.

Mostly of people. But they didn't look natural. Cheeks and eyes out of line. Noses like bulbs and twisted mouths slanting the wrong way. Dizzy colors. Was there some kind of message the artist was sending? They were pictures of people you wouldn't trust for one minute.

I walked around the room looking and came to a small telephone table. There was a little white card on it and my fingers picked it up.

Arnold Silverstein, M.D.

Psychoanalysis

334 Beacon St. LA3-4004

So Joey Gordon was seeing Arnie Silverstein! Him I knew from the Myrtle Drug, a good-natured doctor who lived on Mount Vernon Street. He used to talk to me about the cases in *True Detective,* too. A psychiatrist was a kind of detective, Arnie told me. So what was it with Joey, he had to see a head doctor? I put the card back.

In the middle of the floor was a large easel with some cloth draped over it. I went over and picked up a corner of the cloth, it was covering a big square canvas. So I threw the cloth back to see what was there.

It was the picture of a young girl lying stretched out, long honey-colored hair tumbling over her shoulders. All natural as life, no crazy shapes. Right away I knew that face with those cheekbones and those pouting lips. No question. It was Jeanette Laval.

Only this time she was naked.

I couldn't look away. Her blue eyes were looking into mine in a knowing way. I know all about you, they said. I couldn't help it, I gave a shiver.

Then I heard a noise and turned around quick. Joey Gordon was standing in the doorway, staring at me.

"Who are you," he said, "and what in hell are you doing here?"

SIX

"I'm your Aunt Belle," I said. My heart was pounding, I hoped he couldn't hear it.

Joey closed the door. His brown velvet Tyrone Power eyes stayed fixed on me. He took a cigarette case out of his pocket and lit a cigarette with a fancy gold lighter. "I don't have an Aunt Belle."

"Are you positive?" My voice sounded breathless, even to me.

The brown-eyed stare turned into a Tyrone Power half-smile. "Besides, you're too young to be my aunt."

It was hard to believe that baby face belonged to a murderer. "Thanks." I could breathe again. "It's what I told the janitor, so he should let me in."

Joey nodded. "I don't blame him. Any man would let you in."

See, Jim Connors, I said to myself, maybe women detectives can do things men can't.

"Don't you remember me?" I asked. "We met in the factory office when I came to fill out work papers."

He studied me. "You're the new one. Yeah, I remember your hair. But what are you doing in my studio?"

I gave him my Myrna Loy look. "I wanted to talk to you—" I motioned to the painting "—about her."

For a minute the brown eyes filled with a kind of misery. Then he just said, "Why?"

"I was the one that found the body yesterday. Me and Nate Becker."

"*The* body," he said, drawing out the words. "Funny how gender disappears with death. No one ever says *his* or *her* body, just *the* body."

He wasn't looking at me any more, just staring at the painting. What was he thinking about, I wondered. What was in his head when he painted those breasts and those thighs? Was it just getting the right colors and shapes? After all, he was a man.

How should I begin? "Could I sit down, please?"

"Sorry," he said, "but I'm not in the habit of finding intruders here." His hand motioned me to one of the wicker chairs and pulled up another to sit opposite me. He took one more puff and ground out his cigarette in an ashtray. "Why did you want to see me?"

"She was your—model?" I took a deep breath. "You must feel terrible—"

"I didn't even know until this morning," he said. "I picked up the Sunday paper and there it was, along with the funnies—" He got up and went over into the Pullman kitchen.

"On page five," I said. I watched him take a bottle of whiskey out of a cabinet and pour a drink.

"Some for you?" I shook my head no. He tipped the glass up and swallowed the whiskey in one gulp.

"The police know something else," I said, "that wasn't in the paper." He refilled the glass and turned. "It wasn't suicide, someone murdered her." I watched his fingers tighten around the glass. He didn't drop it, he didn't seem surprised. Did the color of his skin change?

"How do you know what the police know?"

"I have a connection on the force." I decided to stop beating around the bush. "Look, Mr. Gordon, they'll begin checking right away. It won't take them long to find out she was your model. And if they see that—" I waved at the painting "—you know what they'll think."

Joey gulped the second glass down. "So now I'm a prime suspect, huh?" The brown eyes had a glitter in them now. Was he a *shikker,* a drunk, too? He put down the empty glass and came back to his chair. "Okay, Belle Appleman, what brought you here? What's in it for you?"

I gave him my Bette Davis glare. "In it? Nothing's in it! Except I'm the one who found her. I only want to know why it happened. And who did it. And believe me, I'll find out!"

"So you came here right off." He was talking soft, but his fingers were gripping the chair arms. "How come Joey Gordon was the first name that popped into your head? Just like my family. Blame Joey for anything and everything!" His jaw seemed to tighten.

I could see that if I wanted to find out anything, I would have to calm him down. I watched him light another cigarette before I said, "I was trying to figure out why the people in your paintings look so funny."

His expression changed, he almost smiled. "Funny? You're the first one who ever used that expression about them. But you're absolutely right on the button! People are funny on the inside, and that's what I try to put on canvas. Not what a person would see looking in a mirror, but what's inside, under the skin."

"Except for her," I said, pointing to the painting of Jeanette. "Her you painted like she was the same outside and inside."

He got up and walked over to the easel. I could see the whiskey made him a little shaky. He bent forward and peered at the canvas. "Aunt Belle," he said, turning to me, "you have the makings of a number-one art critic." He came back and sat down. "Yeah, you're right." His voice got softer. "She was the same inside and out."

"Listen, Mr. Gordon—"

"Joey."

"Joey, then. You got to believe me, I'm on your side. The police'll want to know where you were and what you were doing Friday night. And maybe Saturday morning. I didn't find out yet what time she died. Maybe you could tell me something about her to help figure it out?"

He looked puzzled. "I don't get it. You work in the factory?"

"I'm a tacker in the pants shop."

"And you play detective on the side?"

"Call it a hobby," I said. "So where were you Friday night?"

"Friday night?" He blinked a couple times and tugged at one ear. "Friday night—" It was like he ran out of breath, a record running down. "I can't even—" He broke off.

"What do you mean? You can't even remember?"

He frowned. "Friday night was a million years ago—"

I tried to catch his eye. "We're talking only the night before last."

He squashed his cigarette. "'But that was in another country, and besides, the wench is dead . . .'"

Goosebumps popped out on my arms. "What?"

"Christopher Marlowe." His shoulders drooped. "I worked all day Friday in the factory."

To follow Joey's mind was like tracing one of those mazes on the puzzle page. "Okay, you worked all day Friday in the factory. Five o'clock you left. So where did you go?"

"That's an easy one," he said. "Grocery shopping."

A bachelor, was he maybe expecting company? "So where were you at night after the groceries?"

"Right here."

"You got a witness?"

He shook his head no.

"Jeanette wasn't with you here?"

He ran his fingers through his hair. "What makes you think that?"

"Come on, Joey," I told him, "I wasn't born yesterday. Jeanette wasn't just your model, was she? A girlfriend, too, maybe?"

He gave a sigh. "She was my model at first. Good models aren't a dime a dozen, you know. Especially for working in the nude. But she was as natural as a child that way. Clothes or no clothes, it made no difference to her. No inhibitions."

"About standing around naked—or—about everything?" I was taking a chance. Such a question could make a man mad. But how could I learn if I didn't ask?

He looked out at the sky through the glass wall. "What you want to know is if we were lovers, right? Well, we were." His tone was matter-of-fact, but he was moistening his lips with his tongue.

"So how come she wasn't here Friday night, on a weekend?"

He got up and went over to the whiskey bottle. "It's none of your business!"

"But it's what the detectives'll ask," I told him.

He poured a half glass of whiskey.

"Take it easy with the schnapps, Joey," I said. "You're too young to be a *shikker*."

"Now you sound like a real Aunt Belle," he answered, and drank. "If you want to know," he went on, "the last time I saw Jeanette was Friday afternoon. We made a date for dinner here. That's why I bought the stuff—steaks, wine, the works. Then she called me around six-thirty to say something had come up, she'd be a little late. A little late? She never showed! By ten o'clock I gave up. Couldn't stand being in the studio without her. I went to my folks' house to sleep over. Got there about a quarter to eleven."

"In Brookline," I said. "So you had a visit with your parents?"

"No, they were out," he said. "How'd you know where they live?"

"A little announcement in the Society pages," I said, "about a certain Felice Leah Nadler who got engaged to a certain Joseph Gordon."

"Oh, that," he said.

"*That*," I told him, "is going to sound pretty fishy to the police. A date with a murdered girl on a Friday night and a notice to be engaged to a different girl on Sunday."

"I was plenty teed off at Jeanette. My mother and father have been bugging me to marry Felice for a couple of years now. We grew up on the same street. Went through puberty together."

"But you were in love with Jeanette?"

He banged the shelf with his fist and the whiskey bottle rattled. "Goddammit, I wanted to marry her! But my father wouldn't hear of it. And when I told my mother, she acted like she was going to have a heart attack!"

"Mothers do a lot of worrying," I said, "especially a Jewish mother who finds out her son wants to marry a *shiksa* that's a factory girl."

"Jeanette made me so damn mad," he said. "And my father was on my back. And Felice—well, she's a good kid, really. So it was easier to say okay to the engagement. Couple of weeks ago. At least I hoped it would make Jeanette jealous. And if she came around, well—" He shrugged.

"You'd break it off, right?"

He nodded.

"Look," I went on, "let's talk better about Friday night. You didn't call Jeanette's house to see where she was? Or call her mother the next day?"

"No. I was too angry."

"You know, I believe you, Joey," I said. "Honest. But with the cops it'll be a different story."

He shook his head. "I could never dump her in any river—"

"That wasn't how she died," I said. His jaw dropped. I told him what Jim Connors said about the water in the lungs. "So if it happened Friday night, you might be in trouble."

Joey looked at his whiskey glass, picked it up, and let what was left in it roll into his mouth. "Maybe they'll believe me like you do."

I decided to change the subject. "How come your father didn't let you finish college?"

His eyebrows went up. "You've sure been doing your homework, haven't you? Well, it's not hard to explain. To a businessman like my father, art isn't real honest-to-God work. It's the kind of profession a lazy good-for-nothing would take up. He wanted me to become a carbon copy of Victor Gordon, self-made business success."

"So what's so bad, working in the office? You can paint after work, no?"

"You don't understand. I need to learn a lot more. Go to France, study under a master painter. I hate the damn factory!"

"But it's—"

"You think just because I'm the boss's son," he interrupted, "I'm wise to what goes on there? Well, I've got news for you, Aunt Belle. I'm an outsider! Something's cooking in those offices around me, but do they give Joey the lowdown? I don't even know what I'm supposed to be doing, except shuffling papers around. They all have secrets. Something's in the air right now, I know. But does my father tell me anything? Will Karsh talk to me man-to-man? The boss's son is the last to know!"

Listening to him, I thought, if that's what it's like to have a child, maybe it wasn't so terrible Daniel and I never had one. So much bitterness already. We sat quiet a minute.

"Does that nude painting offend you?" Joey was leaning back in his chair, he spoke all of a sudden. To tell the truth, it did make me feel funny, but I shook my head no. "Did you ever swim in the ocean at night," he asked, half to himself, "wearing nothing but your own skin?"

Such a crazy question, it floored me. He didn't seem to notice. His eyes were seeing something over my head, and he went on talking. "There's the quality of moonlight, it doesn't flood the landscape like the greedy sun, all the colors are soft. And the feeling of the water on your naked body, it's so different. It's as if you and the ocean were one, not two bodies struggling against each other. The waves enfold you. You get a flash of pure joy, maybe better than lovemaking. Better because you're not depending on another human being. It's just you and the elements themselves."

It sounded nice but mixed-up all at the same time. I didn't really understand but I wanted to say something. "I never swum—I mean, swam—" my Evening English lessons came back, all those irregular verbs "—that way at night, no. But I did it once in the daytime." I couldn't help it, I felt my face getting red. "No bathing suit at all."

Joey laughed, a real laugh this time. "You're an Aunt Belle full of surprises," he said. "Tell me about it."

What's to be ashamed of, Appleman? Two grown people talking, that's all. "You know that beach in South Boston, it's called L Street?"

He grinned and nodded. "Yeah, but I never went there."

"One time I went with a friend. A girlfriend," I added real quick. "Nobody wears bathing suits there. Only there's separate sections for men and women, with a fence between that goes way out in the water." I hesitated. "At first I felt a little funny, I didn't want to go out of the bathhouse. Then I peeked out and saw all those shapes—fat, skinny, all kinds. It made me giggle, and I wasn't afraid after that. Besides, I was young and slim, nothing to be ashamed."

"You've still nothing to be ashamed of," said Joey.

Did that need an answer? I just gave a little smile. "But you're right, Joey, once I got in the water, it was a nice feeling."

"But you never went back?"

I laughed. "No, never again. Someone said some boys were trying to swim around the fence, so we were scared to go."

"They teach us early in our culture," he said, twisting his lips a little, "to be ashamed of our bodies. Even the word *naked* upsets people."

It was getting late, time to get back to business. "You know, Joey," I said, "Jeanette was real nice to me when I started. But in the factory she didn't exactly win any popularity contest. The little time I'm in the pants shop, I heard a lot of talk."

My words made him get up and go to the whiskey bottle again. There wasn't much left to pour in the glass, but he drank it to the last drop. "I'll bet you did," he said, his voice bitter.

"They said she went dancing with Sam Rothberg. A married man."

He came over and waved his finger under my nose. "Sam Rothberg? That was nothing! You don't know what she was doing me! She used to come and stay all weekend and swear she'd never look at another man. And the next time I'd call? Gone with the wind!" He gave a hiccup. "'Busy,' she used to say. Busy, my eye!"

"So what was she doing?"

He shook his head. "Never mind. What's the use? She's gone. Makes no difference now. 'S what the poet wrote—'the past is a bucket of ashes.'"

"Listen—" I began, but he cut me off.

"'Nuff gossip. Anyway, bottle's empty. Got to go to the liquor store now. C'mon, I'll drive you home."

Just dandy, with him tanked up. "You're a doll, but it's so close by, I'll walk."

"No!" He waved his finger. "Lesson one, gentleman sees a lady home." He took my arm and led me down the stairs.

On the first floor Mr. Sandowski stuck his head out and gave us the once-over. "Everything all right, Mr. Gordon?"

"Absolutely hunky-dory, Fred," said Joey. "This is my Aunt Belle. You can let her in any time."

Joey's car was a black sedan. He managed to drive okay and we were in front of my door on Allen Street in no time. He got out and opened the door on my side. "Gonna see you right to your door," he said with a wave.

"Thanks, Joey, you did enough. And thanks for being a good sport when I invited myself."

Before I could move he leaned over and gave me a big smack on the lips. Mrs. Wallenstein's window banged open.

"Too bad you're not really my Aunt Belle," he said. Then he added, "I wish you'd been my father."

That made me laugh. I was going to tell him the old joke about if your grandmother was a grandfather, you wouldn't be born. But he gave a lopsided grin and got back in the car. A second later he was flying down Allen Street.

The sun was getting red over Cambridge. I didn't realize how long I was talking to Joey. How much did I learn? One, he was nuts about the Laval girl. Two, he even wanted to marry her, but his father put his foot down. Three, she was driving him crazy, fooling around with other men.

Three reasons. Was Joey Gordon *meshugge* enough to kill on account of them?

SEVEN

It was about a quarter to eight in the morning when I pulled open the big front door of the Classic Clothing Company and walked up to the landing where you punched the clock. Sitting at his desk next to the clock was one of the factory guards, Ed Bandy, another ex-cop. I hardly ever talked to him, because usually when I was coming in, he was going off his shift.

For the first time, I took a good look at Bandy and noticed his nose was covered with a fine network of thin red veins. I knew what that was—the nose of a hard drinker. The girls told me he wasn't really retired, he was kicked off the force for being *shikker* on duty. This morning, his nose was buried in the pages of the *Advertiser,* the morning paper. His jaw was working up and down, chewing gum. Even sitting, part of his stomach stuck out from under his belt. His jacket was open, and I could see part of a leather strap that went over one shoulder and held a holster with the handle of the gun sticking out. When he heard the noise my heels made on the hard wood floor, Bandy looked up.

"Good morning," I said. I took my card and punched in.

He nodded and put his nose back in the paper. I had to walk past the desk to get to the elevator, so I tried again. "I'm Belle Appleman."

He didn't even look up, but just muttered "Yeah?" and left me standing there like a dummy. Who needed him? "Excuse me," I said and went to the elevator. While my finger pushed the button, my eyes saw him reach under the desk and pick up a dark, flat bottle.

I went into the locker room to stick my lunch in my locker and found Mary Castaldi doing the same. She gave me the big hello I got from her every morning, and we walked into the pants shop together. Tillie came running over to us, her face red and her mouth open. "Hey, Belle, Mary, 'dja hear? Jeanette Laval's dead! Got drowned in the Charles! It was in yesterday's *Globe*. Musta killed herself!"

"Holy Mary, Mother of God!" exclaimed Mary, crossing herself. Her eyes filled. "Drowned? Seems only a little while ago I was trainin' her! So pretty, an' young like my Angelina. I didn't read the paper much yesterday, I was out in the yard helpin' Frank."

All of a sudden a voice roared, "What's going on here, anyway? Five minutes past eight, and all I see is a regular hen party!" It was Sam Rothberg. "Come on, ladies, break up the kaffeeklatsch or we'll all be out on the street together!"

Everybody hurried to the machines, including me. Unnatural quiet changed to the clacking our ears were used to. I knew I'd have to tell them about Saturday's awful business, but better later. Meanwhile I wanted to wiggle out more information.

"Too bad about Jeanette," I said to Gertrude. She bent her head over her machine, adjusting the loop, and mumbled something.

"What?" I asked.

"Some people go looking for trouble," Gertrude said.

"What do you mean?"

"Thought she could wind every man around her little finger—married or whatever—" She didn't look at me, just kept tacking on pant loops.

"Even Sam Rothberg, imagine," I said.

"Says who?" she snapped back. "Can't believe everything you hear!"

"And besides," said Tillie, "d'ya see in the *Globe* where Joey Gordon got himself engaged to some rich girl in West Newton? Boy, if that isn't just like a man, after the way he was foolin' around with Jeanette. You shoulda seen the way he was makin' eyes at her, even last week." She pursed her lips. "Gee, d'ya think that's why she done it—jumped, I mean? Gosh, and he seems like such a goody-goody, not fresh at all. Cripers, go trust a man!" She clucked in disgust.

Better tell them and get it over with. "Listen, everybody, I was the one found Jeanette's body." All of a sudden the machines around me stopped.

"You what?" Gertrude said, staring at me.

"I found the body in the river Saturday. But it wasn't suicide, she was murdered."

Mary crossed herself. "Holy Blessed Virgin!"

"Murdered!" Tillie's face screwed up like she couldn't believe her ears. "How d'ya know?"

"I got connections on the force."

She digested that. "Gosh, why didn't ya tell us right away? Did she look somethin' awful?" She gave a shudder.

Sam Rothberg came our way and the machines got busy again. I was glad. I didn't want to paint pictures for them. Who wants to talk about drowned bodies? I pulled the ticket off the pile of loops I just finished and tackled the next pile.

While my fingers tacked, my mind was running in circles about the whole business. How many people right around me were mixed up with Jeanette? Joey, one hundred percent. Sam, too. I saw how he looked at her right in this room. And Gertrude, why did she talk about her like she was mad enough to—maybe kill her? It couldn't be such a big deal, the other girl getting promoted, could it? Wait a minute. Why did she get so sore when I just mentioned Sam Rothberg going out with the girl? Almost bit my head off. Only one thing gets a woman that worked up.

A man.

Besides, Gertrude all of a sudden didn't know from nothing about the gossip over Sam and Jeanette. How come?

One answer. Gertrude didn't want to know because she was sweet on Sam herself. But how could that be? Sam was married, and he sure was trying to finagle something with Jeanette. Was he also finagling with Gertrude? A busy guy. I looked over at him, he was just leaving the room.

Right now it looked like Joey had the best reason to be mad enough to kill. But in *The Thin Man* movies Myrna Loy found out that the one with the best reason wasn't always the killer. Still, I wasn't *meshugge* enough to think Hollywood was the real world.

All of a sudden Gertrude mumbled something, got up, and left the room. And Sam just left. Maybe this was a good time for me to get a little something from my locker, I could always take out half a sandwich for a snack.

I pushed open the door of the locker room and stopped. Voices, all right, on the other side of the row of lockers. I closed the door real quiet and just stood. Listen, a sneak I'm not. But it's a detective's job to listen, no?

"Holy mackerel," Gertrude was saying, "she's a regular Nosy Hogan. Making cracks about you and Jeanette."

"Whaddaya mean cracks?" Already Sam sounded worried.

"I don't know, she kinda tricked me into saying something about Jeanette vamping other people's husbands. Cripers, a few weeks on the job and she knows everyone's business!"

"Keep your shirt on." Sam's voice got a little lower. "Doesn't know about us, does she?"

"Nobody around here knows a thing—unless you let on." Gertrude sounded mad.

"Don't worry, I can keep my lips buttoned." I heard a creak that meant Sam was getting up from the bench they were sitting on. "Listen, walls got ears, let's get outa here, babe."

"Say, hon, when should we—you know—" The atmosphere was heating up. Made me feel funny, like a peeping whatsis. Scared, too. I opened the door real careful.

I couldn't hear Sam's answer, he must've whispered. But as I got out of there, a little giggle from Gertrude followed me.

So, Appleman, you made a right guess about Gertrude.

Back at my work, I began to wonder why I ever took up this detective stuff, anyway. The pants shop wasn't the classiest job, but at least it seemed friendly. Now I felt up to my ears in a regular *tzimmes,* the whole mixed-up stew simmering on that second floor.

Why would a smart girl like Gertrude be lovey-dovey with a married foreman, anyway? The more stuff I dug out around here, the crummier it all made me feel.

When the bell rang for lunch, we all grabbed our bags from the lockers and walked down to the nearby Charles River Embankment.

There we could sit on benches or on the grass in the sun and enjoy. But this time I had to answer a million questions about Saturday.

"Murder!" said Selma Weiss, rubbing her arms. "Gives you the willies, don't it?"

"You never knew Jeanette that good, didja?" Tillie shaped her mouth into a Cupid's bow with lipstick.

"How could she?" Mary answered for me. "Jeanette got transferred from tacking to inspection before Belle got here, remember?"

"Yeah, that's right." Gertrude swallowed a hunk of chocolate roll. "Jeanette sure got pushed ahead fast, ahead of other people who were here a lot longer. People who did their job better, too."

"That's right," said Selma in a sympathetic tone, "you shoulda got the promotion, Gertrude."

Everybody looked uncomfortable. It didn't seem nice to be saying bad things about the dead. Then we all got up and started back, the jabbering going on all the way to the locker room.

"Jeanette didn't seem to have many girlfriends, did she?" I asked.

"Hah!" Tillie snorted. "Girl like that, what did she need girlfriends for?"

"Jeepers creepers," said Selma, "if the cops lined up all her boyfriends, they'd have to hire a hall!"

"God rest her soul," said Mary, crossing herself.

Just then the factory bell rang, it made me sort of jump. That was one thing about the factory I hated, those bells. Made me feel like I was some kind of machine, too, telling me to sit, stand up, go to work, stop talking, don't daydream, hurry up, watch those stitches. Wasn't that what they did in prisons, ring bells all the time?

We hurried back to our places, and I was just going to begin working when that same ripple of excitement, kind of like a breeze moving through the leaves of a tree, told me

Paul Warshafsky must've come in from the cutting room. But this time he wasn't smiling. He walked over to Sam Rothberg and said something. Sam went over to the main switch and cut off the power, leaving the room dead quiet.

Paul walked up to the long table in the front of the room where the boys stacked finished bundles and asked us all to leave our machines and come over. His voice was kind of low and smooth, and he spoke so good. If he asked would we follow him and climb down the outside drainpipe, we probably would. Was it just his looks or was it something in his personality that made you want to do what he said?

We all gathered around the big table. Some of us sat on the edge and swung our legs, it was a nice change from our routine. He didn't talk till everyone got settled.

"I know how shocked we all feel at the loss of our fellow worker Jeanette Laval," he began, putting some papers in his pocket. "But life goes on, and our work has to go on. We need a shop steward to represent the pants shop in dealing with our employers." He looked around. "Before you nominate anyone, take a minute to think about the qualities a representative should have. She has to be tactful, whether she's dealing with a worker who's upset or a boss who's stubborn. But she also has to be strong enough to stand by her convictions, and that's not easy to do when a worker's facing the bosses. What we're looking for, I guess, is an iron fist in a velvet glove."

"Superwoman, we need," said a voice in the back. Everybody laughed, Mr. Gorgeous also.

"I couldn't have put it better," he said with a smile. He looked around. When his eyes caught mine, his smile got bigger. I made myself turn away, I wasn't looking for complications.

"Well, can we have some nominations from the floor?" he asked.

People whispered to each other, but no one spoke up. Someone said under her breath, "If that's what the job did for Jeanette—"

More mutters. Then a dark-haired young girl called out, "I nominate Anna Iaconna."

Everybody looked at Anna, a pretty woman with a round face. Her cheeks got red. Someone seconded the nomination. Anna shook her head. "No, no, I can't do it." She got redder. "For personal reasons."

Whispers all around. "She's gonna have a baby."

Next to me, I heard Tillie say to Gertrude, "I'm gonna nominate you."

"Are you nuts?" Gertrude sounded mad. "Take her place now? Don't you dare!"

"Come on, everybody, how about another nomination?" Warshafsky was really pushing us now. "We've got to elect a shop steward!"

Silence. More buzzing. Then Paul eyed me. "How about Belle Appleman, ladies?" He looked around at the girls. "How about her, everybody?"

"Sure," said Selma, "why not? She's famous, she's the one found Jeanette in the river!"

"Second the nomination," someone called out.

I slipped off the table and stood. "Wait a second," I said real loud, "I'm new here. What I know about unions you could put in a fly's ear."

"Never mind," said Mary. She turned around to face the gang. "I know, I taught her tacking, she catches on quick!"

Everyone laughed and Paul said right away, "Nominations closed. All in favor of Belle Appleman as shop steward signify by saying aye."

Loud cheers.

"Nos?"

Silence.

"The ayes have it." Paul leaned over, took my hand and raised it in the air like I just won a prize fight. "Congratulations, Shop Steward Appleman!"

More cheers, like a crowd at a baseball game. My first thought was, thanks for nothing. What was I letting myself in for? But wait a minute, look who'd be leading me by that hand that felt so big and warm and cozy, clasping mine. Maybe this union business wasn't so bad, after all.

The meeting adjourned and everyone came around to congratulate me. Mary and Tillie hugged me. Then the girls all straggled back to their work, jabbering. Paul Warshafsky came over and shook my hand with that grip of his.

"Wonderwoman," he said with a grin. He was sizing me up and I was giving him the once-over, too. His collar was open at the neck, with the tie pulled down. Looked like the Arrow shirt man, just the same.

"Now I'm going to take you around to introduce you to the employers," he said. "You'll have to deal with them, that's part of your job. Don't let 'em scare you, they're just people." I glanced at Sam Rothberg standing nearby and he nodded okay, though he didn't look too happy. Paul ushered me toward the door.

I could feel all the women's heads turning behind us. All of a sudden my job became a real pleasure.

What woman wouldn't want to waltz out the door with Paul Warshafsky?

EIGHT

We went down the long hall, past the elevator, and came to the office section where I filled out papers my first day. The offices were separated from the corridor by partitions, some with glass on top, so you could see what was going on. The first one didn't look too exciting, the girl who gave me the papers that day was sitting there typing. We walked to the next office where big white letters on the dosed door told you it belonged to VICTOR GORDON, PRESIDENT. This door was solid wood, but I could hear loud voices inside, like an argument. Just when Paul lifted his hand to knock, the door opened and out came Joey Gordon. His face was set like he was mad at the whole world.

"Hi, Paul," he said, not very enthusiastic. But when he saw me he smiled. "Hi, Aunt Belle," he said and gave a wink.

Paul looked at him kind of funny. "You two know each other?"

"Friends from the old country," said Joey and walked away down the hall.

Paul eyed me. "A woman with unknown depths," he said. Then he knocked on the door.

"Come in, come in," called a deep voice. It belonged to the man sitting at the big desk, waving a hand holding a cigar. He was a stocky man in his fifties, hair white at the temples, a fleshy face with pouches under the eyes. Brown eyes, like the son's. But these eyes didn't look like they ever winked, they were narrowed now, like he wasn't crazy about having us around.

"Afternoon," said Paul. "Mr. Gordon, I want you to meet Belle Appleman. She's been with us for only a short time, and she's already been elected shop steward of the pants section."

"That so?" The president's bushy eyebrows went up while he pushed out his lower lip like he didn't believe it. He swiveled in his armchair to look straight at me but just then his phone rang. He motioned for us to sit down. Whoever was on the other end of the wire must've been doing the talking, because all Mr. Gordon did was give a series of grunts, leaning back in his chair like he was studying the ceiling.

A handsome ceiling, too, paneled in knotty pine like the walls. Pale gray Venetian blinds were on the windows and soft wall-to-wall carpeting was in the same shade. We were sitting in chairs that matched a black leather settee, long and wide enough for a big man to take a nap on. Large standing fans whirring on each side of the room made you feel like a breeze was blowing. Some difference from the stuffy pants section.

You'd think a person with the *mazel,* luck, to work in such an office would be happy. But Mr. Gordon seemed edgy, fiddling with the cigar and moving around when he wasn't staring upwards. Finally he snapped, "Andretti, I'm paying you to figure things out. So figure it yourself." He banged down the receiver like it was a hot iron burning his fingers. Then he gave us a blank stare like his mind was a mile away.

"Belle's taking Jeanette Laval's place," Paul said.

Mr. Gordon cleared his throat. "Not an easy job," he said, looking at me like I was a sample of material too cheesey for him to buy.

"Not very healthy for the last steward, neither—uh, either," I corrected myself, remembering Evening English. "Ending up murdered."

Both men stared.

"Murdered?" Paul looked like someone hit him on the head with a hammer. Gordon said nothing, just stabbed his cigar out, grinding it into the ashtray.

"How do you know it was murder?" Gordon swivelled back toward me.

"I have connections on the police force."

Paul had a funny look on his face. "Curiouser and curiouser," he said, "deeper and deeper."

Gordon cleared his throat again. "I suppose the police will look into it . . ." His voice trailed off.

"Maybe," I told him, "but I'm looking, too. I want to know who did such a thing." Now Paul's jaw dropped, leaving his mouth open. Mr. Gordon picked up his cigar and put it back in his mouth but his eyes never left my face. "It's like this," I explained. "A long time ago, my Daniel—my husband, may he rest in peace—told me about a thing they do in China. If you save a person's life, that person owes his life to you forever. So maybe that's the way I feel about Jeanette Laval, only backwards. I found her, so since she was murdered I should find who was the murderer, see?"

"Well," said Paul, "let's not get off the track, shall we?" He was frowning. To Mr. Gordon he said, "I'll show her the ropes." His voice was like silk.

Mr. Gordon looked at him, his expression never changed. "I'm sure you will, Warshafsky," he said. Then he turned to me. "Good luck. My office is open to you any time, Mrs. Appleman." He began to shuffle some papers on his desk. Paul and I got up, the meeting was over. Well, bosses are bosses, they make the rules. We left.

The next door where Paul knocked was marked MARVIN KARSH, VICE-PRESIDENT. "Yes, yes, come," called out a voice that sounded like it didn't have much patience. We went into an office that was a twin of the president's, only this one was beige, with a tan leather settee. It seemed smaller, but that was on account of all the filing cabinets. I noticed a photograph on the desk, silver-framed, a woman with a little girl. Next to it stood a small statue made of iron or some kind of metal. A knight in armor, like from the olden times, on a thick marble base.

The man behind the desk pushed aside a pile of papers. "Sit, sit," he barked, twitching around in his swivel chair. He groped under a ledger, pulled out a pipe and filled it. A droopy moustache didn't do much for a long, angular face. We sat.

"Mr. Karsh, this is Belle Appleman," Paul began. "She's just been elected shop steward. You know, taking Miss Laval's place."

Karsh gave Warshafsky a sideways look. "Shop steward, eh?" he mumbled, glancing at me over the top of his rimless glasses while he fussed with his pipe. Hard to tell if he was younger than Mr. Gordon. Thinner and he didn't hold himself as straight, his shoulders drooped. "Steward, that's a big responsibility. You got to keep a cool head on your shoulders." He finally pushed the tobacco down and picked up the statue. It gave a click and surprise, the head of the knight opened up and fire came out. Karsh tipped it sideways and lit the pipe. A cloud of smoke swallowed us.

"I'll do my best," I told him, and coughed.

"I'll fill her in on the duties, Mr. Karsh," said Paul.

"Sure, you'll give her the low-down," snapped Karsh. "Why not? Aren't we one-hundred-percent modern around here? Union, closed shop, the whole shmeer. Eight-hour day, forty-hour week, pretty soon there won't be any time left for making suits! Then what happens to the workers, tell me that? Now if I was running the show here—" He banged the pipe down on a big glass ashtray, leaving the sentence dangling. Then he tapped his fingers on the desk a minute. "Naturally, I'll cooperate with you," he told me, swinging around in his chair again.

"Thanks," I said. "I hope I'll do as good a job as that poor Laval girl. I was the one who found her in the river. She was murdered, you know."

Karsh sat up straight. "You what? Murdered?"

"I found her," I said again, "and I'm going to find the person who killed her, too."

Paul put in his two cents. "Miss Appleman is a very determined woman," he said to Karsh.

"It's Mrs. Appleman," I corrected. "I'm a widow."

"Sorry. Well, Mr. Karsh, you can see that she's the right one for the job."

Karsh grunted and blew another cloud of smoke at us. "Well, good luck, Mrs. Appleman," he said. "Just don't waste too much company time. We're in business to make suits, not to run unions."

Paul and I didn't have to get up because Karsh hadn't ever asked us to sit down. "Fine," I said, "I'll get back to my tacking."

"That's right," said Karsh, waving his pipe, "back to work. Time is money, never forget that." He sounded like he was singing his favorite song.

"He's a real doll, that one," I said as we walked down the corridor. "A regular adding machine."

"You've got him sized up, all right. Karsh sees the world through dollar signs." Paul shook his head. "When he said time is money, he meant it. He's the production manager, does time-study, all that stuff. Figures out how many seconds it takes for each part to be cut out, put on the tables, and held under the needle—nothing but figures in his head."

"He sure has it in for the union," I said. "They say he hates Roosevelt, too."

"Curses him at least three times a day," Paul said with a grin.

"So Hoover was better?" I was mad. "Look what happened, the Depression just got worse. At least Roosevelt came up with the WPA to make jobs."

Paul took my arm like we were going for a stroll through the park. He made sure we were walking with little steps, we shouldn't get back to the shop too soon. "That's not the way the bosses see it, Belle. They don't want any regulation of wages or hours, anything that might cut down on their profits."

"Did you hear how Gordon talked on the telephone?" I asked. "What a temper!"

Paul stopped us walking. "You'll soon learn, Belle. Bosses don't regard workers as people." He was still holding my elbow, making me feel a tingle all over.

"Karsh did us a favor, he actually smiled when we left. But I got the feeling he'd like to give a wave of the hand like Houdini, the union should disappear in a cloud of his pipe smoke."

"You said it!" Paul exclaimed. "That's a trick he'd love to do! But he can't. Tough as he is, Victor Gordon at least accepts the union. Karsh may be a boss but Gordon calls the shots. And that's to our advantage, when the bosses are against each other. You know the old saying, divide and conquer."

It was the first time I heard it but I didn't let on. I just nodded.

Paul moved closer and spoke in a confidential tone. "Listen, Belle Appleman, I just had a great idea. You're coming to the union meeting tonight, aren't you?" I nodded yes. "Why don't I pick you up a little earlier, say around six-fifteen or so, and we'll have a quick supper and go to the meeting together. Give us a chance to get to know each other. Now that you're shop steward, we're going to be seeing a lot of each other. What do you say?"

So what happened to Belle Appleman, the cool customer, who was so quick to figure things out and come up with the answers? All of a sudden she turned into a dummy and couldn't even say yes or no. With my lips stretched in an idiot smile, I just looked at that handsome face and nodded my head up and down.

"Good," he said, "it's a date. Where do you live?"

That I could say. Then he remembered what he was telling me before his wonderful idea.

"You see, Belle." His hand pressed a little harder on my arm. More tingling inside me. "The fact is, we have a running war on. Workers against the bosses, pure and simple. They're always trying to put something over on us, so we have to be on our guard all the time. Even now they're trying to—"

A woman's voice broke in. "Hi, Paul." We were standing a little past Gordon's office, she must've come out of there. A tall skinny blonde with a chest like a boy's. And my drug store experience told me the blonde came out of a bottle, you could see dark roots. But she was dressed real snappy in black pique. First I thought she was young, but when she came closer you could see little lines around her eyes.

"Hello, Lillian," said Paul, dropping my arm. "This is Belle Appleman, the new shop steward in the pants shop. Belle, this is Lillian Lewis, the executive secretary here."

"Hello," I said, holding out my hand.

She took it like it was a flounder filet from Mr. Milstein's fish store on Spring Street that wasn't real fresh, so she dropped it quick. "You're taking Jeanette Laval's place?"

I tried to make a joke. "I'm taking it here, not in the morgue."

But Lillian Lewis didn't laugh. "I'll see you later," she said to Paul, and went into one of the offices.

Just then another door opened and a big man backed out, carrying a fedora. I knew whose head that hat belonged to. Jim Connors.

"Thanks for the information," Jim was saying. I heard Joey Gordon's voice mumble something back. Then Jim turned around and saw us. "Belle, my friend, is this where they've got you working now?"

"Guess what, Jim, I just got elected shop steward! Meet Paul Warshafsky," I said, "he's head of the union here."

"Well, congratulations," Jim said to me. "Sounds as if you'll be running the whole shebang soon."

I got red. "Paul, this is Sergeant Jim Connors from the Joy Street station." They shook hands.

"I'm not the head of the union, just the secretary," said Paul. "And I can see that you know the real Belle Appleman." He and Jim grinned, while I got redder.

"Mr. Warshafsky," said Jim, "we're asking everyone where they were on Friday night of this past weekend. I'd be getting around to you eventually, so if you'll just tell me now, we can save time."

"Friday night?" Paul's brows came together for a second, and then his face cleared. "No problem. I went bowling with Sam Rothberg, the foreman of the pants shop. You can check with him."

"And just where did you bowl?" asked Jim. He was scribbling in his little notebook.

"Arrow Lanes," said Paul. "On Mass. Ave., near Symphony Hall."

"Thanks," said Jim, putting the notebook back in his pocket.

And before I could stop to figure out how come someone like Paul Warshafsky was so chummy with Sam Rothberg, Paul said, "Well, I've got to be getting back to the cutting room. Nice to meet you, Sergeant Connors. Oh, and Belle, if you have any questions, you can always find me there." He left.

Jim watched him go. "Shop steward, huh? Does that mean you're taking the Laval girl's place?"

"That's right." I didn't have time to waste. "Listen, Jim, what did Joey Gordon have to say? You know the Laval girl and he—"

"We know all about that," he said. "Now, listen, it's an official case of murder this is now. Strictly police business. Not *True Detective* stories, remember." He was talking maybe to a ten-year-old girl who snitched a lollipop.

"Okay, Jim," I said, "you win, I won't butt in. But I had a long talk with Joey Gordon yesterday in his studio. You know he painted a picture of that girl with no clothes on? And maybe he told me things he wouldn't tell a detective. It's possible, no? So why won't you let me help?"

Jim groaned. "Belle, what'm I going to do with you?"

"Don't do nothing," I said, "just tell me what you found out, and I'll tell you what I found out. Is it a deal?"

He groaned again and put the fedora back on his head. "Must have bats in my belfry," he sighed. "Okay, it's a deal."

So I told him about my visit with Joey while he made notes in his little black notebook. And then he let me in on what he found out.

Jeanette Laval had been pregnant. Three months gone.

NINE

Sam Rothberg gave me a dirty look when I got back to the pants shop. "So," he said, straightening up from a machine near mine he must've been fixing, "you decided finally you got time to do a little work? The loops are piling up on your table."

I just went to my machine. He was right, a million loops waiting to be tacked. I checked the needle and thread and began stitching.

"Gee, you was gone a long time," said Mary. "Sam was getting mad."

I shrugged. "The bosses wanted to talk. Who was I to stop them?"

"Holy mackerel," said Tillie, "with that hunk of man for company, why rush back?" She gave a giggle and bent over her work.

Only Gertrude didn't laugh, she had a kind of sour expression on her face. Listen, I wanted to say to her, if you wanted the union job, why didn't you speak up? I didn't go asking for it. All of a sudden she got up from her chair. "Two-minute break," she said.

After she left I looked around for Sam Rothberg. No sign of him. So I went to the ladies' room, also. Gertrude was standing at the sink fixing her lipstick. I went over and stood behind her so she could see me in the mirror. "Listen, Gertrude," I said, "are you mad at me or something? I didn't ask to take Jeanette's place in the union. If it's making us enemies, I don't want the job."

She turned around. "Who's mad? You've got another think coming—"

"Look, Gertrude, I got to tell you something. I heard you and Sam talking before." Her mouth opened. "Let me finish. Look, what's between you two is none of my business. But you got to remember Jeanette was murdered, so the police are going to question everybody. Everybody who had anything to do with her. Now, they all say there was something between her and Sam. And you know what it was. So why don't you get it off your chest?"

"To you?" She put her lipstick back in her bag. "Why should I tell you anything?"

I gave her my Myrna Loy look. "Because I'm helping the police. It's a secret and you shouldn't tell the others, okay?" Her eyes got wider. "And it's easier to talk to me than a detective giving you the third degree. Those guys can twist around anything you tell them. But if I tell them what's going on, they'll get it straight. And you and Sam won't be in any trouble."

"Sam and I—what kind of trouble?" Her voice was shaky, she fastened her handbag shut. "What're you getting at?"

I tried to remember things Jim Connors taught me. "All kinds—like withholding evidence—and also—hmm, what's that word? Accessory. Accessory to murder. You wouldn't believe what they can think up! And they'll find out about Sam and Jeanette, don't worry." I let my words sink in. "So let me help you, Gertrude. What's the story?"

There was a little bench in the ladies' room. Gertrude sat down with her bag in her lap and I sat down beside her. For a minute she bent over with her face in her hands, her body hunched. I put my hand on her shoulder, and after a while she sat up again and gave out a big sigh.

"Sometimes I could die from shame." She bit her lower lip. "Sam used to be so different, you can't imagine—full of fun, young." Her fingers fiddled with her bag. "I met him three years ago. At a picnic. By the time he took me home we were crazy about each other. Right away we went steady. At first sight, like in the movies, do you believe it?"

I nodded. Love I believed in.

"That's the way it was." She stopped and looked around. "What if someone comes in—maybe—"

"Nobody's here, don't worry."

She swallowed. "What's to tell? We wanted to get married. But when I met his mother it was no soap. Who was Gertrude Scharf? A nobody. A poor girl, an orphan with no family. They talked Sam out of it. Overnight he was engaged and married. A girl with connections—a cousin of a cousin of the Gordons. And with her came—"

"Sam's job, naturally," I finished for her.

"Naturally." Gertrude fished in her bag, took out a hanky and blew her nose. "So then, he had a guilty feeling, he got me the job in the pants department."

"And his marriage, it's happy?"

She rolled her eyes. "Are you kidding? Happy? You should live so! His wife's no bargain, nags him for not going higher in the firm, he'll stay a foreman all his life, that's all he hears."

"They have children?"

She shook her head. "No, she's a sickly type, yet."

Things began to fit together inside my brain. "So when you came here to work and found out what kind of life he had, you felt sorry, right? And you and Sam—?"

She fixed me with a heartsick face. "I was still wild about him. And he felt the same way. Don't you see, we're only human—" She grabbed my hand. "You won't tell on us, will you, Belle? We managed to keep it a secret all this time. Nobody here knows a thing. You won't tell, promise?"

"Listen, Gertrude, a snitch I'm not. What you two do, that's your own business. But what about Sam and Jeanette? Wasn't he two-timing his wife and you also?"

"Oh, her!" Her lips twisted. "That little—I shouldn't say it, she's dead now—made a play for everyone in pants that could give her a step up. So she played games with Sam, too. She didn't know about us, of course, not that she'd give a damn. And wives were the last thing on her mind." She shook her head. "And poor Sam fell for her line like a ton of bricks."

"Remember," I said, "she was a regular Jean Harlow." It was Nate who said that. But Nate didn't tumble.

"I guess so. But after her promotion she gave Sam the cold shoulder. You saw them Friday morning."

I nodded. Sam and Jeanette in the far corner of the room. Sam waving his hands. Jeanette shaking her head. So Sam was getting what Edward G. Robinson called the kiss-off.

"Naturally, you were all upset about Sam and Jeanette," I said, trying to wrap things up; we had been in the ladies' room a long time.

Gertrude's eyes flashed. "I hated her! For what she was doing to poor Sam, I coulda killed her—" She stopped and put her fist against her mouth. "I didn't mean it like it sounds—" Her eyes were wide.

"Don't be so jittery, Gertrude," I said. "People always talk like that. But wasn't Sam sore when she brushed him off? Nobody likes to be made a fool of."

"Sam?" Her hand gave a wave. "He wouldn't hurt a fly. Sure, he was plenty aggravated. But kill someone? That he couldn't do, honest!" She clutched my arm.

"Listen to me," I said. "The police are checking to see where every one was Friday night—the night Jeanette was killed. You were with Sam that night, no?"

Gertrude's face got white. "How did you know?"

"Because Paul already told them he was bowling with Sam. To me that didn't sound kosher."

"Paul was helping us," she said. "It was a cover-up, in case Sam's wife, you know—" Her hold on my arm tightened. "My God, do you think they'll find out—?"

"Take it easy, Gertrude," I told her, moving the fingers that were digging into me. "Who can remember who came into a big bowling alley?"

"*Alevai!*" she muttered.

"Look, let's go back before they fire us."

Sam Rothberg was at the other side of the room, but his eyes followed us all the way in. I knew if Gertrude was with me, he wouldn't blink an eye. I was right.

Gertrude's story I sure didn't expect. This detective business was like peeling an onion, you never knew what you'd find inside. And she always acted so full of moxie. It was hard to see what she got out of hanging on to Sam, a married man with a roving eye yet.

Now, Appleman, I said to myself, you got two more people chock full of reasons to hate that girl. Besides Joey. And the Nadler girl.

Wait a minute—somebody you didn't think about before. Who was it who took around the new shop steward, said he'd show her the ropes? Made a dinner date with her? Did he do the same with the last shop steward?

Who never said a word about Jeanette, good or bad, the whole time?

And who didn't go bowling Friday night?

Mr. Paul Warshafsky, that's who.

TEN

My sewing machine was whirring its head off to make up for lost time when a voice over my shoulder said, "Congratulations on your election, Belle."

My head went up. Nate Becker was looking down at me from the top of his stringbean shape. "You heard already?" I asked.

"Warshafsky told us in the cutting room."

I gave him a faraway Greta Garbo look, remembering how Saturday night supper ended. "Well, thanks, Nate."

He cleared his throat. "About the meeting tonight, I'll pick you up about seven, okay?"

"Oh, I'm sorry," I told him. "After the blintzes I figured you didn't want to bother with a buttinsky, so I made other arrangements."

"Other arrangements?" Why did he sound so surprised? He never even called Sunday to say he was sorry.

"Paul Warshafsky asked me—"

He didn't let me finish. "So he caught you already! I thought you had more brains. That guy has some reputation—"

"Just a minute." My neck got warm. "It says in the Talmud Belle Appleman needs written permission? What am I, sixteen and on my first date?"

Nate's eyes glittered behind those thick glasses. "Belle, can't you see he's a regular ladies' man? Don't let him put one over on you!"

"Thanks a million. Belle Appleman can take care of herself," I let him know.

Nate kept on like he didn't hear a word I was saying. "And another thing. It's already spread over the whole factory, you're running around to hunt for a killer. I told you before and I'll say it again. Let the police do it! Stop mixing in!"

"You'll excuse me, Mr. Becker," I told him in a frosty Joan Crawford tone. "See this pile of bundles to finish? Sam Rothberg wouldn't like it, you're keeping me from getting my work done."

Nate shrugged. "I should know better. Talk to you, talk to the wall." He turned and walked out of the pants room.

I looked around. All the girls heard, naturally, they sure got an earful. Now they all got real busy with their work. Me, too. Who needed Nate Becker, anyway?

When we punched out at five o'clock Gertrude was behind me in line. "Remember," she whispered, "I'm counting on you—"

"I don't know from nothing," I whispered back.

By the time I got home my kitchen clock told me Paul would be coming in less than an hour. No jitters, Appleman, it's only union business with him. What should I wear? He didn't say where we'd be having dinner. But the union meeting was at seven-thirty, so I shouldn't be fancy-shmancy. My dotted Swiss, it gave me a nifty waist line.

It was while I was in the bedroom putting a drop Coty's Emeraude behind my right ear that I had a flash about Joey Gordon. Sure, he had a fling with Jeanette, but so did plenty of other men. But that three-month baby that died inside her, was it Joey's? I remembered a movie I saw with Sarah—*An American Tragedy*—with that pretty actress, Sylvia Sidney.

She's a poor girl, works in a factory, and she falls in love with a young man who loves her also. Then he meets another girl, richer and better educated than the first. Naturally, he decides to marry the second girl. But he made one bad mistake, the first girl is pregnant with his baby. How does he get out of it? He takes the poor girl out in a rowboat on a lake and drowns her. In the end he gets caught.

So, did Joey know about Jeanette being pregnant? Did he see the same movie and get an idea?

A ring of the downstairs doorbell snapped me out of it. I pushed the button to buzz the door open and went to open my front door. I could hear Paul's footsteps on the stairs and Mrs. Wallenstein opening her door to see who was coming. A minute later Mr. Gorgeous himself was leaning against my doorway and handing me a single long-stemmed American Beauty rose.

"I thought that after a day in the Classic Clothing Company, you'd enjoy this."

I took it and gave a sniff. "Lovely, mm," I said.

"Lovely women deserve lovely things."

"For that you can come in," I told him. "Thanks, I'll go put it in water." He came in and closed the door. He wasn't wearing a necktie so I knew we weren't going to the Copley Plaza. "Back in a second."

In the kitchen I fixed the rose in an old vase that didn't hold a flower for a long time. Then I dashed into the bedroom to touch up the left ear with Coty and get my handbag. When I turned around, there he was in my bedroom doorway, eyeing me up and down.

"All ready!" I sang out, walking toward him. I expected him to let me pass and then follow. But he didn't make a move.

Instead, when I got close, he said real quiet, "The beginning of a beautiful friendship," put a hand on each of my shoulders and kissed me, very soft, on my lips.

So did Appleman do what she should have? Give him a good smack in the face and tell him she wasn't that kind of girl? No, she just stood there, tingling all over. But when his hands moved from my shoulders to lower down, I snapped out of my trance and pulled away.

"Listen, Paul," I said, "take it easy. The truth is, I didn't go on a date since my Daniel, may he rest in peace, died. So I'm out of practice with this kind of business, it's a whole new ball game."

He looked surprised for a minute, then he dropped his hands and grinned. "Belle, that's what I noticed about you from the first—you never beat around the bush. You come right out with what's on your mind. That's refreshing in a woman—lets a man know where he stands. Now, shall we go?" he asked, smoothing back hair that was already brushed smooth. "My car's right outside."

Car! I was used to subways and streetcars, what a welcome difference. I floated down the stairs, I had to move slower anyway, my new pumps were a little tight. Paul's car turned out to be a black sedan. He opened the door and gave a flourish with his arm. I stepped in, it felt like a royal coach. He walked around and got in the driver's seat. Before he turned the key to start, he turned to me and said, "Belle Appleman, I like your style. We're going to make a great team."

Was he talking just about this union business? 1 didn't ask any questions. What woman wouldn't want to be on Warshafsky's team?

When I did ask where we were going, he winked and said only, "You'll see."

We drove past Bowdoin Square and down toward Faneuil Hall. When he parked the car, he got out and went around to open my door. Like before, a real gentleman. Then he took my arm and walked me across the street. "Boston's old reliable—good food and quick service. We want to get to the meeting on time."

I looked up at the restaurant sign. DURGIN-PARK. As Paul opened the door for us to go in, I stopped with my foot half across the doorsill.

"What's the matter, Belle?" he asked.

What could I tell him? Already I was drowning in memories of Daniel on our first dinner date bringing me here. Leaning across the red-and-white-checked tablecloth to tell me he loved me and wanted to marry me. It became our restaurant. Lunches every Saturday, sitting with a State Street banker on one side and a butcher from Faneuil Hall Market on the other. Sawdust on the floor. Strawberry shortcake in a soup plate. Daniel holding my hand under the table and smiling. That's what was the matter.

But how long can you live with ghosts? I ran my fingers through my hair and shook the ghosts out of my brain. "It's nothing," I said, and started up the long flight of stairs.

Like usual, the place was crowded. But a waitress took one look at Paul and found two places right away at the end of one of the long tables. Women's eyes followed us to our seats, and it wasn't me they were noticing. It made me wonder about extra-good-looking men: did they always get things their own way?

"Real New England cooking," Paul remarked as we scanned the menus. "I always have clam chowder and Yankee pot roast. How does that sound?"

The menu I knew by heart, but I only nodded. "Sounds perfect." I kept trying to remember how you were supposed to act on a first date. What was it those *Ladies' Home Journal* articles always harped on? To be a good listener? But reading that stuff and sitting across from a real life Paul Warshafsky wasn't the same. And as if all that wasn't enough, I had to remember about my detecting.

Before I could even start, Paul began to tell me all about what a shop steward is supposed to do. It sounded plenty complicated and I had lots of questions to ask. Listen, working in a factory is no joke—the girls there need all the help they can get. So I wanted to do the job right.

By the time he explained the whole business, we were already finishing our Indian pudding and our coffee. Paul glanced at his watch. "If you're ready, I think we'd better get started."

It was just as Paul opened the door for me to step into the car that it suddenly dawned on me.

I didn't get to ask him a single question about Jeanette Laval.

ELEVEN

Paul parked the car on Kneeland Street near Meltzer's restaurant, and we went into a building that looked like a big factory. The giant meeting hall on the first floor was already half full, maybe a hundred people or more.

He left me in the arched doorway. "Forgive me, Belle, I've got to get a few things done before the meeting starts. You go ahead and find a seat. I'll see you afterwards." He pressed my hand and went over to a side room on the left, carrying a little briefcase he took from the car.

"Hey, Belle!" It was Tillie and some of the girls from the pants shop, waving for me to come over. There was an empty chair on the aisle next to them. I sat.

Pretty soon a little procession of men came down the aisle, led by Paul Warshafsky. A real surprise, Nate was one of them. I didn't realize he was such a *macher*, a big shot, in the union. They went up on the stage and sat on the four chairs arranged there. Paul got up to begin the meeting, and I couldn't keep my heart from giving a little flutter.

First was the report of the last meeting, then the treasurer's report. It seemed like it was going to be shlepping on all night. So I sank back into my chair and began to think about the way Jeanette Laval was murdered. First drowned in—what, a bathtub? A sink? And then put in the Charles River. What kind of person would do a thing like that? A jealous lover, mad enough to kill? I remember once Daniel, may he rest in peace, read me a poem, it was beautiful and terrible at the same time, about a man in jail for killing a girl. I forget the name of the poem, but funny how a line sticks in your head, even after years: "Yet each man kills the thing he loves—" Now the thought made me give a shiver all over.

Paul was speaking. I sat up and began to pay attention.

". . . the terrible tragedy that happened to one of our members last week. Let us have a minute of silence in memory of Jeanette Laval of the Classic Clothing Company."

All the heads in the hall bent down, mine too, and for a minute it wasn't a hall, it was a graveyard. Then Warshafsky gave a bang with his wooden hammer and everyone looked up again.

"Now I would like to introduce the new member of our Local who was elected to take over as shop steward in the pants shop of the Classic Clothing Company—Mrs. Belle Appleman."

His words caught me by surprise, I sat frozen. Tillie jabbed me in the ribs. "Stand up!" Everybody was clapping. I stood, gave a quick smile, and sat down. My cheeks felt hot.

Paul gave another bang and went on. "We now come to the most important announcement of the evening. The United Clothing Workers of America is pledged to support the re-election of President Franklin Delano Roosevelt this November!"

Loud clapping and cheers. But when the applause died down, a voice in back called out, "Roosevelt is a stooge for the capitalist pigs!"

Warshafsky gave a couple bangs with the hammer, but another voice yelled, "Roosevelt is for the American worker!"

"If you're Socialists," yelled back the first voice, "why isn't the union supporting Norman Thomas?"

Voices began to yell from all parts of the house.

"Communist *dreck*!"

"Socialist bums!"

"*Fascisti*!"

"Long live the Revolution!"

A few rows behind me, two men began to hit each other with their fists. Others began to fight on the opposite side. Men were standing up and yelling, girls were screaming. Warshafsky was banging away with the hammer but nobody paid attention. I didn't know what was happening. It was like watching a saloon fight in a cowboy movie.

Nate jumped off the platform and came running over. He grabbed my arm and pulled me up. "Come on, let's get out of here!" Tillie and the girls scurried along, but they got separated from us in the crowd. Nate yanked me along behind him, pushing people out of the way, to a side door. A minute later we were outside on Kneeland Street. I could here the arguing and fighting still shaking the walls inside.

Nate groaned. "Oy! Every time! Every meeting!"

I didn't understand. "What was that all about?"

"The usual," said Nate, "happens all the time. Nothing but fights between the Socialists and the *Linke.* The Leftists, Belle, the Communists. Don't you remember, I told you about them in Barney's, on Saturday?"

"Sure. But about politics I never paid much attention," I told Nate. "I only knew what Daniel used to talk about. The Republicans were okay until Hoover made such a mess. And the Democrats are better, no? That's why I voted for Roosevelt."

Nate groaned again. "Oy, a regular baby in the woods!" He gave a wave with his hand. "You want to ride back on the El or walk?"

All of a sudden we were friends again. "It's a nice night. Why not stretch our legs a little?" It was cooler, my shoes felt better.

"Okay," said Nate. As we walked toward Washington and Boylston, he began to explain more about Socialism. A man named Karl Marx wrote a book way back, *Das Kapital.* He was a German who saw there were two classes of people, the bosses who ran everything and the peasants and workers who got run. The way to end misery, he said, was to get rid of capitalism, where the factories were owned by only a few people. Capitalism didn't work right, anyway, it made depressions all the time. So little by little things would have to change to make everything come out even. Everyone would work, there wouldn't be any bosses, nobody would starve or go in rags.

"Understand?" he asked after he finished the whole story.

"Sure. What I don't get is why the Communists and Socialists want the same thing but keep on fighting with each other. Why don't they join up and fight the bosses together?"

"Communists can't wait. They'd rather kill off people that stand in their way. Like Stalin's doing in Russia."

"To me it's terrible," I said. "Grown-up people, they want the same thing, hitting each other at meetings. And over what? Over nothing!"

"Maybe you think nothing," said Nate, "but it's something. They have these cells to make trouble for us."

"Cells?"

"They break up into small groups, maybe five, ten people, who knows? Each cell has a leader. But the cells don't know each other they stay secret. Each cell gets a different assignment, from where don't ask me. And they make trouble in the union."

We were already in front of my apartment. My feet hurt. "You'll come up for a cup coffee?"

Nate peered at his watch. "Tomorrow's a work day, we got to get up early. I'll take a rain check, okay?"

"Okay." I put my hand on the doorknob, then turned. "Nate, why were you so mad that I went just for supper with Paul Warshafsky? He didn't get fresh, he acted like a gentleman. Just explained about the shop steward business."

Nate shrugged. "Maybe I got a little bit upset. He has quite a reputation with women. I still say, watch out."

Advice like that makes me mad, naturally, but I decided to play it cozy. "What do you mean, Nate? That maybe Jeanette didn't watch out? That it's maybe dangerous to be shop steward?"

Nate got red. "Look, Belle, I didn't mean anything like that. I meant—you know—sometimes a wolf wears sheep's clothing."

"So next time a sheep goes ba-a-a, I'll remember. Anyway, you sure got me out of there in a hurry tonight. Thanks, Nate."

Later, getting ready for bed, I wondered what was making Nate so excited all of a sudden. Could he be a little jealous? Look how he took care of me there. And maybe he knew more about Paul than he wanted to tell.

No matter what, that Warshafsky was some guy. No wonder all the girls in the pants shop sat up and looked when he came in. Well, as the new shop steward, I'd get to know him better.

It was a thought to bring nice dreams, maybe . . . those eyes, that deep voice . . . I was smiling when I fell asleep.

But in the morning I woke up late on account of forgetting to set the alarm. Barely time to dress, make my lunch, and swallow a glass of milk with a hunk coffee cake. Apple-man, I told myself, see what happens when you let a man go to your head?

When I got to the factory everybody was already work-ing away. My tacking machine just sat there, the only quiet one in the shop. And a table full of belt loops to be tacked onto pants. Sam Rothberg was at the other end of the room, but his mad look traveled all the way across to me.

"Gee whiz," muttered Gertrude, "where ya been?"

"Forgot my alarm." A dumb excuse. I sat down, turned on the power, and checked the needle. The thread wasn't in right, and I bent to hold the needle to fix it.

All of a sudden out shot a flash of sparks. Before I could say a word, I felt like somebody hit me over the head with a baseball bat. Then, as my mother used to say, it got *shvartz* in front of my eyes .

TWELVE

I opened one eye.
My one eye saw two eyes behind a pair glasses looking down. They gave a little blink. Right away I knew what happened. I was dead and in heaven.

"Daniel?" I asked. I opened my other eye.

It was a white heaven with white walls and a white ceiling. I was in a white bed under a white sheet. An angel dressed in white was bending over me. The features swam a little.

"Daniel?" I asked again.

"What's your name?" asked the angel back. Answering a question with a question, I knew it was a Jewish angel.

"Belle Appleman."

The angel held his hand in front of my face. "How many fingers do you see?"

"Three," I said. "We're playing some kind game? I didn't know they played games in heaven."

"You're not in heaven," said the angel. "This is the Mass. Memorial Hospital." He adjusted his glasses. "I'm Doctor Goldfarb." He took one of my hands out from under the sheet and counted on his watch. I took out the other hand, it had a white bandage on it and it hurt

"What happened?" I asked. My head was a balloon floating around.

Two faces appeared on the other side of the bed. Sarah and Nate. "Your machine had a short circuit," said Nate. "You got shocked."

"Ooh, was I scared!" said Sarah. "When Nate called, I grabbed a cab over right away."

"You took a taxi all the way from the store to Harrison Avenue?" I said. "Sarah, you're a doll!"

"What do you mean!" She sounded indignant. "I told Mr. Klein I couldn't wait on another customer till I came to see with my own eyes how you were!"

Meanwhile Dr. Goldfarb moved the sheet back, helped me turn sideways, and put his stethoscope on different places on my back. Then he turned me back and listened for a second to a couple places on my chest. When he took the earpieces out, he looked pleased. "You're a very lucky woman," he said. "Despite what happened, all your parts seem to be in good working order."

"Except my head," I told him. "And my hand."

"Yes, you have a burn on your right index finger," he said. "That's where the electric current entered. But apparently the shock knocked you away from the machine, so that the current didn't do the damage it might have if you had held on to the needle."

"What's with the top of my head?" I asked, moving only my eyes.

"Now, that's from the fall," he answered. "You must have hit your head on the floor or against a table. At any rate, the worst that's evident is a big bump. If you had any symptoms of a concussion, they seem to have gone."

"Plenty lucky, Belle," said Nate. "When I heard the girls screaming, I ran in. You were lying right on the floor. Angelo, the stock boy, was pushing in and out on your back. He said he was just passing by when you got shocked. And he learned only last night at his Boy Scout meeting what to do—"

"He was giving artificial inspiration—" put in Sarah.

"Respiration," corrected Nate. "Anyway, if anybody saved your life, it was Angelo."

Funny, some of the girls called Angelo a fresh kid. A skinny Italian boy, maybe fifteen, sixteen. A crooked grin. While all the older people were screaming, he knew what to do. Only saved my life.

Dr. Goldfarb gave my hand a pat and put it back under the bed sheet. "I think a day's rest here will be enough, Mrs. Appleman. I'll have you discharged tomorrow morning." He turned and went out the door.

"Don't worry how much it costs, Belle," said Nate. "The union has an arrangement with the hospital."

I heard the door open and a minute later a head wearing a fedora bent over the bed. Jim Connors. "How d'you feel, Belle, m'darlin'?"

The "m'darlin'" part didn't fool me. I knew he was mad. "Dr. Goldfarb thinks I'll live," I said.

"No thanks to your foolishness," he let me know.

"I told her she shouldn't mix in—" Nate began, but stopped when Jim fixed him with a look.

"If you two don't mind, I'd like a word with Belle alone, please."

"Listen, Belle," said Sarah, "I got to get back to the store. But I'll give the hospital a ring later." She bent over and gave me a kiss on the cheek.

"Yeah, I got to get back, too," said Nate. "Oh, here's your pocketbook, the girls told me to bring it. See you later, Belle, get well quick." He laid the bag on the table, put his hand on mine for a second, and turned to go.

"Just a second, Nate," I said. "Was Paul Warshafsky in the factory when it happened?"

"No. He was before, but he had some union business to take care of and he left."

"Oh," I said. "Thanks. See you later."

After they left, Jim took off the fedora and put it on the end of the bed. He pulled up a chair, sat down, and scratched his thinning hair with one hand. "Belle, you've got to know the truth. That accident of yours was no accident. Someone rigged your machine up to short circuit through your body. The minute you touched that needle—pow!"

"Aha," I said, "so it worked."

"What worked?"

"My idea. To tell everyone in the factory I was going to find who killed Jeanette. So someone got scared, right?"

He put his fingers together and cracked his knuckles. Outside, the siren of an ambulance coming to the hospital screamed and then stopped. "Belle, solving a homicide isn't a game you play for fun. And what good did it do, except to nearly get you killed? The chances are whoever it is will try again. That is, if you keep on playing detective." His chin jutted forward. "I want your solemn promise that you'll give up on this Laval business. What's more, that you'll let the factory people know it."

A nurse walked in. "Time for your medicine," she said. She had a little paper cup with two white pills. She cranked up the head of the bed, poured a glass of water from the pitcher on the table, and I swallowed the pills. That made her happy and she left.

"Tell me, Jim," I asked. "You checked who was in the factory early this morning, before I came?"

He sighed. "Of course, Belle. But it wasn't much help. Almost everyone came in before you."

"But who was first?"

"Well, according to Ed Bandy—" he fished out his book. "First, young Gordon. Bandy said he came in about six-fifteen, red-eyed and hung over. Went right upstairs. At six thirty-five Mr. Karsh came in. Then Mr. Gordon, right afterward. About seven-ten, that fellow I met yesterday—Warshafsky, is it? At seven-twenty a Mr. Rothberg and one of the girls, named Gertrude—er, Gertrude—" He began to fish in his pocket.

"Scharf," I told him.

"That's it, Scharf." He closed the notebook. "That list tell you anything?"

"Plenty,"' I said. "Joey Gordon's got the strongest connection with the Laval girl. And Sam Rothberg and Gertrude didn't exactly love her. Karsh I don't know about except he hates the union something terrible."

Jim scratched his head again. "Well," he said, "you've got a point about young Gordon. In fact, I went to the factory this morning to bring him in for more questioning. That's how I found out about what happened to you."

"You mean you already arrested Joey for murder?" I forgot I was supposed to be dizzy and sat up. My head still felt funny.

"No, we couldn't arrest him. Not enough real evidence. But I thought it would be a good idea to let him cool his heels at the station for a few hours of questioning."

"Everybody who could fix my machine came in early," I said. "You'll have to arrest the whole gang." I gave him my Marie Dressler grin.

"Now, Belle,'" he said, "behave yourself." But he was smiling. He picked the fedora off the bed and clamped it on his head. "Better be getting back," he said. "You get a good rest, now. And remember—I want you to tell everyone at your place that you're off the case!"

"Thanks for coming, Jim," I said. He gave me his I-know-what-you're-up-to glare and left.

Things began to go around in my head. How come Paul left the cutting room so early? Who has a meeting at eight o'clock in the morning? Sam Rothberg was the one who always went around fixing machines that broke. Who would know better how to fix one up to give a shock? What about Joey, with those brown velvet eyes? *Nu*, Baby Face Nelson was a killer.

Could Jim be right, somebody tried to electrocute me? Just on account of the word got around I was chasing down Jeanette's murderer? Sure, I was trying, only who would take me so serious? The more I thought about it, the more itchy-pitchy I got lying there. The nice, soft mattress and the cool sheet started to feel like a prison, I had to get out of that hospital room. So I swung my feet out from under the sheet and slid them down to the floor. Next, I stood up. The room went around for a second, then it stopped. Not bad. One step, then another. My head was okay. Appleman was in business again.

In the little bathroom I looked in the mirror, oy, plenty of room for improvement. I splashed cold water on my face with one hand and straightened my hair. A little closet was hiding my clothes. Just as I was pulling my dress over my head, a voice behind me barked, "Mrs. Appleman, what do you think you're doing?"

I jumped. The nurse, naturally. "Getting dressed," I said, tying the belt, "so I can go home."

"But the doctor hasn't discharged you!"

"So I'm discharging myself," I told her. She gave me a mad look and ran out. I could hear her yelling for Dr. Goldfarb. By the time he came I had my shoes on.

"Really, Mrs. Appleman," he said, like he was scolding a naughty little girl, "you should be in bed."

"What for?" I asked. "I feel one-hundred-percent fine." Already I learned how to tie my shoelaces with one hand in a bandage.

"In all honesty, I can't discharge you until tomorrow," he frowned.

"Tomorrow's too late," I told him. "I got things to do."

He threw up his hands. "All right, you win. But you'll have to sign a waiver disclaiming any responsibility on my part or on the part of the hospital."

"I'll sign anything to get out." So I signed and the nurse made me get in a wheelchair. A hospital rule, she said, wheeling Appleman to the front door like she was a baby. So I rode.

Harrison Avenue is noisy. It'll never win a prize for the best-looking street in the world. But believe me, after the hospital it looked better than the fanciest street in the Back Bay. Just to stand there listening to the auto horns blare was a pleasure. On my own two feet.

Should I go back to the factory? Absolutely not, I decided. If I was supposed to stay in the Mass. Memorial Hospital for the day, then I was free. Meanwhile I could get something done.

The M.T.A. got me back to the Charles Street Circle station and I walked back to Allen Street. With each step I felt better. But my head was still stuffed with questions. Who could have done such a thing to my machine? And when was the tricky business done? In the morning, probably, real quick before anybody else came. Wait a minute, somebody could've stayed there all night. Sam Rothberg, maybe? And then come in with Gertrude early like nothing happened? But he would've had to punch out and sneak back later, not so easy.

Someone like Joey could stay on after everyone left the pants shop, easy. Ed Bandy, that *shikker,* could be downstairs, he wouldn't hear a thing if the whole building fell down. So, maybe Joey.

And what about Karsh? I told him straight out I was going to find out about Jeanette. He could've stayed, no question.

Who else was left? Paul Warshafsky and Victor Gordon. For them I couldn't figure a reason. Nate told me Gordon wasn't fighting against the union. And Paul? Why should he start making up to me so lovey dovey if he really wanted to get rid of me?

Back in my apartment, the little people hammering inside my head already went away and left me hungry. I found a bagel, sliced it, and put it in the toaster. There was still some cream cheese and a couple slices of lox left in the icebox. Along with hot tea and an apple, it made a nice, quick lunch. Way better than any hospital mishmash.

While I was eating, my eye caught the Society page of the *Sunday Globe.* I'd saved it for the part about Joey's engagement. There was another announcement, that Mrs. Morris Nadler was hosting a Hadassah tea today at Temple Shalom in Newton. My brain gave a click. Felice Nadler was Joey's fiancee. How did she fit into this whole picture?

THIRTEEN

It was a cinch to find the Nadler number in the phone book and dial it. A girl's voice answered.

"Mrs. Morris Nadler, please," I said.

"She's not at home. Can I take a message?"

"I'm speaking to her secretary?"

"No, this is her daughter, Felice."

"I'll call later," I said, and hung up. A chance to catch Felice Nadler at home alone, just what I wanted. Where was she Friday night when Jeanette was murdered?

A quick change into my navy blue shirtwaist with the white pique collar. Sitting on my bureau was a Helena Rubenstein sample case, a souvenir of my drugstore days. I grabbed it, put my bag over my shoulder, and clapped on my straw hat. A check in the hall mirror. Okay, Appleman, go be a snappy saleslady.

The El took me to Park Street, the streetcar to Cleveland Circle, and the bus to a block away from the Nadler house. Just what I thought. Big white columns in front, a two-story brick set way back. My apartment would fit inside maybe ten times. I rang the bell.

Felice was something like what I expected. About a size 8, suntanned, with smooth brown hair pulled back and tied with a ribbon. An athletic type, dressed in white Bermuda shorts and a white shirt. You could tell right away, a college girl.

"Yes?" she asked.

"I'm here to see Mrs. Morris Nadler," I said. "We made an appointment."

"Oh, I'm sorry," she said, "my mother isn't home."

"We had an appointment." I held up the cosmetic case. "Helena Rubenstein."

"There must be a mix-up," Felice said, "because my mother is at a Hadassah tea this afternoon."

I gave her my Fay Bainter disappointed look. "Oh, and I came all the way from town." I moved closer to the door. "Listen, maybe I could come in and leave some things for her—?"

Felice frowned. "Well, I don't know—"

"And a note," I added quick, "so we wouldn't get mixed up next time."

"I guess it's all right." She moved aside and let me come in. "There's a desk in the library you can use." She led me into a room with books and sofas and stuffed chairs. Fancier than the West End Branch of the Boston Public Library.

I turned and faced her. "Felice, I didn't come to see your mother. I came to see you." Her eyebrows went up. "You know about Jeanette Laval?"

After her dropped jaw got back in place, she said, "Who are you, anyway?"

"I'm Belle Appleman," I said. "A friend of Joey's."

I had to give her credit. She got over the first shock right away, like a champion fighter. "Please sit down," she said, pointing to one of the chairs. She sat across from me. "I don't understand why you're here."

"I'm the one who found Jeanette's body in the river. And I'm trying to find out who killed her."

She jumped up from the chair. Felice was either a good actress or she was really surprised. "Killed? What do you mean? Didn't she jump?"

I shook my head. "No, Felice. She was murdered. So why I'm here is to ask what you knew about her."

"Me? Absolutely nothing!"

I gave her my Myrna Loy smile. "Nothing? Come on, let's talk. It's good to clear the air." She sat. "First, did you know that Joey is at the Joy Street police station right now?"

She shot up again. A regular jumpingjack. "Police station? What for?"

"On suspicion he killed Jeanette, that's why."

"Oh, that's horrible!" She sat down and held her cheeks in her hands.

"Do you think he did it?"

She took her hands away and looked at me mad. "How can you even ask such a question? Of course not! Joey could never kill anyone!"

"But you knew about him and Jeanette, didn't you?" I asked.

She opened her mouth and closed it again without saying a word.

So I said right away, "Joey told me everything."

"Okay, I did know," she admitted, after a minute. Her chin went higher. "I came to the studio once without calling. There she was, naked as a jaybird, and Joey painting away. I hated her the minute I saw her." She stopped to take a big gulp of air. "After I came in, she got dressed and left. But the way she acted, as if she belonged there—" She wiped her forehead with the back of her hand, like she was sweating.

"So you could tell—" I didn't finish, she looked so miserable already.

"Joey and I had a terrible fight about it."

"When was that?" I asked.

"Oh, I don't remember exactly. About three weeks ago—"

"But you made up with Joey right after?"

She swallowed. "Look, Miss—I forgot your name—"

"Mrs. Belle Appleman."

"Mrs. Appleman, I've known Joey all my life. I guess I've been in love with him from—well, from the time when I figured out what the word 'love' means. Kindergarten, maybe. I just assumed that he loved me, too, and we'd get married after college."

"But the business with Joey's painting and his father—?"

She bit her lip. "That didn't help. But it was all working out, honestly. When he came here Saturday, he insisted that the affair with that—that girl was over."

"Listen, Felice," I told her, "the police are going to come and ask you questions. Did you see Joey Friday night? Or talk to him on the phone?"

She shook her head. "No, he just called up Saturday morning and said he was coming over."

"So you don't know where Joey was Friday night?"

She shook her head again. "No, I don't. Why? Is it important?"

"Because Joey needs an alibi for the night Jeanette was murdered."

She wrapped her hands around herself, like she was feeling cold, even though the room was warm. "I could say I was with him," she said half to herself.

"No," I said. "Lying is the worst thing you could do." I looked straight at her. "Where were *you* Friday night?"

"Right here, at home. One of my girlfriends was supposed to come over, but she had a last-minute date."

"Were your father and mother here?"

"No, they went out about seven-thirty."

"And they came back?"

"Late probably, I was asleep."

"Anybody call you on the telephone?"

She shook her head. "I don't think so. I did my hair and read a book."

"Oh?" Would a classy young girl spend a weekend night alone reading? "What was the name of it?"

Her eyebrows gave a twitch, she only hesitated for a second. "*The Thin Man*," she said, in a voice that got a little snooty, like she didn't expect someone like me to know from books. "By Dashiell Hammett."

"One of my favorites," I let her know. The movie, naturally. "The nifty way Myrna Loy figures things out."

She moistened her lips. "Mrs. Appleman, are you a private detective?"

I gave a little laugh. "Me? Maybe. But I also work in the factory." I reached out my hand. "Good-bye, Felice. I want to wish you and Joey the best. And don't ever let him stop painting," I said, "even if he has to keep working in the factory."

She had a strong grip, the grip of an athlete. Strong enough to keep Jeanette Laval's head underwater somewhere Friday night? I looked back after I walked down the street a little. She was still standing in the doorway, watching me.

Now, what did I find out after all that? Plenty.

First, Felice Nadler hated Jeanette like anything. With good reason. She knew Jeanette was stealing Joey away from her. Maybe for keeps.

Second, Felice had no alibi for Friday night, neither.

FOURTEEN

When I came downstairs from the El at the Charles Street Circle, I meant to go right home and take it easy. But crossing West Cedar Street, I looked at the buildings that crept up the sides of Beacon Hill. That reminded me of the card I saw in Joey's studio. Arnie Silverstein, M.D. Joey's doctor, my old friend from the Myrtle Drug. He lived right up there on Mount Vernon Street. So, why not? Of course, he might still be in his Back Bay office, but what did I have to lose, a few steps extra up the Hill? All of a sudden I felt peppier.

Naturally, a lot of people would raise their eyebrows at the idea of a woman going alone to a man's apartment. If Sarah knew I was doing that, she'd have a fit. Especially someone like Arnie Silverstein, already divorced twice. But that cut no ice with Belle Appleman, Detective. I made a right turn and headed for his house.

When I rang the bell, his voice asked who it was.

"Arnie, it's me, Belle Appleman. You got a minute?"

"Belle? The Madonna of the Myrtle Drug?" He sounded surprised. "Sure, come on up." The buzzer buzzed to let me in. His apartment was one flight up.

Arnie Silverstein was fiftyish and fat. Two more reasons I didn't worry about going to his apartment by myself. How fast could he move? He opened the door and gave me a big hug and kiss on the cheek. "Belle, no see long time already!"

That was Arnie, always saying things backwards. I wondered if he would still be so lovey-dovey when he found out why I came. He ushered me into the living room. Psychiatrists make a good week's pay, I don't have to tell you. Some fancy-shmancy apartment. In the front hall, a big Chinese vase with umbrellas sticking out of it. Wall-to-wall carpets you sunk in up to the ankles. In the living room, everything cream-colored. Lots of mirrors. All the furniture velvety and squashy. Another thing I noticed on the coffee table and on every table in the room, bowls filled with nibbles—mixed nuts, raisins, chocolates, Jordan almonds, stuffed dates, Hershey kisses, bonbons, and fruit. I wondered if this time Arnie married a hungry decorator. I sat on the sofa.

"It's nice to see you again, Arnie," I said. "You're married now?"

He shook his head no. "After two strikeouts, I thought I'd better sit on the bench a while." He held out a silver bowl. "Have some mixed nuts." I took a cashew. "It's good to see you, too, Belle. What have you been up to? Can I get you something to drink?"

"You got maybe a glass ginger ale?" I asked.

"Cliquot Club, what else?" He grabbed a handful of nuts, crammed them in his mouth, and chewed his way to the kitchen. For a man his age and shape he moved pretty good. In a minute he was back with a tall, bubbling glass.

I took a sip. "Thanks, Arnie."

He came over, sat beside me, and munched a stuffed date. "So, to what do I owe the pleasure of this visit, Belle?"

"I'm glad I found you home, Arnie," I said. "Listen, you remember how we used to have arguments about the cases in *True Detective*? With Jim Connors?"

A little light came in his eyes. Still chewing, he leaned over to a bowl of fruit. "Have an apple, Belle?" I shook my head, but when he kept on I took a small bunch of grapes. He bit into his apple. "Ah, those were the days. Nothing relaxed me more after a tough day than those arguments." He made a tsk-tsk sound with his tongue. "Too bad about the Myrtle Drug. A regular home-away-from-home."

"Hard times," I sighed. "So, where do you go now?"

"Charles Street Pharmacy," he said. "You know, Harry White's place. I see Jim there sometimes, having a cribbage game with Harry."

"Harry I know, my Daniel was once his pharmacist." So now I knew where Jim Connors played cribbage. Was he still trying to stay away from his family? From his wife? He never mentioned a thing about his personal life. Arnie could know, but that I wouldn't ask.

"Listen, Arnie," I began, "don't laugh, but I'm working on a case."

"No kidding." Arnie finished his apple, put the core in an ashtray and scooped a handful of raisins. "What kind of case?"

"Murder," I told him.

That made him sit up straight. "Anyone I know?"

"Maybe," I said. "You got a patient named Joey Gordon, right?"

His face tightened up a little. I didn't blame him. Doctors don't like to talk about patients with someone on the outside.

"Why, is he mixed up in it?" He chomped on the raisins.

"Hoo-ha!" I told him about my job in the factory and Jeanette Laval in the Charles River. "She was Joey's model, posed for him naked. And did more, also—" I took a swallow of ginger ale. The bubbles went up my nose and made me give a little sneeze.

"*Gezundheit!*" Arnie bit a Jordan almond in half. "So—?"

He waited for me while I took out a handkerchief and blew my nose.

"So," I said, tucking the handkerchief back in my bag, "I want to know why Joey is coming to see you."

Arnie frowned and finished crunching up the Jordan almond. "Why?"

"Because he's being questioned by the police in the Joy Street station. The number-one suspect in the Laval murder case."

I gave Arnie credit, he had good control. Are psychiatrists also actors? He reached over and began to work on a handful of mixed nuts. "Belle, you know I can't violate physician-patient confidence. So forget it. Have a chocolate cream."

"No, thanks." I drank up the ginger ale and put down the glass. "What'll happen when the police find out Joey's your patient? It's murder, Arnie. They'll be here with bells on. To ask you the same question like I am."

He finished the last pecan and dug into the raisins. "I've had plenty of experience with the police, Belle. Believe me, I can handle it. So let's forget Joey Gordon and have a nice visit, shall we?" He patted my hand. These brain doctors know their onions. Arnie managed to say it in such a nice way with a chummy patting like a brother. But you couldn't mistake the voice underneath. No dice, sister, it said.

The telephone rang. "Excuse me." He hopped up to go into what looked like study and closed the door.

Some detective you are, Appleman. So far you managed just to tell Arnie what he didn't know yet, instead of the other way around. Was I just going to spend this visit watching Arnie grow fatter?

Use your bean, now, it only got a bump on top. Of course, Arnie was nobody's fool.

"Sorry to keep you waiting, Belle. Have you tried the glacéed fruit?" He came back and sat down.

"No, thanks." I watched him sampling a ring of candied pineapple. "Listen, this story you'll remember from the old days, we all argued about it. The Chicago case, the crazy who chopped his wife in little pieces? The judge ruled his psychiatrist *had to* testify. Remember? On account of the doctor-patient relation didn't hold. Because it was a homicide." He was leaning back, listening. "So, you'll see, it won't hold here, neither. The girl was murdered, Arnie. Jim Connors'll be here asking questions. You know him, he's a regular Johnny-on-the spot. Fat chance you'll have to finagle with him! You'll just have to tell him what's what with Joey."

Arnie was chewing his lower lip instead of the raisins. "Have a heart, kiddo—"

"Listen," I said, "this is your old friend, Belle Appleman, speaking. You know I'm not a blabbermouth. And I'm working with Jim on the case, honest. Right now Joey's in trouble. He's got no alibi for Friday night, that's when she was killed. And there's something else. She was carrying a baby—three months pregnant. Even though they don't really know, the police probably figure it's Joey's."

He scratched his head. "Look, Belle, I just can't—"

"Arnie, anything you tell me, it stays private. I'll only tell Jim the part I think is important. You got a *mezuzah* on your door? I'll swear on that!"

He laughed and picked up a stuffed date. "Belle, I sure get a kick out of you! There's nothing terribly the matter with Joey. He's suffering from too much family pressure. Trying to be something he doesn't want to be, that's all. Like lots of young people."

"I know all about that," I said. "Look, does he have sometimes spells, he can't remember things he did?"

Arnie gave me a sharp look and bit into the date. "Oh, come on, Belle, you know I can't tell you things like that."

"Listen, Arnie, all I want to know is, could he do something and not remember he did it?"

Arnie shrugged. "There are cases of people who have fugues." He swallowed the rest of the date.

"What?"

"It's nothing uncommon, you know."

"Hmmm." I thought for a minute. This gave Arnie a chance to pick up a Hershey kiss and undress it in a split second. "What about something else he told me? That in the factory office everyone has secrets and they're not telling him a thing? You think he's making that up?"

Arnie scratched the hairs still there on the back of his head. "Fact is, I'm not sure he's even my patient anymore."

"What do you mean?"

"I got a call from him. Drunk as a skunk, said he didn't need me, wasn't coming back. Didn't want all his secrets uncovered by a prying head doctor." He studied a chocolate and bit into the filling. "Hmm, nougat."

"What I want to know—" I leaned toward him. "Could Joey do something—like killing that girl, for instance—and not even remember he did it?"

He kept munching till the nougat got swallowed. "Sorry, I'll have to pass on that one." He straightened up. "Say, let me get you some ice cream. Two kinds in the freezer, mocha and frozen pudding."

Before I could say no, thanks, the phone rang again and Arnie went to answer it. I hopped up and went over to some bookshelves in the alcove and hunted up a big fat dictionary. I pulled it out and found the word *fugue*.

"In psychiatry, a state of psychological amnesia during which a patient seems to behave in a conscious and rational way, although upon return to normal consciousness he cannot remember the period of time nor what he did during it. A temporary flight from reality."

Okay, Arnie, I said to myself, you don't have to answer no more questions, you already gave me the important word. When Arnie came back, the dictionary was on the shelf and I was sitting down.

He looked at his watch. "Hey, it's almost five o'clock, I'm starving. How about my taking you out to dinner? Sort of a welcome-back party. A chance to wine and dine a mysterious detective from my past. What about the Copley Plaza? Let's live it up!"

How could he be hungry after setting a record for nonstop nibbling? Anyway, my head wasn't up to a night out. "You're a sport, Arnie," I said. "It's the nicest invitation I got today. But I just can't tonight. You'll maybe give me a rain check?"

He brightened up. "Sure. Here, write down your phone number." He found a pen and a prescription pad on the desk. "I'll give you a ring, and we'll have a night on the town."

Nu, Appleman, you got a new admirer. "Sounds terrific, Arnie," I said. "And thanks a million for the dope on Joey."

His hand reached out and grabbed a bunch of grapes, which he popped into his mouth one at a time as he walked me to the door. "So long," I said, and gave him a peck on the cheek.

He gave me back a hug. "Be seeing you." A big Teddy bear, gobbling up goodies.

On my way down the Hill I turned over in my head what Arnie told me. Temporary amnesia. So was that why Joey answered like he did when I asked him where he was Friday night? Was he covering up on account of he couldn't remember? Boy, this was something for Jim Connors to grab hold of.

When I got near my place on Allen Street a car was standing in front of the house. A black sedan. A man got out and waited for me.

Paul Warshafsky. "Belle! Where've you been? I've been waiting nearly an hour. I didn't hear about your accident till this afternoon. And when I called the hospital, they said you'd checked out. Are you all right?" He grabbed both my hands in his.

"Ouch, my finger—"

"Oh, I'm sorry!" He dropped the hand with the bandage. "Didn't even notice—"

"It's nothing, I'm really okay," I said.

"Boy, you sure had me worried." He let go the other hand and looked at his watch. "Tell me, have you had dinner yet?"

"No—"

"Good. I'm taking you out."

Out. With Paul. All of a sudden my head didn't feel funny no more. "I have to clean up a bit—"

"No rush." He opened the front door of the house for me.

"It'll only take me a minute." Upstairs I didn't exactly trust Mr. Warshafsky. "You'll wait here? I'll be down in two shakes—"

"Sure." He sounded disappointed. "Take your time."

I heard an upstairs window slam shut. Mrs. Wallenstein was keeping track of the men in my life.

FIFTEEN

You want good Jewish cooking, you go to Meltzer's, where else? Only you got to bring two stomachs. Meltzer's restaurant is down on Harrison Avenue in the garment district. The menu is a list a mile long—sweet and sour stuffed cabbage, potato *latkes,* brisket, stuffed *derma,* noodle *kugel,* pot roast with prunes, chopped chicken liver, pickled herring— go make up your mind. The most dangerous thing that could happen to a person at Meltzer's, you could die from overeating.

So that's where Paul took me, not to the Copley Plaza. Entering the dark paneled room on his arm made lots of heads turn, especially women's. It was almost like going out with a movie star. Right away I was Jeanette MacDonald with Nelson Eddy.

And I didn't have to stand around and wait ages for a table, like when I came for supper with Sarah. At once the headwaiter came over. The place was crowded but we were seated in a flash. Believe me, the whole world acts different when you're out with a man.

The waiter appeared, a skinny guy in the regulation black suit and bow tie. "What'll it be, ladies and gentlemen?" he asked, as if there was a bunch of us.

Paul wasn't the kind who waits forever, he made up his mind fast.

"Something light for me, the baked salmon sounds good, in this weather."

He looked at me. Right then it didn't matter one bit what I ate. What Bette Davis said in one of her movies came into my mind.

"Why don't you order for both of us?" I suggested, handing my menu back to the waiter, who almost dropped it, he was so surprised. Most ladies in Meltzer's worry over every item in the meal, this he wasn't used to. He just stared at me. But it was easy to see Paul enjoyed my idea, it made him feel he was running the show. So Bette Davis was right.

In the car we already talked over all the details of my accident. Naturally, I didn't mention what Jim Connors told me, that it was no accident. So, to figure out more about Paul Warshafsky, I got him started telling me about his early years in the union.

So I tried to be a good listener, like the *Ladies' Home Journal* advised. With Paul it was easy, he was a good talker. After a while I said, "The union's your real work, all right. But to tell you the truth, Paul, I feel a little funny about being shop steward so quick. It was only a couple days ago Nate and I found Jeanette Laval's body. What I noticed was people in the pants shop were shocked, absolutely. But nobody cried, hardly a tear came out of anyone's eyes. Nobody seems to miss her, do they?"

Paul sat up straighter. "What kind of question is that? Of course we miss her. But there's bound to be jealousy when a woman's as beautiful as she was."

"She was shop steward, so you knew her pretty good, right?"

The waiter's hands thrust the steaming salmon under our noses. I picked up my fork, waiting for Paul's answer.

He just shrugged. "You could say that."

I stabbed my salmon. "But is being jealous reason enough to make somebody want to kill? Gertrude Scharf, you know who she is? Well, she was plenty jealous of Jeanette. But enough to murder—?"

Paul shook his head. "That's for the police to figure out, isn't it? That detective friend of yours, what's his name—Conroy?"

"Connors. Jim Connors. Talking about Jim, remember what you told him—about where you were the night Jeanette was killed?"

"Sure. Bowling with Sam."

I shook my head. "No, you weren't, Paul. Sam was with Gertrude."

His eyebrows went up. "How'd you know that?"

"Gertrude told me herself. You were covering for each other. So why did you tell a lie?"

"A white lie," he corrected. "Just helping to smooth the path of true love."

"So where were you really that Friday night?"

"Well, if you must know—" He took a sip of coffee. "I was home. Painting my kitchen."

"What color paint?"

Paul laughed. "You certainly do ask questions. Well, light blue, actually." He shook his head. "You got that out of Gertrude—I'll be damned!"

"I took some lessons from Connors," I told him.

He picked up his knife and fork. "Come on, Belle, let's not spoil a nice evening. Try the salmon."

I took a bite. Paul was smart, it was delicious. While I ate I looked around the room. Some of the women were still sneaking glances at Paul. And sizing me up, also. I was glad I made him wait downstairs long enough for me to put on a new face.

For a while we just enjoyed our food, smiling at each other now and then. Returning Warshafsky's smile came easy, I thought, buttering a piece of roll. But getting him to open up about that girl was going to be no cinch.

In the middle of dessert, raspberry sherbet, he put down his spoon and took my hand. "You know how important the union is to all of us, Belle."

"I know, all right. When I first came to this country, a young girl, I worked in a shirtwaist factory." I told him about the sweatshop, all of us crowded in like hens in a coop, stifling. Three dollars a week for ten hours a day. Always afraid you'd find that pink slip in the envelope: Your services are no longer required. After I married Daniel I never went back.

He gave my hand a squeeze. "So you suffered, too, Belle. You understand. But there's trouble here at Local 135. You saw what happened at the meeting."

I nodded. "Some *tararam*! Nate came over and got me out."

"I'm glad. I tried to find you but you were gone. Well, as secretary, I've begun to see things going on that I don't like. Things that could destroy the union we've all worked so hard to build. And you know what that means."

He knitted those handsome eyebrows to make lines in that tanned forehead.

"Back to the sweatshops," I sighed.

He nodded. "Right. And that's what I'm trying to fight." He leaned toward me and his voice took on a confidential tone. "Belle, you're going to be taking on the duties of shop steward. You can help the union in a very important way. But first, I want you to promise that what I tell you is just between us, understand?"

I gave him my Joan Crawford look and told him I understood.

"Belle, listening to the way you talked to Gordon and Karsh, I knew right away you were a very special person. The union needs someone like you to help keep an eye on what's going on, someone with detective skills. It's impossible for me to do it alone, along with my work in the cutting room."

I gave a sympathetic nod.

He kept those green-flecked eyes on mine. "It's just a question of keeping your eyes and ears open for me. And if you hear talk about breaking the union, you report it. Does that sound like the wrong way to go about it?"

My sherbet glass was empty. I took a sip of tea. "Why wrong? You're trying to save the union, no? So what could be bad?"

Paul turned on that smile that could change a woman into a bowl of Jello. He reached in his pocket and took out a package of cigarettes. Raleighs, with the union label, naturally. "D'you mind?" He offered me one but I shook my head no. Then he lit his cigarette with a small silver lighter. Maybe he was for the working class but he sure liked nice things.

"What you mean is," I said to him, "you want me to be a spy. Like Greta Garbo in *Mata Hari*."

He threw back his head and laughed. "Belle, you're terrific! I'll bet you'd make a better Mata Hari than Garbo." His tone became serious. "In a way you're right. It's a real war and we're all soldiers. The enemy's out there, the bosses. Something funny's going on in the front office—typewriters get used at night. Are Gordon and Karsh up to something?"

"How'd you find that out?" I asked. "Besides, if the bosses own the typewriters, why can't they use them?"

He smiled. "Good point. But why should they be typing letters at night when there are secretaries around during the day? And remember, the bosses have their spies, too. Besides, things are going on among our own that I don't like."

A picture came into my head of Joey Gordon saying something was cooking inside the offices, but nobody was telling him anything. Was there a connection with what Paul was saying? And Paul was making everything sound so mysterious and exciting. At the same time a little bell was ringing in my ear, singing careful, careful, careful. It sounded like Nate and Sarah together. That made me decide.

"Okay, Paul," I said, "I'll join your—what do you call it? You have a special name?"

He smiled. "No name. And you don't report to me. Someone will contact you. The fewer direct lines between us the better, you understand?"

I understood, all right. He expected me to say yes, he had a place all set up for me. And I sure fell for it. Never mind. How else could a detective find out what was really going on?

But on the way home, I realized I never knew a man like Paul before. Open but filled with secrets. Flirty but serious. A puzzle. To figure out what made him tick would be a pleasure. At least till I found out where he stood with Jeanette Laval. And if he was away from the factory on purpose when I had the accident.

But to be alone with him in my apartment, that I wasn't ready for. Not yet, anyway. So when the car came to a stop in front of my apartment house, I said, "Don't bother getting out, it's late," and hopped out.

"I never leave a lady in the street," he said, getting out and coming around behind me. So much for your brilliant plan to get away, Appleman. He held the door open and then followed me up the stairs.

Again he was making me feel like a flustered teenager. Better I should've paid my own dinner check. Did I owe him something in return? No, that would be like selling your company for the evening, payment for services rendered. Relax, Appleman, you're behaving like a dope in the man-woman game. You're out of practice. And you're dealing with a specialist.

Ask him in for coffee? And then? Better not. It was late, tomorrow was a work day, we'd had tea already in Meltzer's. I could think up a million reasons. In a minute we were on the landing in front of my door. I began to fish wildly around in my bag for the key. "It's here someplace," I said nervously.

"Take your time." He smiled and leaned against the doorframe.

I found the key and held it up to show him. "Thanks for the dinner, Paul, and the lesson about unions."

He picked the key from my hand and put it in the lock. I caught my breath. Was he coming in? Then he put his hand out and I put mine in his, thinking he wanted to shake hands goodnight. But he pulled me to him, and all of a sudden he was kissing me. Hard, on my lips. And my other hand was creeping all by itself around his neck.

Just then the heads of Mr. and Mrs. Wallenstein appeared, coming up the stairs. That woke me up enough to grab my hand back like it was on a hot stove. I pulled myself out of Paul's arms, twisted the key in the lock, and flung open the door.

"Goodnight, Paul," I threw over my shoulder as I dashed in and closed the door behind me. I leaned against it to catch my breath and heard him call softly, "Goodnight, Belle. Sweet dreams."

Oy, the Wallensteins were on their way to the third floor, listening to every word. I could hear Paul's footsteps going down the stairs, it seemed to me he was humming.

Standing there, I realized I was shaking a little. I went in the bathroom, put on the light, and looked at the feverish woman in the mirror.

What is it with you, Appleman, all this because a man gave you a kiss?

Don't start with alibis, the mirror shot back. What was your hand doing while he was kissing? It didn't push him away.

It happened too quick. Who had time to do anything?

Cut it out, kiddo. You're falling for this guy.

Hoo-ha, I told the mirror, I'm only checking him out. Like with Sam and Gertrude. Like with Felice. He's a suspect, that's all.

Clark Gable should be such a suspect.

In the bedroom first thing I did was to set the alarm for the next day. One morning late, look what happened. Pulling off my earrings, I began to wonder about what he asked me to do in the factory. Why me? It would be nice to think it was on account of my *saichel.* But he didn't hardly know me yet, wasn't he taking a big chance? He sure was no dumbbell, just the opposite. But spying for him I wasn't so glad about. Was that the best way to help the union?

And look how fast he steered our talk away from Jeanette Laval. "Of course we miss her," he said. We. Meaning the whole gang, not Paul himself. Not one word about how he felt when he picked up the Sunday *Globe* and read about her. Nobody's made from stone, didn't he get all upset? Or how come? On account of he already knew?

Listen, Appleman, I told myself, a real detective wouldn't get all mixed up right away with someone that's sort of involved. What's with you, anyway? You know he's just another smooth operator, the kind you always ran from. You know what he's like, he expects a woman to tumble into his arms, bing, bang, just like that.

And you tumbled.

SIXTEEN

Thinking about what I promised Paul at dinner made me mad at myself. No use trying to sleep, I went in the kitchen. When I get excited and mad, I get hungry. So, in spite of the Meltzer dinner that was still getting digested somewhere inside me, I made a cup tea, took some *mandelbrot* out of the cookie can, and nibbled.

That got me calmed down. I was sipping my tea when the phone rang.

"Belle!" Sarah's voice spluttered. "Where were you? I went to the hospital and what did I see? An empty bed! I thought, God forbid, something terrible happened! Nate came also—you should've seen his face. How come you didn't stay overnight like the doctor said?"

"Sarah," I apologized, "I'm so sorry, honest. To make you go there again, for nothing! I feel terrible."

"Some terrible," she snapped. "All evening I'm trying to call you, you're not even home! That shock maybe did something to your head? What's got into you? You couldn't even telephone, you already forgot my number?"

"Sarah, have a heart," I begged. "I couldn't call tonight early on account of I got taken out to dinner. I'm only home a few minutes."

"Nate took you out?"

"No, somebody else. He's from the factory, the union also. See, I got elected shop steward, so—"

"I heard already, Nate told me," she said. "So from the hospital you went out on a date?"

"Not to a nightclub, we only had dinner in Meltzer's. Look, I'm home, already in my nightgown." That didn't sound right. "I mean, he's real nice, Sarah, honest."

"*Mazel tov,* congratulations."

"What? It's just business!"

"Listen, it's okay by me," she remarked.

"Look, Sarah, can we talk about the case? A million new developments already, I'll fill you in." I told her everything. "But meantime, you wouldn't forget, you're gonna talk to the girl's mother after the funeral. Mrs. Laval, remember?"

"I remember," she sighed. "I'm not crazy about it, neither—"

"Don't worry, Sarah, you'll be terrific. Like always. Listen, I'll call you, okay? And I'm awful sorry about today—"

She said it was okay before she hung up. Sarah's a good sport.

Tired like anything, I still couldn't help dialing the Joy Street station. Jim Connors was there, like usual. Didn't he ever go home?

"Jim, it's Belle."

"Belle, what's going on? I called the hospital, and they said you'd checked out. Tried your home phone, but nobody answered. Where've you been?"

"I'm fine, Jim, honest. Just out gadding around, that's all. Listen, what's with Joey? You still suspect him?"

"We let him go. But he's got no alibi at all, says he can't even remember. Pretty lame excuse, if you ask me. Say, it's none of my business, but should you be running around, just out of the hospital?"

"Hospitals give me the heebiejeebies," I said. "Guess what, I had a talk with Joey's psychiatrist."

"He goes to one of *them*? How'd you manage to worm that out of young Gordon?"

"Who wormed? Just happened to see Arnie Silverstein's card in Joey's apartment."

"You mean he's Arnie's patient."

"That's what I said. Anyway, it was some business trying to get Arnie to give me the dope on Joey. But he finally let fly with one of those fancy words they throw around to mix people up."

"What're you talking about?"

"So I looked it up in his dictionary. It's simple. Means Joey might not remember what he did Friday night. Maybe—"

"Hold on. What was that word, Belle?"

"Fugue. It's spelled funny, f-u-g-u-e."

"Nice work, Belle." He sounded surprised. "For someone who just got a knockout punch, you sure snap back fast."

"Also, I had a little talk with Joey's girl. That he's engaged to, Felice Nadler."

"All this today?" He gave a groan. "I suppose she confessed to the murder?"

"I'm getting important information and he's making wisecracks," I sighed. "You're paying attention? Two things I got from her. First, she knew what was going on with Joey and Jeanette. So she hated her something terrible. Second, she's got no alibi for Friday night, neither."

"Hmph, another one. All these people, all by themselves on a weekend night," he remarked. "But that Nadler girl doesn't sound too hot as a suspect. It's pretty normal for a young girl to be jealous over her fiancé's yen for another woman. Can't make much of a case for murder out of that."

"But a detective has to consider every possibility, no?"

His brogue came back. "Belle, darlin', you're full of trump cards. Now, will you behave yourself and get some rest?"

"G'night, Jim," I said. "Don't worry, we'll cop a murderer yet."

Now he got real serious. "After that close shave this morning, I do worry about you. Be careful, now, I'm not kidding. Let us do the work, we're getting paid for it. Promise?"

"Whatever you say, Jim."

"Mmm. You take care of yourself, now. Sleep well."

Fat chance Appleman would quit. Still, Jim shouldn't be worrying, he had his own troubles. All of a sudden all my bones began to ache like they were ready to fall off their hinges. My head, too. It didn't take ten seconds before I crawled into bed. My brain felt all blurry, full of pictures of Paul floating around, his eyes across the dinner table, his hand pressing mine, his smile as my fingers fumbled with the keys . . . stop, better think about what he said . . . but before I could even think about what to think, I feel asleep.

After breakfast I fixed a clean bandage on my finger. It was a little burn, all white around the edges, it only hurt if I banged it. When I came into the pants shop there was a regular *tarrarom*, the girls all crowding around asking questions. I said thanks, I was okay, about twenty times to different people. For some reason Sam Rothberg and Gertrude were extra nice to me. Made me wonder, were they sorry for something they did?

Nate came in a little later from the cutting room. He didn't smile. "I went after work to the hospital. Where were you?"

"I know, I know," I said, "I already heard from Sarah last night. I'm sorry you had a trip for nothing. But after I left the hospital, I got busy talking to people about—"

"Don't tell me," he interrupted, "about who killed Laval, yes?" The light bouncing off his glasses hid his eyes. "You're still mixing in, Belle, there's no stopping you. So maybe the accident yesterday was fixed up on purpose?"

"Have a heart, Nate," I said. "Don't start in."

He shrugged and turned to go, then he stopped. "And I was tickled pink to get you a steady job." He turned around and went back to the cutting room.

Gertrude heard the whole conversation, she gave me a look over her machine. I paid no attention and picked up my work where I left off.

Later I had to go to the ladies' room. While I was at the sink a voice said, "Golly, you've been doing all right for yourself from what I've been hearing."

I grabbed a paper towel and turned around to see who it was. Lillian Lewis, the head secretary to the bosses. She fished a comb out of her handbag and pushed in front of the mirror over the sink to start fixing her blond pageboy.

"What do you mean?" I asked.

She put her comb back in her purse. "Can I talk to you a minute?"

My hand was already on the doorknob. A kind of funny place to gab, just white tile and a small wooden bench against the wall. "For a minute, why not?" I answered.

"Here, let's take a load off our feet." She sat down on the bench. I sat also. What did she have to say to me, she looked so cool and sure of herself? She'd never ask for my advice. I found myself picking threads off my plaid gingham dress.

"Actually, it's lucky we met here, this is a good spot while no one's around," she began. "Maybe we should have all our meetings here."

All our meetings? What was she talking about?

She crossed her legs and leaned back. "I'm your contact," she said, pronouncing every word slow, like I was deaf.

I stared at her for a minute. Then I got it. "You're the one I'm supposed to report to, in case I hear anything funny, you mean?"

"Gee, you catch on quick," she said. It didn't sound like no compliment.

"I was surprised when Warsh—" I began, but she interrupted me right away.

"We never use names, remember that." She reached in her bag, took out a small white card, and put it in my hand. "Here's my phone number in case you need it." Her eyes got narrow. "Just because he took you out to dinner," she said in a nasty voice, "don't get any ideas."

I was too surprised to answer. Did she have her hooks into Paul? What did she mean by that crack? Did she maybe say the same thing to Jeanette Laval? And did Jeanette maybe pay no attention?

"Got to get back now," she was saying, standing up. "Old man Karsh'll have a stroke. Listen, if you want me for anything, come by the office and give me the eye. Then come in here and wait, okay?"

"Okay," I echoed, following her out the door. Her high heels tapped in one direction, my sporty sandals the other way. The whole business wasn't one bit like I'd expected. First of all, I wanted to know more about what I was supposed to do, like what was important to tell and what wasn't. Then, I figured my contact would be someone more like Paul, his words about the union sounded like a rabbi's sermon. This ritzy secretary was the last person you'd expect to help fellow workers.

What a funny way to help the union! Meeting Lillian Lewis in the middle of all that white tile, with the strong smell of Pinesol and the sound of a dripping toilet, didn't sound like what I'd seen in spy movies, exactly. Paul believed in what he said. That you could tell. But to be a tattle-tale for Lillian Lewis, it just made me feel sneaky. I stuck her card in my right-hand patch pocket to think about later.

During lunch a bunch of us straggled over to the park on the Embankment. Sometimes it was a surprise to see that the sky was still there, cloud-sprinkled blue, and the grass and trees just the right shade green to cool you off. It made me wonder lots of times, which was the real world, the factory or the park? Or was the real world what you carried around in your head, wherever you were? Because right now I wanted to forget that high-toned secretary and enjoy my pastrami sandwich. But her words stuck in the back of my head like one of those burrs that clings to your stocking and leaves a snag when you pull it off.

Paul must've got in touch with her last night after he left. Or this morning. So he must know her pretty good. What did he say to put her on her high horse about my not getting ideas? I chewed angrily on my sandwich. *Nu*, Appleman, I said to myself, why should you care how many women he's chummy with? Let him run one of those harems, what do you care. Only you're not going to join it.

Right after lunch, while I was tacking away on my loops, Paul Warshafsky came in the pants shop. The same restless thrill among the girls. He asked Sam to shut off the power for a minute. "Listen, everyone," he announced, "I just want to remind you Jeanette Laval's funeral is tomorrow afternoon. The factory will close down at noon so we can all attend. The time and place are posted downstairs next to the time clock, so please make a note of them when you leave tonight. Let's show her family how the union sticks together. I'd like to see one hundred-percent attendance at the services. Thanks, everyone."

Sam pushed the handle of the power switch down and the machines came back to life. Paul spread that smile around to all the girls and gave a wink in my direction before he left.

A little later Selma Weiss came over to me. "Gee, Belle, look at this bundle of pockets, there's something wrong with them. No matter how I try to sew them on, they don't come out right, they pucker all up at the top. See? I got to make an extra fold to get them on." She showed me one.

"Hoo-ha," I said, "they're all like that?"

She nodded. "Jeepers, what should I do? They'll blame me if they're lumpy like this." Her usual sallow complexion was mottled with red, she was aggravated. "You're the shop steward now, you're supposed to know."

Hurray for getting elected shop steward so quick, this was one of the blessings that came with the job. *Nu*, where to begin? I looked around. There was Sam Rothberg down at the other end, repairing a machine for one of the girls.

"You got something else you could do now, Selma?"

She made a face, squashing the end of her nose with a finger. "Well, I could do some waist linings. We're behind on them on accounta these pockets."

"So work on them and don't worry. I'll find out about this." It was easy to tell her not to worry, I wasn't sure what to do myself.

Selma handed me a pocket. "Gee, thanks, Belle, I sure wouldn't wanna lose a day's pay. Here's the bundle tag, too." She rubbed her nose again and left.

So where should I start? I was gazing at the well-filled rear view of Sam Rothberg bending over. It seemed as good a place to begin as any. I walked over.

"Say, Sam," I told his backside, "there's a big problem with these pockets." He straightened up fast, very red in the face from being upside down. I waved the pocket under his fleshy nose. "Selma says the whole bundle's cut wrong, she can't work on them."

It was like waving a red flag in front of a bull. "Listen," he snarled, "I got plenty to do here today, I gotta get this machine fixed somehow, or we'll get way behind." He took out a blue-printed bandanna from his back pocket and wiped the sweat off his forehead. "Don't bother me with that stuff! Go find Karsh, he's in charge of production, let him handle the headaches. Or go in the cutting room, that's where they musta loused it up, that bunch of *knockers,* big shots. They think they're the brains of the place! Me, I got enough trouble right here." He got down on his knees again, cursing.

A swell beginning. *Nu,* I decided, maybe better go up the ladder a little at a time. First the cutting room, then maybe Karsh. I'd find Nate—no, he was sort of mad at me. Paul, then. He had a head on his shoulders, he'd know what to do.

Before I even got into the cutting room I heard loud voices. It was a room with long tables where thick piles of material were spread out and electric cutting machines cut through a bunch of layers all at the same time. The knives were sharp like razors, they had guards to keep you from cutting off a finger. You had to be good to be a cutter. Any little mistake and all the garments would fit wrong, a lot of expensive material would be wasted. That's why the cutters got higher wages than most of the other workers, on account of so much depended on them.

Once, while I was in training, Nate took me in the cutting room and showed me how things were done. There were two big doors in the back wall that opened outward over the alley two floors below. Nate pressed down on the bar of one door to show me how easy they opened. That was where the big bolts of cloth got lifted by chains from the loading platform downstairs. The cloth for the suits was rolled out, one layer at a time, by a machine you could move from one end of the long table to the other. How many layers, you'd be surprised. Some times over a hundred, Nate told me. Then the patterns were put over the top layer of cloth. The lines of the patterns were really made of little holes cut with a wheel, like the kind they sell in the five-and-ten for pie crusts, only bigger. The cutters sprinkled a kind of chalk powder through the holes, and the pattern lines came out on the cloth. The hardest part was figuring out how to lay out the patterns so you wouldn't waste material, just like when you're making a dress at home. Of course, there's always some left over, they sold it for rags or used it to replace little parts which didn't turn out right.

I was surprised, the loud voices belonged to Nate Becker and Marvin Karsh. They were standing facing each other near a table at the other end of the room, and none of the other cutters was doing any work, they were all watching what was going on.

SEVENTEEN

Nate and Karsh were facing each other like two boxers in the ring. I took a few steps into the cutting room, holding Selma's wrinkled piece of cloth. Appleman, you picked a great time to come asking about pockets.

"You guys screwed up a whole unit of our most expensive worsted," Karsh was hollering, his voice high and thin. "You got any idea what that's worth? What do you care, you get your salary just the same, we get the heart attacks!"

Nate pushed his glasses up on his nose. "Every man here knows his job," he said, talking loud but extra slow, like he already said it before. "A mistake like that just ain't possible, even a greenhorn wouldn't do it. I told you yesterday and I'm telling you now, it was the pattern that was wrong." His voice was hoarse.

"We've been using Meyers' patterns for years, we've never had any trouble with them!" Karsh screamed, and waved his pipe around. "You guys are full of excuses! The same old story every time, it's always somebody else's fault. But when it comes to raises and hours and benefits, then you're all Johnny-on-the-spot, ready to fight the whole world. Especially the company that feeds you!"

Nate ran his hand through his hair, it was sticking up in back. "What are we, a bunch of lazy slobs?" he asked, his voice getting hoarser all the time. "We spend our whole lives here, stooping over these tables. But in your mind we're not people, we're just a lot of wage-hour schedules, to figure how much you'll get out of us."

"We put the food on your tables!" shrieked Karsh. "It's a Depression on, suits don't sell good, we got the real headaches! But no, you're so full of that union baloney, brotherhood and solidarity. Before the unions came in, we got along fine! What can you expect, we got a president in Washington acts like a regular Bolshevik. You can't run a business today, you got to ask the government what to pay the workers!"

"Before the unions, there was nothing but sweatshops," answered Nate. "Children worked for pennies a week, I saw it myself."

"To hell with your unions!" yelled Karsh. "If I had my way, I'd throw out every union worker in the place!"

"Better I should see you dead first," said Nate, his voice so low it was almost a croak. He turned his back and walked out of the room.

Every eye, mine too, watched him go. And what we saw also was Victor Gordon standing in the doorway. How long had he been there? Nate just pushed by him without a word and went out. For a minute nobody moved. Then Gordon turned around and left.

"Lousy union agitator," sputtered Karsh, pulling on the ends of his moustache. He looked around the room with all those watchful eyes. "You're all the same, every goddam one of you!" He stuck his pipe between his teeth and marched away.

Without a word the cutters went back to work, spreading patterns over layers of fabric or lifting piles of cut pieces. The bundle boys got busy, also. I spied Paul Warshafsky holding up a pattern, studying it. I walked over, pretending not to notice some of the men eyeing me.

"Belle!" Paul laid the pattern down. "Welcome to the cutting room. What brings you here?" He sounded like we were meeting at a party.

"I came to see Karsh. Tell me, do arguments like that go on all the time? I never heard Nate talk like that. Could he maybe lose his job over it?"

"Don't trouble your curly head over it," Paul said easily. "Sure, we workers have fights with the bosses all the time. Remember, I told you it's a real war we're waging, we all have to take sides. But that blow-up didn't mean a thing, just hot air. Karsh is a nervous Nellie. Nate's one of our best cutters, no one's going to fire him."

"Thank God," I said. "Bad enough to fight with Karsh, Mr. Gordon had to hear, also."

Paul rubbed his chin with his fist. "That's nothing. Our union contract doesn't permit firing without agreement of both sides." He gave me a funny look. "Why, is Becker a special friend of yours?"

Why did he want to know? And what was the answer? "Depends how you mean," I said, kind of slow. "A friend he is, he got me this job when I couldn't find a thing. It would be awful to see him fired in these times."

"Forget it, the whole thing'll blow over by tomorrow. It's only Karsh's way of letting off a little steam, that's all. He's got a jealous wife at home, she's just about what he deserves. She'll get his mind off the class struggle."

"All wives aren't like that," I let him know. I turned to leave, but he grabbed my elbow.

"Wait, Belle. Do you have anything special on for Saturday night?"

That was an easy one. "Nothing special."

"Tell you what, supposing we drive out to Swampscott for a shore dinner. We can eat at the Cliff Manor, there's dancing, too. How about it?"

Dinner on the North Shore. Even the drive sounded snazzy, I loved seeing the rocks and the ocean. And dancing, that was something I didn't do in years, just floating around to music.

Besides, a terrific chance to dig out some answers.

"What time would we go?" I asked.

He smiled, sure of himself as ever. "Pick you up about six-thirty, okay?"

"Okay, it's a date."

He reached over and gave my hand a little squeeze before I hurried back to the pants shop. *Nu*, Selma's pockets better wait till tomorrow. Who could talk to Karsh after that fight? Selma said okay but not to forget.

But the rest of the day, little thoughts kept sneaking into my head. If Paul was such a big shot in the union and such a great speaker, why did he let Nate do all the arguing with Karsh? Why did Nate have to take all that by himself? I couldn't believe it, the way Nate stood up to a boss that way. All of a sudden, right in the middle of the Depression, here was easy-going Nate taking on one of the bosses. A regular David with Goliath.

A little after four o'clock I thought of something. Sam wasn't around and I was caught up with my bundles. So, from a stop at the ladies' room it was a cinch to hop downstairs where Al Pallotti, the guard, was sitting.

He grinned when he saw me. "Hi, carrot-top, so ya finally gave in, huh? Couldn't stay away from handsome Al!"

"How did you guess?" I said. "Listen, I got something to ask. You knew Jeanette Laval, didn't you?"

He whistled. "Who didn't? Boy, the way she used to shake her fanny when she went by. Too bad she went in the river. Some looker."

I gave him a Mae West wink. "So maybe you and her used to—you know—?"

He chuckled. "Boy, I'd a made her mighty welcome. Well, she had a short life and a merry one, like the resta them kind."

Them kind, I thought. What about the men so willing to make a woman "them kind"?

"So tell me," I said, "did she ever come in after hours?"

"Not when I was here." He licked his lips. "No such luck." He reached over to make a grab for my hand. "How's about you comin' in after hours, baby? I'd show you a good time!"

I ducked and he missed. "So you never saw her here at night?"

"If she was here," he said, "she never came my way." He looked at me kind of funny. "What's with all the questions, kiddo?"

"Thanks for the invitation, Al," I said, heading for the stairs, "but you got a wrong number." His laugh chased me all the way back upstairs.

So, more loops to tack. And what did I learn from Pallotti? Nothing much I didn't know before. But in my mind was a nutty notion about Jeanette in the factory at night. Was there another way to come in besides the front door? I knew each floor had a door leading to the fire escape outside, but you could only open them from the inside. She didn't have wings to fly up through the big doors in the cutting room. Besides, they also opened just from the inside.

The last hour of the day shlepped along extra slow, but finally it was over. Together with the other girls, I stamped my time card, swept past Al Pallotti's desk, he gave me an extra wink, and clattered down the steps out into the sunlight.

"Why are we rushing like the place is on fire?" I asked.

"Get her," snorted Gertrude. "Who wants to stay cooped up in that place one minute extra? You'd have to be nuts altogether!" She thought a minute. "Unless it was overtime."

"Holy cats!" Tillie wiggled her head around. "My neck is so stiff from bending over, I can't hardly move it."

"Tough apples," said Selma. "Whatever you do, it just comes back tomorrow."

"You're a big help," Tillie complained. Then she brightened up. "Say, d'ja hear about the big fight in the cutting room?" The way she described it, it sounded like Nate actually took a swing at Karsh.

So where was Nate now, anyway? I looked up and down the street. No sign of him.

"Who are ya looking for?" asked Tillie. Those droopy eyes never missed a trick.

"If it's Paul Warshafsky, forget it," said Gertrude. "I saw him drive off with a couple of guys."

"That smoothie?" I said. "Not my type."

"Talking about types," said Tillie, "guess who I saw in the corridor today. Mrs. Karsh, dressed to kill in a white suit. I was coming back from the ladies' room and she was pestering Lillian Lewis, where was her husband."

"What does she come to the factory for, anyway?" I asked.

"Oh, brother, what do you think?" Tillie said with a groan. "When you got a husband who don't come home from work on time, you go checking up."

"That old goat!" Gertrude snorted. "Better for the union if *he'd* got knocked off!"

"Listen, he's loaded, a regular old moneybags. Betcha ya can't guess what Al Pallotti told me about him." Tillie sounded all puffed up with her secret.

"So what could be exciting about Marvin Karsh, that dried-up prune?" I asked.

"Well, some nights he comes back to the factory to work after dinner and he stays all night. Sleeps on the settee in his office, c'n you imagine?"

"Jeepers," said Selma, "no wonder his wife goes running around looking for him." The corners of her mouth turned down in disgust. "Call that a husband?"

"Who knows?" Gertrude looked thoughtful. "Maybe he has company. It's a big settee."

We all giggled.

EIGHTEEN

Did it pay to stand up for your beliefs if it meant losing your job? It was hard not to worry over Nate's argument with Karsh on my way home. Even if Paul said it was nothing. Quiet Nate, with his bristly thatch of hair and his thick eyeglasses. Stubborn like me, maybe that's why we always fought with each other. Just the same, I made up my mind to call him up when I got home. He must be feeling rotten.

My walk had to be by the Spring Street markets on account of there wasn't much for dinner in my icebox. First, Mr. Schechter's butcher shop. It was late, he was sweeping the floor already.

"So, Mrs. Appleman!" He put the broom aside and went behind the counter. "You're maybe becoming a vegetarian these days? I don't see you so often."

"A vegetarian? I should live so! With a butcher like you handy?"

He beamed and stroked his neat little beard. I bought some chopped meat fresh ground, and a spring chicken for Friday. And laughed at the jokes he told me. Next to a husband, the most important thing in a woman's life is a good relationship with her butcher.

Next, Schipper's fruit and vegetable store for plump blueberries, a solid head lettuce, and some oranges and bananas. Then Mr. Danberg's bakery, who could resist? Half a rye sliced, two poppyseed rolls and a bagel, and a good hunk *bobke,* his special coffee cake filled with nuts and raisins.

In my apartment at last, it was already too late for "Portia Faces Life" on the radio. Should I call Nate right away? No, better give him a chance to have his supper. Besides, I was hungry. I made two hamburgers out of Mr. Schechter's chopped meat, sizzled them and ate them on a halved poppyseed roll with a salad tossed with sour cream. Blueberries for dessert, just a little cream. With my hot tea I sneaked a piece Mr. Danberg's *bobke.* Only a sliver. Listen, I wanted to stay a size 12.

When I put the stuff back in the icebox I realized I forgot to get anything for my lunch the next day. Barney's delicatessen was only a couple minutes away. Should I run down now or call Nate first? Better get the errand done and then call, he might even want to come over and talk out his *tsoriss,* his troubles.

It was a decision I was going to regret bitterly. But at the time, who knew?

Like usual, Barney's was busy, every table taken. Lucky all I wanted was some sliced meat to go. I ordered a quarter pound tongue and corned beef each. "A half-sour pickle, too. Pick a nice one, Barney."

"Only kind I got."

Barney handed over the package, and I handed him the money. A voice behind me said, "Hi, what're you doing here?" I turned and looked into Joey Gordon's eyes, they were kind of bloodshot.

"Buying *nosherai* for lunches, what else?" I answered.

"Sliced brisket and noodles with coffee ready!" called out Mrs. Barney, looking to see who ordered.

"That's mine," said Joey, shoving a bill across the counter. He turned to me. "Can I buy you some dinner, too, Belle?"

He was wearing a yellow polo shirt and white duck pants, real sporty, but his face was pale. Naturally, all that time being questioned by the police.

"Thanks, Joey," I said. "I already ate at home."

He bit his lip. "I hate to eat alone." He picked up his change and shoved it in his pocket. "Look, how about having some dessert with me? Barney's cheesecake is one of the finer experiences of this world."

"On that you don't have to sell me," I told him. Here was real luck, a chance to talk with Joey. "Bring on the cheesecake. And a glass hot tea."

Joey gave the order. When it came, he found a table by the window. I tried the cheesecake. What language had words to describe it? Joey stopped chewing brisket and began to laugh.

"What's so funny? Did I get some on my face?" I quick dabbed with my napkin.

"No, no, you're fine. It's just that right after that piece of cheesecake went into your mouth, you looked as if you were seeing a vision of angels or something, with your eyes half closed." He rubbed his chin with his knuckles. "I'm a painter, remember, I notice people's expressions. But then, you always look happy, even at the factory."

"You hate the factory so much, Joey, why do you stay there?"

He looked past me, out the window. It was still light, though the sun was already down, and people were walking by, peering in at us. "I'm an only son, it's expected," he said. His words sounded like he was repeating a lesson he'd learned by heart.

"So how's the brisket?" I asked.

"First-rate, like everything they make here." He attacked it.

"So enjoy, Joey." I went on with my cheesecake, thinking what kind questions to ask and how to get started.

"I'll bet you're a good cook," he remarked all of a sudden.

"My Daniel, may he rest in peace, used to think so. But maybe he was a little bit, you know, prejudiced. Now I don't fuss much, just for myself."

"Sure, but you work all day, it's not easy," he said. "I paint when I get home from work, but the light goes fast, it's not the same."

"What about weekends?"

"That's what I live for. Or used to. Until all this—" He waved a hand.

"The Laval business," I said. "No wonder." Right then I hated to begin with questions and spoil his meal, so I just gave him a Fay Bainter understanding smile and sipped my tea.

Sure enough, Joey worked on his brisket and finished it. Then he looked at me over his coffee cup. "Say, Aunt Belle, you got anything on for tonight?"

"Tonight? Why?"

"I've got a great idea. My car's parked right outside. Let's go back to my studio and shmooze, okay?" He sounded peppier.

"I got this package of cold cuts—"

"No problem, we'll stow it in my refrigerator. What do you say?" A pile of noodles stayed on his plate, he pushed it away.

What did I say? A God-sent opportunity. "Let's go."

In the studio I noticed right away the picture of Jeanette without clothes was still covered up. He put my package in the icebox and took out a bottle wine. I let him give me a little in a glass this time. He filled his glass up and sat down next to me.

"*L'chayim,* to life!" I toasted.

We clinked glasses. "Yeah," said Joey, "what would we do without it?"

I took a sip. It wasn't sweet like my Mogen David at home. "They gave you a bad time at the Joy Street station, Joey?"

He eyed me. "You hear about everything, don't you?" He took a gulp of wine. "Talk about Jimmy Cagney getting the third degree—it's lousy, all right—makes you feel like you're some kind of degenerate—a bunch of strangers asking you questions you wouldn't believe—" His shoulders hunched up for a minute, then he gave a long sigh and leaned back.

Time to change the subject. "You heard about my accident?"

He nodded. "Yeah, your friend Connors kept asking me about it. Do you really think I could do a thing like that to you?" He got up and took a package of cigarettes from the bookcase, shook one loose, and lit it. Then he sat down again.

"No, I don't think you did it. But somebody wants to stop me asking questions. Listen, Joey, Jim Connors is having trouble believing you can't remember a thing about Friday night. That's your big trouble, you got no alibi."

"You're telling me?" He gave a couple of furious puffs and stubbed out his cigarette in the ashtray.

"What's with this not remembering?" I asked. "Did you maybe fall and hit your head sometime?" I couldn't mention the fugue business, he'd right away smell a rat about Arnie Silverstein.

He jumped up and began to walk up and down. "The cops wouldn't believe me! They said it was the oldest dodge in the world."

"But if you maybe saw a doctor about it, he could tell the police you weren't faking."

"Tell them?" He stopped and stood over me. "You must be kidding! That's all I need, for them to know I went to a psychiatrist. They'd be sure I was crazy enough to kill!"

"You told me before, you bought groceries for Jeanette to come to dinner. And she didn't come. Then you went to your folks' house in Brookline. So when did you stop re-membering?"

He threw himself into a chair and sat slumped down, his mouth working. "When she didn't show, I got madder and madder. I was hungry, but I couldn't eat. Just kept drinking. She'd been taunting me, you know, about not being man enough to get my father's okay for us. I began to hear her voice in my head . . . and that's all I remember. Woke up in my folks' home."

"But you told me before that you left your apartment at ten o'clock."

He tugged at an ear. "Did I say that? I wish to God it was true! You can't imagine what it's like, a fog coming down. It's been driving me absolutely nuts. Could I have done some-thing terrible and not remember at all? Let me tell you, this is the real hell, not the lousy cops' third degree."

"This never happened before, you couldn't remember what you did?"

"Oh, God!" The skin on his face seemed to tighten, he sucked in his breath between his teeth. "A few years ago I got knocked down by a kid on a bike, got a concussion. It started after that. Only happened twice, never lasted more than a couple of hours. Both times I was pretty upset about something."

"It's a hard thing to prove without a doctor's word." But, I thought, a doctor's word might make him seem like a loony.

Was he? Aloud I said, "So tell me, Joey. Do you know—was there anyone else from the factory Jeanette was going out with?"

He drank the whole glass of wine before he answered. "She was always busy. Busy, busy, busy. But I found out where."

I leaned toward him. "Where, Joey?"

He got up, went over to the bottle, tipped it up, and emptied the last drops in his glass. "Old guy you wouldn't believe. Disgusting!"

"What old guy? Anybody I know?" I hoped the wine would keep him talking.

He drank what was left in his glass and bent over my chair. "No names. Too late for anything. She's gone, let the dead be dead. No gossip."

"It's not gossip, honest, I got to know—"

He moved away from me and picked up the empty wine bottle. "Goddammit!" he yelled, and threw the bottle against the wall. By some miracle it didn't break, just fell with a thud. Next thing I knew, Joey was slumped on the rug, head in his hands, his shoulders heaving. He was crying.

I got up, put my glass on the bookcase, and went to him. "Joey, don't—" I bent down and tried to put my arms around him.

He shook me off, mad. "Go away, Aunt Belle. Go home. Too many questions. Too damn late—"

"But, Joey—"

He didn't move. "Just leave me alone."

So I took my package from the icebox. When I stopped for a minute by the door to look back, his face was still hidden in his hands. He didn't answer when I said goodnight.

It seemed like a long walk back to Allen Street. Just getting dark, the air was close. Then a little breeze sprang up, the east wind, with that salty smell from the ocean. The smell of Boston, I wouldn't ever want to live no place else.

I kept thinking over what Joey said. About the fog that came down on everything Friday night. Like what the dictionary said about a fugue. But Arnie wouldn't tell me if a person could commit murder and not even remember.

It was hard not to feel sorry for Joey. So young and already so messed up. Not a very professional way to make a judgment, Jim Connors would say. Don't be letting that sob stuff run away with you now, Belle.

This detective business was no cinch.

At home my bed welcomed me. Maybe it was the whole *megillah* with Joey that got me wilted, but it was a pleasure to pull up the light summer blanket and stretch out. Then my memory gave me a sharp needle prick: Nate, you forgot to call him.

I jumped out of bed and went in the hall to the telephone. Never mind it was a little late. But after I dialed, no answer. After it rang and rang, I hung up. So where could he be? Out? So fast asleep he didn't hear the phone? Some friend you are, Appleman, forgetting what you promised yourself to do.

Nu, too late now. Tomorrow I'd make some excuse to go in the cutting room and see him. First thing in the morning. Stretching out didn't bring back that drowsy feeling I had before. I padded into the kitchen and fixed myself a glass of warm milk with honey.

Did Joey really forget what he did Friday night? Or did he just want to forget? And who was the old guy I wouldn't believe?

While I was sipping, an old saying of my mother's, may she rest in peace, came in my mind: after a good cry, your heart feels lighter. But I wasn't sure it was true in Joey's case.

Do murderers cry afterwards?

NINETEEN

What made me wake up extra early? A guilty feeling over Nate? But the lump on my head was gone and the finger burn was healing. Cheer up, Appleman, I yawned to the bathroom mirror, a little cold water, a little makeup, it won't be so bad.

After breakfast, who wanted to hang around the house? So it was only seven-fifteen when I came in the factory door and went to punch the time clock. Ed Bandy was sitting at his desk. I thought for a second he was asleep, he was leaning back, head against the wall. But as soon as he heard my footsteps, he sat up and pushed some of his stomach back under his belt.

"Oh, it's you." He rubbed his hand over his red-veined face. "You're early."

It was the first time he said a halfway friendly word. I saw my chance. "Good morning!" I put my card in the clock and it gave a *klop,* then I went over to the desk. "Say, Mr. Bandy, I heard you used to be a regular policeman."

His bleary eyes opened a little wider. I could smell the whiskey on his breath. "What's it to you?"

"Nothing, only it must be hard on you, doing this kind of work, after the other."

He snorted but didn't say nothing.

"I mean, I got a friend on the force, maybe you know him. Jim Connors?"

Bandy's mouth opened and he straightened. "Jim? You know Jim?"

I put two fingers together. "We're like that! So how come you left the force?"

His face collapsed into its usual glum expression. "None a your business."

"Listen, people working together should be friends. And sometimes it's good to talk things over with friends. We all got troubles, no?"

He looked at me with those eyes of a *shikker.* "Twenty years on the force," he said, drawing out every word, "and they give me the heave ho. Just like that! You talk about trouble."

Suddenly Bandy became a talker, I had to keep him going. "Say, you knew that Jeanette Laval, didn't you?"

"They all come in when I'm goin' out," he said. "Can't tell one broad from another."

"Come on, Ed," I said, "she was the girl who was killed, the shop steward. You know."

"Sure," he mumbled. "I knew her." He half-closed his eyes and leaned back. "What's it *to* you?"

"Who do you think could do such a thing?"

"Who died and left you in charge?" he said, without moving. Then he added, "I could tell plenty—"

"About that girl?" I asked.

He didn't answer. *Nu*, I'd try again another day. So I went on upstairs. Maybe he just wanted to make out he knew something. Be a big shot again.

The pants shop was empty. No people, just machines waiting to be made alive. I went to the locker room to put my lunch away and came back to my machine. Bundles of loops were sitting there, but I couldn't start tacking till Sam came in to put on the power. Then I saw Selma Weiss's pocket lying there. It wasn't my fault Karsh was so mad, who could come to him with a complaint yesterday? Better go over to the office and see if he got in yet.

I picked up the pocket and went in the corridor leading to the offices. A few people were already coming into the pants shop, they nodded hello. The factory was waking up. You could hear the little elevator *kvetching* away, taking someone up.

The office corridor was empty, so were the secretaries' offices. I stopped in front of the door marked MARVIN KARSH and knocked. No one called to come in, so maybe he wasn't there yet. Or maybe he was asleep on that big settee? So forget it, Appleman.

Then I noticed something. The door must've been left open, and my knocking made it swing slowly back all the way.

He was there, all right.

Marvin Karsh was slumped over his desk. His head was lying down on his right arm that was sticking out. The other arm I couldn't see, but it must've been hanging down, pointing at the floor. A pool of dark red stuff all over the desk, more on the carpet. Raspberry syrup it wasn't.

The pocket fell on the floor. For a minute I held on to the door frame. I started to choke in my throat, but I fought away the feeling. A detective can't be a sissy. I took a couple steps forward and looked at Karsh's right hand. The fingers were holding something bright like silver, maybe a knife. Then I saw something else. Where the hand was attached to the wrist, there was a dark, gaping hole. A couple flies were buzzing around it.

I didn't need no doctor to tell me Karsh was dead.

All of a sudden from behind me came a terrible scream. Then another. I jumped a mile and turned around. It was

Lillian Lewis. She was holding a hand to each cheek and her eyes were bulging almost out of her head. I yelled for her to stop it but she paid no attention. Then I remembered what they did to screaming actresses in the movies. I gave Lillian a good slap. She gave a gasp and began to cry.

A man came up behind Lillian, turned her around, and put her head on his shoulder. It was Paul Warshafsky. The girls from the shop were standing with open mouths. Nate pushed his way through.

"What is it?" he asked. I pointed. Nate gulped and swallowed. "*Gottenyu*! Better call the police—" He went away.

I became Mrs. Thin Man. "Don't nobody touch nothing!" I warned the people standing around. They all became statues. After all, I was Belle Appleman, authority on dead bodies.

A red face with a cigar sticking out of it loomed out of the crowd. "What's going on here?" The boss, Victor Gordon.

"It's Mr. Karsh," I told him. "I think he's dead."

"Dead? What do you mean, dead?"

He started to push past me through the door. When he saw what Karsh was doing, he backed out quick. I began to tell him about not touching anything, but after three words he turned and shoved away through the crowd. Nate came back and stood with me by the door. "I called the police—Joy Street station," he said. "For the second time, *gottenyu*! They're coming right away, don't worry."

It wasn't so right away. Thank God, Nate stayed by me, leaning against the doorframe like he was just waiting for a bus. If his stomach was heaving he didn't show no sign. By me it wasn't so easy. I was icy in my hands and feet, sweaty on my face.

"You all right?" Nate asked. "If you want to go sit down, Belle—"

Who could sit? "No, thanks, Nate."

"Look," he said, "seeing what's in there, it's no joke—"

"I'm fine, I'm fine," I lied.

Nate shrugged. Then I remembered how I meant to call him yesterday to talk over the argument with Karsh. The call I made too late. Now there was nothing to talk about. Karsh was dead.

All of a sudden a deep voice boomed, "Police, let us through, please." The workers stepped aside and there, thank God, was Jim Connors. Behind him was the young cop, Rafferty.

Jim stopped short when he saw Nate and me. "You two again?" His forehead wrinkled as he tipped back the brown fedora that was his trademark summer and winter. "The Gold Dust Twins—"

"Belle found the body," Nate explained.

"Yeah, she has the gift, doesn't she?" remarked Jim.

"It's—he's right in there," I told him, stepping aside. Jim disappeared inside, and the young cop stood in the doorway, his back to us. A second later he turned around facing us, his face kind of funny. But he spoke up, in a squeaky voice.

"All right, let's clear the place, now."

Sam Rothberg was standing nearby, gaping. Rafferty's words turned him back into a foreman. "You heard the officer, didn't you? Get a wiggle on, they got their job and we got ours." The groups that were whispering to each other broke up. People straggled in different directions. Paul and Lillian Lewis, I noticed, already disappeared before.

"You coming, Belle?" asked Nate, taking his hands out of his pockets.

Detective Connors stepped out of the office. "I'd like a word with Mrs. Appleman," he said.

"Good luck," said Nate, and followed the others away.

"Are you up to going back in there?" Jim asked. "You don't have to, we could talk out here."

"No, no, Jim, I'm already getting used to dead people."

"Full of blarney as an Irishman," he said in a dry voice. "Nobody ever gets used to this stuff. Come on, then." He turned to Rafferty. "Don't let anyone in."

I took a deep breath and followed Jim. He was taking out his little notebook and a pencil. "What time did you find the body?"

"Must've been around seven-thirty. I know, on account of I came early."

"Did you have an appointment with Karsh?"

"No, but I needed to talk to him." I explained about Selma and the pockets. Nate and the argument I didn't mention.

"Hmmm." He pursed his lips. "Was the door closed when you got here?"

"Not really. When I knocked, it opened by itself." The flies were still buzzing. "Then Lillian Lewis, she's the secretary, looked over my shoulder and let out a yell, and everyone came running. Only I didn't let anyone in. Nobody touched nothing."

"They should be putting you on our payroll," Jim muttered, scribbling away. "Did he always come in so early?"

"Lillian Lewis should know, she's right down the hall. Or, wait, also Ed Bandy, the guard."

He wrote some more. "I'll be talking to them later. Let's have a good look around first." He walked over to the desk and looked at Karsh. "Been dead some time, looks like." He bent over the desk. I peeked over his shoulder. There was a piece of paper next to Karsh's hand, one corner brown with soaked-up blood.

"Uh-huh," Jim mumbled. He took a handkerchief out of his pocket and picked the paper up carefully by one corner. I knew what the handkerchief was for. Fingerprints. There was some typing on the paper. "Holy mackerel," he said, half to himself.

"What is it?" I asked.

"Listen to this." He read out loud. "Forgive me, dear Evelyn, but I cannot face you and the family. I'm ashamed to face the world. God help me, I killed Jeanette Laval. I had to, she was blackmailing me. I love you all."

So now I knew who Joey's disgusting old guy was.

Jim put the piece of paper back on the desk. He leaned over the desk again and, with the handkerchief, plucked the piece of metal out of Karsh's hand. He held it up toward me. "Know what this is?"

At first I didn't recognize it. It was long and flat, like a knife blade. Then I knew. "It's from a machine in the cutting room. Nate showed me once, he's a cutter, you know." The minute the words were out of my mouth I wanted to take them back.

Jim nodded, wrapped the knife in his handkerchief, and put it in his pocket.

"So now we know who killed Jeanette Laval," I said.

"Both wrists cut and a suicide note, that ought to wrap it up." He took off his fedora and scratched his head. "Who's Evelyn? His wife?"

"Must be."

He put the fedora back on. "Don't you think she would've been worried enough to call someone, when he didn't come home all last night?"

"Maybe not," I told him. "The girls say he slept over lots of nights, on that settee."

His eyebrows went up. "There?" He stared at the sofa, muttered a "Hmm," then said, "She's got to be told right away."

That job I wouldn't want. "Mr. Gordon would probably do that."

"Gordon? Oh, yeah, the head guy." He called out to Rafferty. "Check the offices and locate Mr. Gordon, the company president. Ask him to come here." Rafferty disappeared.

Footsteps came near and Mr. Gordon appeared in the doorway, clearing his throat. He looked drawn. "You wanted to see me?"

"Right, sir. Someone has to notify the wife."

Gordon nodded. "I'm on my way."

"There's one more thing."

"What's that?" Gordon barked it out, he wasn't used to taking orders.

"Some member of the family has to identify the body, it's the law."

Gordon's expression showed plain what he thought about that law, but he only said, "How soon will—"

"At the City Morgue, probably any time after one o'clock."

"It'll be taken care of." Gordon cleared his throat again. "I told Marvin a hundred times if I told him once, stop worrying yourself sick over the business. But this union stuff drove him crazy." He turned to go but Jim's voice stopped him.

"Oh, Mr. Gordon, I'm sorry we had to have your son over at the station. Just routine questioning, you know."

Gordon waved his hand. "It's routine, I understand. What's going to happen now?"

"Nothing. No charges filed."

"Thanks, Detective—uh—Connors. I worry about that boy, you know. My only son."

"Karsh left a note," said Jim. Then he gave me a look, I got the meaning.

"I've got to get back to work," I said in a little voice, moving toward the door.

"Many thanks for your cooperation, Mrs. Appleman," Jim said.

"You're welcome." I slipped past the young cop standing with his arms folded.

My legs felt like they were made of rubber, they were glad when I sat down at my machine and began tacking. Dead bodies are no picnic, believe me.

"Hey, Belle," said Mary, "you okay? That's some long time you stayed with the cops."

"Yeah," said Gertrude, with a kind of nervous giggle, "what were they doing, giving you the third degree?"

"Whatsa matter, Gertrude? That's what they do to bad guys, not Belle!" Mary took everything real serious. She sounded special edgy, not like usual. Everybody was whispering, Sam wasn't around, and you could see in a minute the usual work quota wouldn't get done this morning.

I just kept tacking, but in my mind a pencil was crossing out a list of suspects. Sam, Gertrude, Felice, Joey, everyone I thought might have a reason to kill Jeanette. Everything was settled by one more body and a letter. So it must've been Karsh who fixed my machine. Imagine, a man that age with Jeanette.

"Jeepers, with his do-re-mi, why should a guy like that end it all?" Tillie said. "You should see how his wife dresses, gorgeous outfits from Filene's upstairs, and Jordan Marsh, new ones all the time."

Funny how people think, you got enough money, you got no *tsoriss.* Tell that to Joey Gordon. Come to think of it, I didn't remember seeing him in the corridor outside Karsh's office. So many faces, so much excitement, who could remember?

"Boy, some place this is getting to be," Tillie went on, tossing her head. "A suicide in the morning and a funeral in the afternoon. Don't seem too healthy around here nowadays!"

"Belle," Mary asked, "you goin' to Jeanette's funeral this afternoon?"

"Positively," I said. "We're getting the time off, we gotta go. Listen, she was a union member, it's like a relative, sort of."

Besides, I thought, I found her body, also. So the funeral was like the last act in a play, you had to stay to see it. And according to our religion, anyway, going to a funeral is a *mitzvah,* a good deed.

"All right, ladies—" Sam Rothberg was making an announcement, the whispering and buzzing in the shop stopped. "—a little less shmoozing and a little more action. Remember, you're getting half a day off for the Laval funeral at two o'clock. Furthermore—" He stopped and blew his nose into a large handkerchief. "Furthermore, in respect for the sudden death of Mr. Karsh, the whole factory will close one hour earlier than planned—not just the pants shop. So we still got a couple hours left, let's get cracking."

The machines obeyed and began to clack. The church would sure be filled today with the whole factory off. Nate would probably go and also Paul, of course. Thinking about Paul brought back the picture of Lillian Lewis wailing and Paul holding her in his arms. Why did that particular picture give me a funny feeling when it flashed on? Appleman, you're jealous, you dope. What's he to you, anyway? A classy date, that's all. Who needed him? Go to a Clark Gable movie with Sarah this weekend, you'll enjoy just as much and you won't get into trouble.

But then the picture changed a little. This time it didn't have nothing to do with Paul holding her. Lillian was an executive secretary, right? And when Paul asked me to help out the union, he gave me a contact. Lillian. But secretaries ain't factory workers, they can't belong to our union. So how come she's my contact? My stitches began to run crooked.

When the noon bell rang, everyone sighed with relief and rushed out. In the street I ran into Nate loosening his tie.

"Some morning!" he said. "They could of closed down right after finding Karsh, for all the work that got done. Talk, talk, talk, everybody had a different idea why Karsh killed himself."

"Likewise with us." It was hard to keep up with Nate's long legs as we walked home. "Listen, I feel bad. I meant to call you last night to see if you were okay. But a million things happened so I forgot. Oh, wait, I did call you real late, but you didn't answer. You were maybe asleep early?"

"No, I went out for a long walk," he said. "But forget it, doesn't matter now. Look, what went on after I left you with Connors?"

I was really dying to tell him about the suicide note. So I did, remembering every word just like Karsh typed it.

"*Gottenyu!*" Nate stopped dead, pushing his glasses higher on his nose. "Karsh killed Laval!"

"She was blackmailing him, that's what it said."

"Oy, that woman!"

We came to my house. "You're going to the funeral, Nate?"

"Yeah. But maybe you shouldn't, after that business this morning—" He inspected my face.

"But we were the ones found her—"

Nate shrugged. "Yeah, I know, you got to be there. So let's go together, nobody should go alone to a funeral. Pick you up a little after one?" He looked at his watch.

"Don't worry, I'll be ready."

"See you then." He loped away.

My hands fished out my key as my feet tapped up the stairs. But my mind kept nagging me.

Paul saw me standing in Karsh's doorway, but it was Lillian Lewis he was holding. Nate rescued me at the union-hall riot, not Paul. And it was Nate who came running when my machine almost electrocuted me, not Paul. And now it was Nate who didn't want me to go alone to Jeanette's funeral.

So where were you, Warshafsky, all those times?

TWENTY

Nate reached up and pulled the cord. "This is where we get off," he said.

The streetcar shook to a stop and we climbed out. Nate was so quiet on the way, maybe he was still thinking about the fight he had with Karsh. I wondered if that was the reason he went walking so late last night, he was still upset. Now Karsh was dead. When people die, it's easy to feel guilty about things you said in anger. But I wouldn't ask. Why hurt his feelings?

The street we were on was lined with houses that could have used some paint. Three-story houses that looked like they were wearing lace curtains to apologize for being so run-down. It was only a few steps to the church. A graystone building with a huge doorway, the front part over the door formed a triangle. It was a little early, people were standing out in front, talking low. A girl waved at us and smiled. It's hard to say hello with a sad face, even at a funeral. Then everyone started going in and we followed.

Nate picked out a place in the back to sit. Familiar faces were turning around up front to see who was coming. I was glad to see them because it gave me a funny feeling to be there, like I was in a country where I didn't belong. This place was so bare, just that big cross up front. The coffin was open, they must've fixed up the face. People went up to look, but not me. It was enough to remember her from the river and from Joey's painting. The organ was playing, it sounded like crying.

The minister was a tall, skinny man with a long face to match. When he began to talk I listened, because I wanted to hear all about Jeanette. But he went on and on and hardly mentioned her at all. When he recited, ". . . To everything there is a season, and a time to every purpose under the heaven, a time to be born and a time to die . . . ," Nate nudged me and whispered, "That's our stuff he's quoting." I nodded, those words from the Hebrew prophet I knew all right, only they didn't seem to fit this funeral, a girl so young and the way she died. Finally it was over, thank God. The minister's only conclusion seemed to be Jeanette was better off than on this miserable earth.

We all squeezed into cars lined up to take us to the cemetery. I caught sight of Paul but he was too far away to see me. More rows of three-story houses bunched together, then farther apart. A dusty road outside an iron fence. The cars stopped and we all piled out. On top of the wrought-iron gate, a scrolled sign said MOUNT OF HOPE. Here there were lots of trees and grass, much prettier than where the live people around there lived.

At the gravesite, a surprise. The minister stepped forward and announced in his high voice that one of Jeanette's fellow workers would say a few words in her memory. I looked around to see who it was, other people were craning their necks. My eyes fell on Joey Gordon. He was standing all alone, swaying like he was unsteady on his feet. While I was watching, he took out a handkerchief and blew his nose.

A tall, broad-shouldered figure, wearing a navy blue suit and dark tie, stepped up to one end of the grave. Paul Warshafsky. His face was serious and thoughtful. Standing very straight, he began speaking in that clear, deep voice that could silence a mob in seconds.

"Mrs. Laval, members of the Laval family, friends, and fellow workers. It was my privilege to know and work with Jeanette Laval as a member of Local 135 of the United Clothing Workers of America. We who mourn her want to pay tribute to her loyalty to our cause. As we bid her farewell, we salute her as a comrade in the war against oppression and injustice."

Nate gave me a little poke and whispered, "It's a good thing old man Gordon ain't around to hear about oppressed workers, he'd love that."

Paul was speaking again. "These words of a great poet express better than any of mine what we all feel:

> 'From too much love of living,
> From hope and fear set free,
> We thank with brief thanksgiving
> Whatever gods may be
> That no life lives forever;
> That dead men rise up never;
> That even the weariest river
> Winds somewhere safe to sea.'"

Paul just stood there for a minute. The only sounds were people blowing their noses. Mrs. Laval, with a dark veil covering her face, was sobbing. In spite of the muggy weather my flesh was all covered with goosebumps. Was it the poem or the man who recited it?

The minister came forward, said a short prayer with the words all running together, and it was over. People raised bowed heads and began to move. A few stopped to throw a handful of dirt on top of the casket. I could hardly wait to get away from that open grave. My legs ached and my hair was getting damp under my hat brim. I turned to Nate to tell him we should get going to one of the cars.

That's when it happened.

Two policemen, they came out of no place, appeared and stood, one on each side of Nate.

"You Nathan Becker?" asked the older of the two, a heavyset man with a dark complexion.

"Yes, that's me." Nate peered at him. "What about it?"

"We'd like you to come with us, sir."

"With you? What for?"

"We're not at liberty to talk about that here. If you'll just come along with us, sir."

"You mean to the police station?" Nate's forehead creased, he sounded like he couldn't believe it.

"Yes, sir. Our car's just outside the gate. Right this way, please."

Nate gave me a look with eyebrows raised and a little shrug of his shoulders. Before I could even say a word he was gone. The crowd parted to let them through, everyone staring at their backs.

What did the police want with Nate? Did they come here to catch him like he was a thief or something? I couldn't think of what to do to help him. The Karsh affair in the morning, the funeral, the heat, and now Nate being led away by two cops, my brain was a head of wilted lettuce. I looked around, trying to spot Paul, or even Tillie or Mary. But I couldn't see them, the crowd was moving toward the gates. So I started to stumble along, but just then an arm grabbed mine.

"What was that all about?" Joey's eyes were bloodshot.

"Who knows? Nate was only standing there with me and the police came. They just took him away, they wouldn't say why. What could it be?"

"My God, what a day!" Joey bit his lip. "Look, let me take you home, my car's down the road."

"Oh, thanks, Joey, the subway would be stifling."

We picked our way across the grass to Joey's sedan. Most of the funeral limousines were roaring away already. I wondered for a second why Paul didn't look for me. But maybe he had to stay with Mrs. Laval and the family. Joey opened the door, I crawled in and leaned my head back.

He got in and started the motor. There was a strong smell of liquor in the car. How *shikker* was he? Could he drive? *Nu*, I was stuck now.

He pulled off his tie and jacket and threw them on the backseat. "Phew! Sorry it's so hot in here, open your window some more. It'll be cooler when we get going." The car started with a little lurch when he shifted.

"You've no idea why the cops wanted Nate?" Joey was keeping his eyes on the road, thank God. Not much traffic yet.

I took off my hat. "Positively not." Then a thought pricked my mind. "You heard what happened in the cutting room yesterday?"

"Who didn't?"

"*Gottenyu*—it couldn't have anything to do with that argument, could it? Karsh didn't kill himself on account of an argument with Nate! You heard what his note said?" I looked at Joey.

He snorted. "Everybody heard!"

"I don't get it," I said. "A man like Karsh, with a business, money, a wife, a family, why should he—"

"Karsh!" he exploded. "Same age as my father! Sneaking around to be with her, imagine. What the hell did she want with him? Selling herself to the highest bidder? She could have had money from me any time she asked, she knew that!" He leaned on the horn so hard it blasted my eardrums. The car in front got out of the way fast.

"Now they're both gone." His voice was raspy. "A regular dime novel on the wages of sin!"

We were in heavier traffic now. "Take it easy, Joey. Listen, you told me last night you knew Jeanette was seeing an older man. How did you find out it was Karsh?"

"It's a wow!" He gave a strangled laugh. "From my own father. Ain't that one for the books? He went back to the office one night and saw what was going on. Couldn't wait to tell me the next morning!"

He was getting too upset. "Well, you know how a father is," I told him. "Always wants the best for his son. He was worried you might get stung, that's all."

"Sure. It was his great victory. Final proof that I was still wet behind the ears, wasting my time with a tramp. Time to get serious with Felice."

"So now, it's all right with you to marry Felice?"

"All right? Well, for once my father's satisfied with *something* I'm doing."

Just like in the old country, I thought, a *shadchen,* a matchmaker, to arrange everything. People could be rich and live in Newton or Brookline, but they couldn't break away from the old ways of doing things. Still, in those days marriages seemed to work out pretty good most of the time.

Joey twisted the wheel and we went around a curve with the tires squealing. Allen Street never looked so good to me before. "That's your house, right?"

"There, where the woman is standing with a bundle." Mrs. Wallenstein, naturally. She waited till the car stopped and she could see who it was before she opened the front door and went in.

I turned to him. "Thanks for taking me home, Joey. It was a big help."

"Other way round. Talking to you helps. Glad I found an Aunt Belle." He gave an apologetic wave of his hand. "Sorry about the way I drove."

"We got here, no?" I pushed on the door handle and got out. "And get some sleep, everything seems worse when you're tired."

He gave another wave with his hand and sped away.

Poor Joey, Jeanette's funeral must've been tough on him. But at least one thing made me feel better.

He wasn't a murderer no more.

TWENTY-ONE

The minute I got back from the funeral I was on the phone dialing the Joy Street station. But no luck, Jim Connors wasn't there. "Coming in later," they told me.

After I hung up, my stomach began to nudge me to the icebox. Too much excitement. So I finished off a bowl blueberries with cream and a poppyseed roll piled with cream cheese, drank a glass milk, and felt better. Still, I kept seeing those special stories in the Sunday papers with headlines like: "Was Justice Blind?" An innocent man sent to the electric chair. Okay for someone in some faraway city. But when it happened to somebody you knew, the shivers and chills down your back didn't go away. It was impossible, they couldn't railroad Nate on account of that stupid argument. Or could they?

When I tried the station again Connors was there, thank God.

"Jim, what's going on with Nate Becker?"

He grunted. "Figured I'd be hearing from you."

"Two cops came to the Laval funeral and took him away!"

"Now don't get excited. He's just in for routine questioning."

"What do you mean, questioning? About what?"

A little sound told me Jim was tapping his pencil. "Well, I can't say much yet, but there's a new development in the Karsh case."

"What kind development?"

"Karsh didn't commit suicide. It was murder."

"But the wrists? The letter—?"

"Anyone can type a letter."

My head was buzzing. "You mean—" Jim wasn't telling me enough. "So what's it got to do with Nate?"

His voice got sharp. "Why didn't you tell me about the argument in the cutting room?"

"A little argument at work, what's the big deal?"

"Come on, Belle, we know Nate threatened Karsh."

A piece of ice slid down my spine. My memory played back Nate saying, "Karsh? There's a name for a man like that I wouldn't say in front of a lady." And then his hoarse voice with, "Better I should see you dead first!"

"Belle, listen." Jim brought me back. "He's just being held while some tests are being made. Nothing'll turn up, probably. It's just routine, you know how it is."

"Some routine. Look, what about the wrists? You didn't tell me—"

"Sorry," he interrupted, "they're calling me, I've got to cut off. I'll let you know if anything develops." He hung up before I could even say good-bye.

I sat huddled in the chair, feeling like I lost my best friend. Was that what Nate was, my best friend? Then it came to me. He probably didn't have an alibi for last night. Maybe if I called him earlier he wouldn't be in jail. Nice going, Appleman.

Then I remembered someone else I had to call. After two rings Sarah answered.

"Belle? Did you go—"

I didn't give her a chance to finish. "Sarah, you'll never guess who's in jail."

"Jail? What do we know from jails?"

"Nate Becker. In the Joy Street station."

Silence for a minute. "Your Nate's in jail?"

"My Nate, your Nate, that's what I said. The police have him by the Joy Street station and they're asking questions."

"Questions? What about?"

I told her the whole story.

"On account of an argument, they're making him a murderer? That's *meshugah*!"

Crazy, all right.

"Belle?"

"I'm here."

"Listen, I didn't talk yet to that Laval woman. But I got time tomorrow morning. You still want I should go?"

"Positively! It's more important now than ever. You never know what could turn up. Remember, just say you're from the union. And call me tomorrow night, okay?"

"Naturally." She sighed. "The police holding Nate, how do you like that! It's a disgrace!"

"You said it! Okay, Sarah, we'll talk tomorrow. 'Bye."

Enough with the sob stuff, Appleman. What Nate needed was action. A lawyer, that was it, a smart one. But I didn't know any lawyers. And lawyers cost money, plenty. Especially for something real serious. Like murder.

Wait. Didn't Nate once mention that one thing the union did was to get a lawyer for any member in trouble? Who paid attention to that kind of stuff? It was the last thing on my mind then. But now it was the first. I didn't have no time to waste.

Paul Warshafsky, that's who would know. I picked up the telephone book to get his number quick, before he maybe went out for the evening. My finger followed the W's down the line. Aha, there were three Warshafskys. Albert, Robert, Samuel. No Paul. Maybe he spelled it different? I looked. No.

So what did that mean? A man so important in the union like Paul didn't have a telephone? Impossible. Maybe he lived outside the city? But how far out? Even Chelsea and Malden were in the book. *Nu*, what are you waiting for? Ask Information.

I dialed and a bored voice answered. The voice got real unfriendly when it found out I was asking for a name that didn't have an address attached. But with a grudge, it agreed to check. Pretty soon it reported with a snappy, "I'm sorry, that number is unlisted."

"Unlisted? But I'm a good friend. This is real important!"

"I'm sorry." The voice sounded glad. "We are not allowed to give out unlisted numbers under any circumstances." Then it cut me off, leaving me listening to a dial tone.

Unlisted number. Funny thing for a union big shot to have. So now what? Who would know Paul's number? Then it struck me—my contact, that was who! That stuck-up Lillian Lewis. And she gave me her phone number in the ladies' room. What did I do with it? I searched through my handbag, down to the loose bobby pins in the bottom, but it wasn't there. Think, Appleman, where did you put it?

Then I remembered. The dress I was wearing that day. I ran in the bedroom, found it in the closet, and searched the pockets. There it was, thank God. I went back to the phone and dialed. Someone answered right away, sounded like a young girl.

"Lillian? Yeah, just a sec." I heard her yell, "Lil! For you! It's not a man, tough apples—"

"Hello." The same artificial greeting.

"Lillian? This is Belle Appleman, I got a favor to ask."

"I can't talk long. I'm expecting an important call." Right away friendly.

"Listen, it's about Nate Becker."

"Who?"

"You know, Nate Becker, in the cutting room. You saw the police at the funeral today? They took him away on account of he had a fight with Karsh yesterday."

"What's wrong?"

"Nate's in trouble. He needs a lawyer, that's what," I said, trying not to sound mad. "Paul Warshafsky'll know what to do, I've got to reach him right away."

"What's the rush, he'll be at work in the morning."

And let Nate rot in jail? Not on your life! My stomach muscles were getting tied in a bow knot. I had to make her jump. So I just said real quiet, "There's not a minute to waste. Because now it's a case of murder."

Lillian must've jumped, all right. "Murder! What're you talking about?"

"Karsh," I told her. "The police found out he didn't kill himself, he was murdered. So I got to get Paul's number. Right away. Please."

She hesitated a minute. "Well, okay." She gave it to me slow, number by number.

"Thanks a lot, I'll call right now." Boy, did she hate to give me that number. Was her connection with Paul just business? I didn't have time to care. But it bothered me that my heart seemed to be beating faster the minute I started to dial Paul's number. Hoo-ha, Appleman, you're worse than the girls in the factory, they get *meshugge* the minute they see him. Relax, it's only a phone call.

The phone rang and rang at the other end. No answer. Wouldn't you know. Out to dinner? Maybe he ate only in restaurants. What kind of place did he live in? It was hard to picture. The union seemed to be his whole life, maybe he lived very plain. But he had a nice car and a fancy cigarette lighter. And he seemed fussy about food. So maybe he lived good. Only where? Come to think of it, in all the times you were with him, he never mentioned his address. Why didn't I think to ask? Appleman, you're slipping.

But the part that seemed fishiest was the Lillian Lewis connection. Someone who wasn't even in the union, yet to her I was supposed to give reports. A kind of secret service. Did all unions have that?

So where did he live, this Nelson Eddy full of union dreams? Could I find out from the telephone number? I picked up the phone and dialed Information again. I explained I had a phone number, could I get the address?

The voice was horrified. "Oh, no, we're not allowed to give out that information!"

"You're positive? Even in an emergency?"

"Would you like to speak to the head operator, ma'am?" If she's anything like you, forget it.

"No, thanks." Give up already, Appleman, the phone company won't give you any help. I leaned my head against the wall and tried to think. Ordinary people like me, they wouldn't tell nothing, no. But who would they tell? What about the police? Right away I was dialing again.

"Jim? It's me, Belle. Sorry to bother you again. But you could do something, maybe it would help."

He sounded doubtful. "And what's that?"

"Well, I got a certain telephone number, unlisted, only I don't have the address that goes with it. The operator wouldn't give it to me. So I thought maybe you could—"

Silence.

"Jim? You're still there?"

"Yeah, and I wish I wasn't." More silence. "This isn't just some sort of hunch, is it?"

"Have a heart," I said. "I need it to help Nate, honest."

"All right, give me the number. I'll see what I can do."

I read it to him. "Jim, you're a doll."

"Yeah, I know," he said. "I'll be getting back to you."

My throat was dry. I went in the kitchen and ate an orange. Where was Nate now? In a jail, with doors made of iron bars. Imagine, Nate in jail. Bad enough to be in jail when you're guilty. But when you're innocent? He was so skinny, anyway, and now what would he eat?

I switched on Station WEEI. Rudy Vallee and his Connecticut Yankees, he was singing that his melancholy baby should come to him. Somehow, three dresses got ironed while I listened and waited for Jim's call. It was almost time for the "Lanny Ross Show" when the ringing came. I hopped over to the phone before I realized it was the doorbell.

When I saw Jim Connors standing in his rumpled suit I got real scared. He must have something bad to tell me, he didn't want to do it on the phone.

"Evenin', Belle," Jim said easily. "Don't you trust me enough to invite me in?"

"Jim!" I stopped being a statue. "Come in!" I led him into the living room. "It's just—" we sat down on the sofa "—I feel like a cook in a restaurant, everything's boiling over at the same time."

He nodded absently, twisting the battered fedora around in his hands. "Now don't be alarmed. But I've got to tell you. Nate's been booked on suspicion of murder."

"Murder! Nate? That's impossible!"

Jim signed. "Sorry, Belle, but evidence is evidence. 'Twouldn't help if he were my own brother. They found a couple of Nate's fingerprints on the cigar lighter on Karsh's desk. Along with those of Karsh, of course. You remember it, the knight in armor?"

I remembered all right.

"And we have witnesses who heard Nate threaten Karsh. Something about seeing him dead."

"But everyone talks like that, it doesn't mean a thing! You know Nate—"

"He's got no alibi for that night, said he went out for a walk. Didn't meet anyone he knew. Didn't talk to a soul. Came home and went to bed. Not much help."

Why didn't you telephone Nate, Appleman? *Nu*, too late for that now. "Jim, you didn't tell me yet. How did you know Karsh didn't kill himself?"

He put his fedora in his lap and pulled at the lobe of one ear. "Funny thing, the M.E. spotted that. Seems a fellow who wants to cut his wrists has to change hands. And people are either right- or left-handed. So when the cuts are made—"

A hundred-watt bulb switched on in my head. "They'll be different! One deeper than the other? Or maybe not so even?"

"Ah, Belle," Jim sighed. "If they only took women on the force! Well, the cuts on Karsh's wrists were exactly alike. And the murderer apparently didn't figure on the M.E. finding the contusions on Karsh's head under the hair. The autopsy report was a blow from a heavy object."

"Wait," I said, "there was a big ashtray right on the desk."

"I know. But it was clean. And Nate's prints on the lighter are all we got."

"But a smart murderer would wear gloves, no? Or wipe off anything he used?"

"Right." He nodded. "I know that. But you know how we work, slow but sure. Getting the facts first and then narrowing things down." He reached in his pocket. "Oh, I almost forgot, here's the address you asked for." He unfolded the piece of paper. "A Paul Warshafsky, 2617C Bay State Road. That the one you wanted?"

I nodded yes. Jim groaned as he handed me the paper. "God help me, I hope you know what you're doing. Isn't this one of the men in the factory?"

"He's a cutter."

"What's he got to do with Karsh's death?"

"Listen, there's so much going on, I can't figure it out right this minute. Especially if Karsh didn't kill Jeanette, neither. But I got to get Nate cleared." That reminded me. "Jim, where's Nate now?"

"He's been remanded to the Charles Street jail, he'll be all right."

"Could I go see him? Maybe on my lunch hour tomorrow, twelve o'clock?"

"Sure, I'll call and fix it."

"Thanks a million." I reached over and touched his arm. "You worked so late, and you still took the time to come over. To tell me yourself. I appreciate that."

He gripped my hand in his. "Works both ways. You've helped me, too." He got up to go.

"Wait!" I jumped up. "What about Joey Gordon and that fugue business? Joey knew Jeanette was seeing Karsh at night. It drove him wild. So maybe he had another forgetting spell."

"Belle, I've talked to Dr. Silverstein. We're not counting the Gordon boy out."

"Okay," I said. "But what about his father? Partners always fight, you know. What about Sam Rothberg? He—"

Jim cut me off with a wave of his fedora. "Take it easy, we're checking everything out. I know how much you want to help Nate. But homicide is a dangerous business. And you've had a taste of that already." He clapped the fedora on his head. "I'd better leave before your reputation's ruined. While I was waiting for you to open the door, a woman was gaping at me over the third-floor railing."

"My nosey neighbor, pay no attention." Mrs. Wallenstein never took a rest.

Jim said goodnight and left me alone with a million thoughts *dreying* around in my head. Should I try Paul's number again? Ah, no use, too late to call a lawyer, anyway. I'd see Paul at work in the morning.

While I was sliding my nightgown on, I began to think. Two murders in the same factory. In the same week. And both fake suicides. Some fancy coincidence. Was there a separate murderer for each one? Or only one murderer for both murders?

I was already in bed when I remembered. So I switched on the night table lamp and got up. The piece of paper Jim gave me was on the coffee table in the living room. I brought it back to the bedroom lamp and read it. 2617C Bay State Road. Wasn't that right next to the Charles River? And wouldn't it be easy to dump a body from there at night?

I filed that question under W and got back into bed to toss myself to sleep.

TWENTY-TWO

In the morning the locker room sounded just like when you get two different stations on the radio at the same time. The girls were bunched in little groups, everybody talking at once. Before I could even stick my lunch in my locker Tillie grabbed my arm.

"Gee whiz, what happened to Nate Becker? The police dragged him away right in front of our eyes, didja ever! Did they lock him up? What did he do?"

"Holy Mary, Mother of God, what a sin!" Mary crossed herself. "Poor Belle, in all that heat, you musta been ready to faint."

"C'mon, give us the lowdown," said Selma, "what's going on?" Everyone stopped talking and waited for my answer.

"Believe me, Nate's in trouble up to his ears!" I threw my lunch in the locker and slammed the door shut.

"What for? What do they have on him?" A million questions, all at once.

"It wasn't suicide, Karsh was murdered." Everybody stared at me. "And remember Nate had a fight with Karsh in the cutting room? From that he's a suspect!"

Silence for a minute. Then Tillie said real slow, "No kidding," like she couldn't believe a word I said. "If that doesn't take the cake!"

"Such a nice fella, that Nate, why do they pick on him?" Mary was clasping and unclasping her blue-veined hands.

"Never mind," I said, "the union'll take care of him, they'll hire a good lawyer. We'll get him out, you'll see."

"Gee, so many real skunks running around and they pick on him!" Tillie shook her head and the others made sounds of sympathy.

"What's going on?" Sam Rothberg stood at the door. "Listen, we're running a business here. Yesterday was one thing, today's a work day, remember?"

The others left to go to their machines but I stopped in front of Sam. "Listen, Sam, the police have evidence Karsh was murdered. It wasn't suicide."

His mouth opened, but nothing came out.

"They'll be checking everyone for alibis night before last," I told him. "You'd better have a good one."

"Night before last?" His face turned the color of beet borsht. "Hey, my wife was at her mother's," he sputtered, "I went to the movies."

"I hope you saved the ticket stub," I said, and went to my seat.

Tacking sure didn't appeal right then, but I had to get a little work done to make Sam happy. One bundle was just about done when a hand touched my shoulder. I looked up into Paul Warshafsky's smile. The girls pretended not to watch him.

"Good morning, Mrs. Appleman," he said. "We have some union business to discuss if it's all right. Only let's get away from this noise."

"Sam wouldn't mind?" I asked.

"No, as shop steward you have a right to the time."

I stood up and we walked over to the locker room. Every eye in the room swiveled to follow us. Just like in a dance hall, I could've sold the girls time with Warshafsky at ten cents a minute. In the locker room we sat down on a bench. Paul crossed his legs. He was wearing cord pants and a white shirt opened at the neck, and somehow he looked more like an executive than a factory worker.

"I understand you tried to reach me last night," he said.

Aha, I thought, Lillian Lewis. "That's right, Paul, I tried to get you, but you weren't home."

"That's too bad. What was on your mind?"

"Nate Becker's on my mind. You know he's in jail?"

He nodded. Of course, Lillian would've spilled the whole *megillah.*

"So that's why I called you. Nate's in real trouble, he needs a lawyer. That's what the union's for, no?"

Paul picked up my hand and pressed it. "You bet that's what it's for! Don't think for a minute that Nate'll be forgotten. I'm calling a special meeting of the Joint Board tonight, this is an emergency. There'll be funds for a lawyer right away."

I pulled my hand away. "He can't wait for meetings. He needs a lawyer today! Right this minute!"

Paul grabbed my hand back and held it more tightly. "Don't worry Belle. It's all taken care of. The best lawyer in Boston will get Nate out on bail right away. Justice isn't only for the rich, you know."

I sighed. "*Alevai,* it should only be."

Paul began to stroke the back of my hand with his other hand "Does Becker mean so much to you?"

"I told you, we're friends. To me that means you help each other." His hands were warm, I could see the little light-colored hairs on the fingers.

"Can't I be your friend, too?" he asked real quiet, still stroking my hand.

A little tingle started to prickle over my skin. I tried not to get red. Would Claudette Colbert get flustered from just holding hands? "Why not?" I said. It came out almost like a whisper.

He slid over closer to me on the bench, I slid away.

"What are you, a Puritan?"

"Puritan-shmuritan, anybody could walk in the door right this minute." I pulled my hand away and stood up. Stay in control, Appleman. "To be real friends takes time, it can't happen in a second."

"You're right," he said, "we'll start working on that tomorrow night at the Cliff Manor. Six-thirty, remember?"

I wasn't sure if it was right to go off dancing and having a good time with Nate in jail. But if I went to visit him and the union got him a good lawyer, then maybe—

"Six-thirty," I said. "So the lawyer's already on Nate's case?"

"Yes."

Paul went back to the cutting room, me to my machine.

Gertrude lifted up her head and sniffed, "What's cooking with Glamour Man?"

I told her they already got a lawyer for Nate. What I didn't mention was that I was beginning to think again about Gertrude and Sam's alibi for Friday night. Could it be they were just covering up for each other?

And what about Paul, was he in with them? Painting his kitchen Friday night, some alibi. What bachelor stays home on a weekend night to make his kitchen prettier?

Of course, it was possible.

So, Appleman, I told myself, you better forget those green eyes and start being Mrs. Thin Man. There's got to be a way to check out that kitchen story.

Maybe I should get him to invite me there, I said to my tacking machine. It would just be business, see?

Go to that man's apartment? clacked the machine. Are you *meshugge*?

Hoo-ha, I shot back, it's not a crime.

How come when he shows up you get all shivery? it whined.

Listen, I'm only thirty-six, I answered. Live people got feelings.

Everybody warned you, it whirred, he's a woman chaser. Even going out with him again, you're looking for trouble.

Enough already, I snapped. I yanked the loop out.

The seams were crooked.

The minute noon came I flew out of my chair. The girls all called over to give their regards to Nate. I stuck on my hat and shoulder bag and hurried outside. It was cloudy and much cooler than the day before. Most people were on their way to lunch.

I was on my way to jail.

I walked up Charles Street past the Elizabeth Peabody House and the Massachusetts General Hospital. Should I bring Nate something, a magazine or newspaper at least? When people are in the hospital you know what to bring. But this was my first visit to a jail. Anyway, there wasn't time to stop now.

The Charles Street jail was a brick building with stone steps in front. A million times I'd passed it and hardly looked. But now I saw the bars on the windows. It was scary, just like in an Edward G. Robinson movie. I climbed the steps and pulled open one of the double doors. The inside was smaller than I expected, with bare floors, kind of dingy in spite of the overhead lights. A man in a blue uniform was sitting at a desk, writing.

"Excuse me, I'm here to visit somebody—"

He waved an arm. "Window over there."

A sign over the window said VISITOR PASSES. The man behind the glass slid the partition open. "Name?"

"I'm Mrs.—"

"No, no, the prisoner's name."

"Oh. Becker, Nathan Becker."

He shuffled some papers and peered at one. "First day, no visitors."

"What?" I was upset. "But Detective Connors said—"

"Who?" His tone was suspicious.

"Detective Jim Connors, he's from the Joy Street station."

"Hold on." More paper shuffling. "Oh, yeah, here it is. Special permission for Mrs. B. Appleman."

"That's me!"

"Okay." He stamped a piece of paper and shoved it at me. "Here's your pass, five minutes only. Give it to the guard at the desk."

The guard took the pass, pressed a button that made a buzz, and the iron door behind him opened. He motioned I should go through and called out, "Becker! Five-nine-six-two! Five minutes!" On the other side a man in a uniform clanged the door shut behind me. Now I knew how Jimmy Cagney felt in *The Big House*. He motioned me over and said, "Open your pocketbook, please."

"You mean this?" I pulled off my shoulder bag.

"Just routine, ma'am." He opened it and rummaged through. I wished it wasn't so full of junk.

"Here you are." He handed it back. With a key he opened a door into a small room. "Wait here, please." He closed the door and went away, his footsteps sounded loud.

No windows, so the small room looked even smaller. Two wooden chairs, tan walls, and a scuffed floor. Another door opposite. Light came from a little bulb in the ceiling. I sat on the edge of one chair. What was it like to stay in such a place?

A key turned and the other door opened. The guard ushered in Nate. His clothes looked like he slept in them. Worst of all, the guard closed the door and leaned against it. He was going to stay in that little room with us.

But that didn't bother Nate. When he saw me a big smile came over his face, just like he was coming in my front door. He came over and held out his hands. I got up and took them in mine. We just stood there for a minute like that, not saying a word.

I found my voice at last. "Nate, how are you?"

He shrugged. "The hotel's not so bad, but the food I wouldn't recommend."

We both laughed. It was a relief to hear him make even a little joke. Then he took away his hands and made a motion we should sit. We faced each other.

"You're here on your lunch hour, Belle?"

I nodded. "Everybody feels just terrible about you, Nate." I had to talk fast, the minutes were running out. "Listen, I spoke to Jim Connors last night. He knows you didn't do it. It's just the *meshuggeneh* business of your fingerprints on that statue—"

"I know, I know." Nate pushed up his glasses. "From such a little thing, who could imagine? I was in Karsh's office the morning before the argument and he got called out. So I picked up the lighter just to see how it worked." His lips twisted in a half smile. "I saw."

"Warshafsky said they got a lawyer, a good one. He came already?"

"Yes," said Nate, "he came. Said he would apply for bail right away." He sounded more confident.

"He'd better get you out quick, or the union'll hear from me!"

Nate's eyes twinkled. "To think, only a little while ago I was explaining to you what unions are. Now Warshafsky better watch out, you'll have his job yet."

We both giggled. Then we just sat and looked at each other. It was like a long-distance call. Little things sounded silly and big things stuck in your throat.

"Time's up," said the guard.

Nate stood up slowly and his smile disappeared. "Thanks for everything, Belle."

He went out the door with the guard, while I called, "See you tomorrow, Nate." The door banged shut.

I sat there alone feeling shivery. Appleman, you forgot to ask did he need anything. Well, tomorrow. The guard came back and let me go.

Outdoors on the front steps I stood a minute listening to the honking of auto horns. Across the way on the Embankment a bunch of balloons were tugging at a vendor's arm. The east wind tasted salty.

The corridor on the second floor of the factory seemed long as I walked back to the pants shop. I walked extra slow, thinking about Nate, my eyes fixed on the floor. Then a pair of well-shined black shoes showed up, sticking out from under navy blue pants cuffs. I looked up. Victor Gordon was standing at the door of his office. Belle Appleman, tacking-machine operator, would've walked by quick. Belle Appleman, shop steward, wasn't afraid of no boss.

"Mr. Gordon," I said, "remember me, Belle Appleman?"

He gave me a look that said he didn't.

"I'm shop steward in the pants shop, I found Mr. Karsh—"

He grunted. "I remember."

"Listen, Mr. Gordon, you heard they got Nate Becker in jail? They think maybe he killed Karsh."

"I heard." He shifted from one foot to the other.

"I just now came from the jail, I went to see Nate. Believe me, he didn't do it."

"I understand the police have evidence—"

"Listen, Mr. Gordon, Nate's been a cutter for the Classic Clothing Company for how many years now? Sure, the union's got him a lawyer." My voice got low like Barbara Stanwyck's. "But you're an important man, you know people, maybe you could help, too?"

Gordon eyed me. "You got strong feelings about Becker, Miss—"

"It's Mrs.," I said. "Mrs. Appleman, I'm a widow."

"Well, Mrs. Appleman," he said, looking at me with those brown eyes that were like Joey's, "I don't know what I can do that a good lawyer can't. And the police—"

"Police-shmolice," I told him, "it takes them a year to figure out anything. But I'm going to make sure Nate gets out of that jail right away!"

Victor Gordon gave me a long look from under his bushy eyebrows. "Good luck, Mrs. Appleman," he said, and went back into his office.

TWENTY-THREE

Dropping in on Al Pallotti always meant dodging those hands, but late in the afternoon I decided to chance it.

"Look who's here—carrot-top!" He tossed his copy of *Life* aside and greeted me with his usual grin. "How about it, you'n me, baby?"

"Sure," I said, "you're ready to propose, I'll marry you." That surprised him so much, he forgot to make his usual move. "Listen, Al, let's talk serious for a change. You saw Karsh come in Wednesday night?"

His forehead wrinkled and he scratched the back of his neck. "Yeah, but I already told Connors all about it. He came in about eight, he done that plenty of times. That was it, never saw him again, never heard a thing." He shook his head. "Jeez, he gets knocked off while I'm sittin' right here, if that don't take the cake—"

"What about when you made your rounds? You didn't see or hear nothing?"

"Hell, kiddo." He ran a hand through his white-streaked hair. "I learned not to fool with them offices at night, specially when the doors are closed. Jeez, it's a good thing the boys down at the station know me, they'd be giving me the works right now. You shoulda seen them goin' over Karsh's office yesterday after everyone went to the funeral."

"So they found Nate Becker's fingerprints," I said bitterly, "what does that prove? Listen, Al, there's the front door, the fire escapes, and the big pushout doors in the cutting room. But there's a back door too, right?"

He nodded. "Sure, there's that fire door exit out to the back alley. Stairs go down from the second floor corridor. You can't open it from the outside 'less you got a key."

"So who's got keys?"

His lower lip jutted out. "How should I know, I'm only the hired help!"

"*Did* Karsh ever have company at night?"

He blinked those heavy-lidded eyes at me. "Hey, I gotta job to keep, see. So I make like them three monkeys, y'know?" He put his hands over his ears, then over his eyes, and finally his mouth.

"Hoo-ha," I told him, "dress it up a little, you got a nice vaudeville act. Listen, Al, I got to find out if anybody besides Gordon and Karsh came in that back door at night. It's serious. Don't worry, it's just between you and me."

Pallotti gave a shrug. "Hey, carrot-top, if it's to help you, sure." He lowered his voice. "Lemme see, I spotted Karsh sneaking down those steps a few times to let someone in. I know, because I heard them both come back up."

"So who did he let in?"

"Dunno. They didn't talk. And the kind of a guy Karsh was, I made myself scarce."

"Anyone else besides Karsh? Gordon, maybe?"

Al scratched his neck. "Funny thing about Gordon. You'll never believe this. Few weeks ago a coupla guys ring the front doorbell at night. I open up, real careful, but they look okay. Said Gordon was expecting them. Talked real Southern-like—y'all and stuff like that. But I know Gordon ain't in his office. So I tell 'em to come in and I call Gordon at home to see if they're kosher. Gordon says he's just leaving, to keep them there. Boy, does he sound mad. When he comes in, he doesn't even say thanks, just leads those crackers to the elevator. Before they get in, I hear one say they didn't come in that way last time. Gordon tells him to clam up. What do you make of that?"

"Sounds like monkey business," I said. "Maybe out-of-town buyers he was going to take to a night club?"

"If he was," said Pallotti, "they sure got a late start. Stayed in Gordon's office about three hours."

Three hours!

"Thanks, Al," I told him, heading for the stairs. "You're a big help."

"Anytime you get lonely, don't forget big Al. I could go for you in a big way, kiddo—"

"You'll have to wait in line," I called back, and went up.

First thing I did when I got home was to dial Sarah. No answer. Meanwhile my stomach was complaining about no lunch at all. So I cut up Mr. Schechter's chicken, sizzled it with an onion in a pan, threw on a splash of wine, and covered it to pot. My mother, may she rest in peace, never put wine in pot-roasted chicken. That I learned from an Italian neighbor, Marie De Nezzo.

Nibbling on celery, I put on rice to go with the chicken gravy and went back to the phone. Sure enough, three rings and Sarah answered. "One second, Belle, I just got in." She sounded out of breath. "Okay, I dumped my stuff. Some busy afternoon in the store, my feet're killing me "

"Sarah, you saw Mrs. Laval this morning?"

She sighed. "Oy, that poor woman."

"So what happened? You found out something?"

"To lose a child, no parent should know from it!"

"Tell me, what did she say?"

"An earful, believe me. Poor thing, she talked like she couldn't stop. No luck at all. A husband—a drunk who hits her and the children. Then he runs away and leaves her to support them. A real no-goodnick!"

"What about Jeanette?"

"She showed me the class book, the daughter got voted the prettiest girl. Graduated Jamaica Plain High School. Always boys around, every night a different date. The mother worried, she wanted her to settle down, get married like the older sister. But Jeanette bragged she wouldn't take just anybody, she was after a 'big fish.'"

"So who was this fish? The mother knew?"

"No. She said he just blew the horn outside and the girl ran. You know how it is with kids today. She only remembers a black sedan."

"What about names? Anything?"

"Not the black sedan. Just that nice man from the union, he recited a lovely poem at the funeral. Used to come right in to call for her like a gentleman. Got her home early, also. Oh, and the boss's son, the girl did extra work for him as a model."

"So what about Friday night?"

"Oy, that night the girl called a taxi and went out by herself, said she had a late date. Last thing, she told her mother, 'You're always nagging me to find a good man and settle down. Well, you may be hearing wedding bells for me pretty soon!' Then the mother started crying something terrible, who could ask more questions?"

"Thanks, Sarah," I said, "you did real good. Listen, my chicken's begging me to come to supper. I'll give you a ring later and tell you about Nate."

When I lifted the lid the sauce was bubbling. I poked the chicken with a fork, it went right through. While I ate, a tenor on the radio was singing that I was getting to be a habit with him. Could I bring Nate some chicken? I pictured the guard unwrapping it, poking to find a gun in it or a file like in the comics. No, better use my brains to get him out.

I poured my tea and thought about Sarah's report. What did she really find out? Of course, I didn't know Paul used to come to Jeanette's house to take her out. But wasn't that for union business? Anyway, I wanted to think so.

Joey, no surprise there. But one thing was new, what she told her mother. Wedding bells. With who? Did she know Joey was engaged to Felice?

A big fish. What did that mean? And a black sedan? *Tsu meine tsoriss*—to make things worse—everybody had a black sedan, even Karsh.

Now Paul's alibi nagged at me even worse. Was he really home painting his kitchen? Listen, if he lied once, he could lie again, no?

Just the same, why would Paul want to get rid of Jeanette? Him I figured for a guy too smart to let himself get all upset over any woman. But he was a man, and when it comes to women, men do funny things.

Besides, he lived on Bay State Road. Right by the Charles River.

Appleman, I told myself, that kitchen you've got to see.

TWENTY-FOUR

On the phone I could hear Sarah's radio. "Sarah, you're done with supper?"

"Just this minute. I'm listening to Myrt and Marge. You too?"

"No, too much on my mind. Listen, I saw Nate today in jail."

"Nate in jail, who would believe it?"

"He's okay. Let's go see him tomorrow. Listen, want to go out tonight? It could maybe help Nate a lot. And I need you to back me up."

"Where? What do you mean?"

"Look, it's a long story. And you'll have to get ready fast."

Sarah was a good scout. "To help Nate, no question."

"So I'll come by your place in fifteen minutes, okay?"

"Wait a second, how should I dress?"

"Like for work, nothing fancy."

"You can't tell me where we're going?"

"I'll tell you on the subway, 'bye."

After I did my face I decided to get the junk out of my handbag, I shouldn't be ashamed in front of the guard in jail next time. A wrinkled handkerchief, a couple bills, a shopping list from last week, a pencil with a broken point, a playbill from the Yiddish theater from April, some torn movie stubs, all got sorted and disposed of. For tonight I added one small item I usually don't carry around.

Outside kids were playing hopscotch on the sidewalk. I stepped over a big pink chalk heart, inside it said Sally loves Mike. Hopscotch and love, it starts young.

Sarah had on a beige dress and she was carrying a matching sweater. When she saw my striped blouse and skirt, a frown knitted her plucked eyebrows together. "No sweater? What if it gets chilly?"

"We won't be out late."

"So where're we going? What's the big mystery?"

"First we're going to the El." While we walked to the Charles Street Circle I told her about a black sedan coming for Jeanette Laval and how Paul Warshafsky had a black sedan, also.

"So what?" Sarah was disappointed. "Loads of men got black sedans!" We went upstairs to take the El to Park Street.

"Something about him don't seem kosher." I told her about the unlisted number.

"My boss has a summer cottage by Nantasket, his phone's unlisted, too. So what?"

"Wait, there's more." I told her about reporting to Lillian Lewis.

Sarah shrugged. "Seems a little funny, maybe. But he's in charge of union business, he's just doing his job, no?" By then we were on the train, it was too noisy for her to talk. At Park Street we waited for a Commonwealth Avenue car, and that's when Sarah found out what we were going to do.

"So what are we going to ask this—what's his name?"

"Warshafsky. Paul Warshafsky." No use putting it off, I had to tell her, even though no Commonwealth car was in sight. "We're not going to ask him nothing."

She stared at me. "But you said we're going to visit—or where are we going, Belle? Who lives on Bay State Road?"

I couldn't stall no longer. "He does. That's where we're going, all right."

"So who'll be there to talk to?"

"Nobody."

Just when it sank in and Sarah's eyebrows began to rise, I grabbed her sleeve. "There's our car, come on!"

We hurried to climb on and get seats. Poor Sarah! She glared at me, dying to ask more questions, but I just put my finger to my lips and shook my head. A streetcar's too public.

When we got off at Kenmore Square she wouldn't budge, she clutched my arm. "Belle! Are we going to—you know—just go in there?"

I nodded.

"But—how can we do it?"

I gave her my Myrna Loy smile. "Remember the time I got locked out of my apartment, the door slammed, my keys were on the telephone table? Well, Mr. Slavich, the locksmith, came over and opened the door with a funny bunch of iron sticks, he called them picklocks. He did it so speedy, I asked him to show me how. He liked me, so he gave me a set for a present and showed me how to use them. I got them in my bag right now."

"How do you know what's-his-name ain't home?"

"He's got an important union meeting tonight. Come on."

Sarah peeked around. "What could we find?" So nervous, her voice squeaked.

"We'll see. We'll just take a quick look, that's all."

"Belle, this is *meshugge*! It's against the law! And we're taking a terrible chance, besides. What if he comes back or something? *Gottenyu*!" She stood there, paralyzed.

I gave her arm a push. "Look, he won't be home. And we got ears, no? So if we hear a step we'll rush out. Maybe the apartment has a back door."

"You're already getting us out, we didn't even get in yet." Some optimist, my partner.

"We'll get in, wait, you'll see how easy." If Mr. Slavich could do it, why not me?

Holding her arm, I walked Sarah around the corner to Bay State Road. Then I stopped and pulled out Jim's piece of paper from my bag. "It's 2617C, let's watch the numbers." A brass plate on a gray stone apartment house, 2408. The next house said 2412, so we were going in the right direction. "Let's cross. Even numbers are on the other side."

Every few steps Sarah muttered, "*Meshugge*" and wet her lips with her tongue. Of course I had to act like it was something I did all the time, but inside my stomach was playing hopscotch.

"Here it is, 2617." We both stopped and looked. My stomach jumped two squares. What if he didn't leave for the meeting yet? Or if the meeting was postponed?

"I know, we'll ring the bell." My voice got high-pitched all of a sudden.

Sarah looked terrified. "What if he answers?" Her fingers were twisting her sweater.

"Listen, we could always say we picked the wrong house. Come on." We walked real slow up to the front door. It was like any brownstone house, nothing special. I opened the front door and Sarah dragged herself in like she was on her way to the electric chair. Under one of the doorbells I found a card: P. Warshafsky, Apt. C, 2nd floor.

I waited a minute for my stomach to come back up, then I rang the bell. We stood there and waited, me studying the bells and Sarah studying me. No answer. Just to make sure, I rang again. He was out all right. We both sighed.

Now another problem. The house had an inside door you had to buzz open from the apartments. I tried it. Locked.

What would Mrs. Thin Man do?

Before I could think of anything, a man and a woman came out of one of the first floor apartments. They were young and laughing like anything. When they pushed the door open to go out I said, "Thanks," and held onto the handle so Sarah and I could go inside. Myrna Loy couldn't have done better.

Up the stairs on tiptoe. A guilty feeling makes you act funny. There it was, his door. In the back. Apartment C.

"What if somebody comes out in the hall?" whispered Sarah. She's a little on the plump side, she was puffing.

"Just stand like you're talking to me, so they only see your back." I took the picklocks out of my bag, my hands were shaking. Could I do it? I found the right size, pushed it in the lock and twisted. Nothing clicked. What was wrong? I tried again, a little slower this time. Aha, the lock clicked, the handle turned! The door opened.

My throat was so dry I couldn't say nothing. I took a step inside and listened, holding the door. All quiet. My hand motioned Sarah to come in after me. Then I heard footsteps somewhere. In my excitement I slammed the door shut with a loud bang. The footsteps came down the stairs, heavy. We waited. They passed by and went on downstairs. Everything was quiet again. We both gave a big sigh at the same time.

Sarah leaned against the wall near the door. "Oy, Belle, this ain't for me."

I should never have made her come, but it was too late now. "Listen, Sarah, you don't have to do a thing. Only, if you hear anyone coming, let me know. I'll just take a couple minutes, poke around, okay?"

She licked her lipstick and nodded. "Okay." I gave her my bag to hold and looked around.

We were in the entrance hall, looking into the living room. Low modern furniture, blond wood with black leather cushions. A glass-topped coffee table. Monks' cloth drapes at the bay windows. Rush matting on the floor. Like those pictures in *House Beautiful* I read in the drug store. Not what you'd expect from a factory worker.

Bookshelves in one corner and a big desk near the window. I went over to look at the books. The first title was what you'd expect, *A History of the American Working Class.* Next to it, *Ten Days That Shook the World,* by someone named John Reed. The title made me curious, but this wasn't no time to go browsing. Now the desk. A magazine called *The New Masses* and a newspaper, *The Daily Worker.* Two books lay open, I glanced at the pages. One was by Lenin, *Selected Works,* and there was a sentence underlined:

> The abolition of classes is impossible without the dictatorship of the oppressed class, the proletariat.

Who had time to figure that one out?

The other was a book of poetry, open to someone called Swinburne. A poem was underlined. I recognized the words he said at the funeral. Then I read some more of it:

> And love, grown faint and fretful
> With lips but half regretful,
> Sighs, and with eyes forgetful,
> Weeps that no loves endure.

Poetry I didn't know much about, but Algernon Swinburne, whoever you are, you sure know Paul Warshafsky.

"Find anything?" Sarah's voice right in my ear made me jump.

"Not exactly." Appleman, no use putting it off. Go find what you came for. I went back through the living room where Sarah was pacing around practically on tiptoe. There was the kitchen, all right, more of a kitchenette. I stopped in the doorway a second and then walked in.

The walls were white, no question. Well, cream-colored. I snapped on the light for a second to make sure. Not blue at all. Didn't even need painting. I just stood there.

My eye caught sight of a few dirty dishes in the sink. Gave me the crazy feeling I should wash them, so I snapped off the light and backed out of there fast. Might as well go home.

Wait, I told myself, you're here already, take a look around. Maybe you'll find something more. After all, the man's been giving out fake alibis all over the place.

Next, the bedroom. A big room with two windows that faced the river. I could see the M.I.T. dome already lighted up across the river in Cambridge. Again modern furniture, light wood twin beds with black and-beige striped spreads. A black leather chair with a matching foot stool held a crumpled tan shirt and a pair of brown socks. A closet that ran the width of the room. I decided to start with the chest of drawers that had a silver-backed comb and brush on top, and a picture of an older couple, must be his parents. The left-hand top drawer had handkerchiefs, tie clips, a clothes brush, a small stamp album, and some coins in a box, old ones. In the right-hand drawer lots of snapshots, mostly groups. Some were of a real young Paul, he looked so cute. A deck of Ace cards and a small chess game.

Then I saw something else in the drawer that made my face burn. A box of those things we sold in the drugstore, three for fifty cents, that men bought so girls wouldn't have babies. Of course, they didn't always work, look what happened to poor Jeanette. Appleman, you idiot, why should you feel embarrassed? You didn't in the drugstore, it was just a part of life.

Nothing else in the chest but underwear, shirts, stuff like that. So I checked the closet that ran the length of the wall. For someone who believed in the poor worker, he had a nifty wardrobe. Well, maybe he got a discount at the factory. Nothing in his pockets: a squashed package of Raleigh cigarettes, matches, a small penknife, coins. Almost as bad as my handbag.

It was getting late. Should I bother with the bathroom? What could be there? Might as well, you never know. The shower curtain was still wet. All of a sudden something touched my hair and I jumped about two feet. My breath stopped while I turned around to see what was there. Only a damp towel hung over the shower rod.

The medicine chest had the usual assortment of shaving stuff and junk like that. I turned to go and noticed his bathrobe hanging on a hook on the back of the door. It was striking, a kind of Chinese design, a black dragon on red. I fished in the pocket on one side. A piece of Kleenex. On the other, a white handkerchief, small and crumpled. I took it out and pulled it smooth. In one corner was an embroidered name, you can buy handkerchiefs made that way in Jordan Marsh. Blue threads on white.

Embroidered across the corner was the name: *Jeanette.*

TWENTY-FIVE

Jeanette and Paul.
It wasn't no business relationship.

A movie began to play in my head. She was lying across one of his beds, wearing the Chinese robe, tied tight with the sash on account of it was too big for her. Paul was standing by the bed, looking at her, smiling. The movie stopped. I hurried back to Sarah and showed her the handkerchief.

She gasped. "It's that girl's! Where did you find it?"

Why did my heart feel like a lump? "In his bathrobe. Here, stick it in my bag, okay?"

She opened my bag and shoved it in. "So now we'll go?"

It was just the kind of evidence I was looking for. So what else did I want? His desk, I forgot to check the drawers. "Wait, just a couple seconds."

The center drawer had mostly writing stuff, like pencils and paper clips, and the top drawer had stationery. The bottom drawer had letters in a file, I looked at one. Union business. A ledger, money spent and received. A small notebook with a place marker, it opened to a list of names:

> ~~Jeanette Laval~~
> Lillian Lewis
> Ralph Ianello
> Herb Raskin
> Belle Appleman?

A line through Jeanette's name I could understand, but why the question mark after mine? I memorized the two men's names, slid the notebook back and closed the drawer.

"Belle, it's getting dark out already." Sarah was fidgety. "Let's go, his meeting could end."

She was right. Wait, there was a piece of paper sticking out of the telephone book on the table. "One second, Sarah." I pulled it out. Handwriting. A note.

P.

Be at home Friday night. I'll get in touch.

Have big news. Get ready to pop that bottle of champagne you promised

J.

J. Friday night. The night Jeanette was killed. So Paul was the last one to see her. And that meant that he—

"Belle!" Sarah's hand was shaking me. "Listen!"

Footsteps on the stairs. We stared at each other. Then Sarah was pulling me along the corridor. Thank God there was a back door. She opened and we fell out.

My brain felt *famisht.* "Wait," I said, "did I put that note back?"

Sarah kept pulling on my arm. "Never mind, we got to get out of here!"

It was no time for an argument. I let the door close real careful, and we crept down the back stairs and peeked outside. No one around. We ran down the stone steps and along the bush-lined walk to the path by the Esplanade.

For a minute I glanced up. No light in the bedroom yet. But he could be standing there, looking down. I couldn't get away fast enough. We rushed to the corner, turned, and hurried up Deerfield Street. Both of us were out of breath and puffing like anything.

A taxi came to the corner and stopped, a woman got out. "Taxi!" I yelled at the driver and waved. He saw me and nodded. "Come on, we're taking that cab." We slowed down to a walk, but my heart was still banging like a hammer.

"A cab—it's expensive—" Sarah was panting. But she sounded glad.

"Expensive-shmensive!" I pushed her in the backseat and gave the driver Sarah's address on Blossom Street. The taxi started, the motor made a beautiful grinding in my ears. The whole trip, we didn't say a word. By the time we got to her street we were breathing regular. When I paid the driver, Sarah insisted on giving the tip.

"Some visit!" she said. Her hair was messed up and her face all shiny with sweat.

"I shouldn't have dragged you there."

Her eyes flashed. "I should let you go alone to take such a chance?" She grinned. "Besides, when do I get to visit a man's apartment?"

"Sarah, you're a sport!" I gave her a hug. "Listen, we'll go see Nate in the morning, okay?"

"Absolutely."

Once in my apartment, I realized my throat was a dust bowl. I peeled an orange and sat down to eat. Oh, boy, Appleman, look what you found tonight! Real evidence even Jim Connors didn't know. That girl came to see Paul late Friday night. What big news was she going to bring him? Why champagne? The only time I drank champagne was at a wedding. So was her news about her catching the big fish? Why would that make Paul want to kill her?

Wait a minute. Her name was in Paul's notebook. That meant she was spying for the union like he asked me to. Was the big news something she maybe found out about the union? Something so bad Paul had to kill her to keep from telling?

Too many questions, Appleman. Maybe you should call Jim Connors. But I decided no, first I had to find some answers. Maybe Saturday night.

And the handkerchief. Why did that bother me so much when I found it? I knew already what Paul was like with women. Come on, Appleman, shpritz away that little black cloud hanging over your head.

In bed, though, it was hard to keep the picture of Paul and that girl from sliding through my mind. So they were lovers, who cared? Worry better about the notebook with your name in it. What did that question mark mean? That he didn't trust you yet? So maybe that's why you got the invitation for Saturday night.

Nu, I could play that kind of game, too. I had to give a little giggle, two suspicious people checking each other out. Is he after you as a worker or as a woman, Appleman? But why should you care? You're only doing it for one reason. To get Nate out of jail.

Thinking of what to say to cheer up Nate, I fell asleep. But I had a funny dream. I was on the beach at L Street, wearing nothing at all. All around, other women were bare like me. Only Sarah was there in a regular dress and she kept telling me it was a *shandeh,* a disgrace, I was naked. To get away from her I ran into the water and started swimming. All of a sudden I saw a man swim around the fence toward me. It was Paul. He called out my name. What should I do? I couldn't swim out farther, the waves were too big. If I went back to the beach he would see me naked. My arms were getting tired and Paul was getting closer. Just as he caught up with me, I woke up sweating. Some dream.

The truth is I never learned to swim.

In the middle of my morning bagel and coffee the phone rang. It was Sarah. "Belle, I'm scared."

"Sarah, what's to be scared?"

"What we did last night. All morning I couldn't get out of my head the police would ring my bell. You're sure it was all right?"

"Sure I'm sure. Nobody knows what we did. Forget it!"

A long sigh traveled over the wire. "Okay So, when should we go to see Nate?"

"Nate? Wait a minute," I said, "Nate told me the union lawyer would get him out on bail. So maybe he's home already. Listen, let me check. I'll ring you right back."

After ten rings in Nate's apartment, no answer. I looked up the number of the jail. A voice told me Becker was still their guest.

"Sarah? Listen, Nate's still there. So we'll go."

"What'll we do later? Want to take in a show?"

"Tonight I got a date," I told her.

"A date? Who with?"

"You don't know, someone from the factory."

A gasp. Sarah was putting two and two together. "You don't mean the one where we went last night?"

"Listen, don't get excited. He already took me to dinner twice. Once in Durgin-Park, once in Meltzer's. A perfect gentleman, you should see."

"Some gentleman! What about that girl's handkerchief in his bathrobe? You're not afraid?"

"Dinner at Cliff Manor? What's to be afraid?"

Sarah got mad. "What's the matter with you? A man you got such suspicions about, you bust into his apartment! You find out he had that girl there! And you make a date to go out with him yet?"

"Take it easy, it's not so terrible." Better she shouldn't know any more.

"*Gottenyu*!"

"Don't worry, I wasn't born yesterday."

Sarah sighed. "I give up."

I did a quick job with the Hoover and pushed a dustcloth over the furniture and window sills. My mind wasn't exactly on housekeeping. Was Sarah right? Was it dangerous to go out with Paul? Maybe he was the one fixed my machine, not Karsh. But why would Paul kill Karsh? Well, it was one way to get rid of the man who hated the union most. And Jeanette? Maybe on account of the baby she was carrying. And look what I found out in his apartment. Paul Warshafsky was moving up on my list of suspects to Number One.

When the bell rang, I grabbed my bag and hurried down. But just as I opened the door I remembered the picklocks. What would the prison guard do if he found them in my bag? "Back in a second," I told Sarah and ran back up.

When I came out, it was cloudy. Sarah had on a jacket dress and she was carrying an umbrella. Sarah the optimist. We began walking down to Charles Street. "How was Nate yesterday? Was he okay?" she asked.

I nodded.

"I never was in a jail before."

"It's like a hotel, only with iron bars. Don't be scared."

"Who's scared? Only—" She looked at me. "—I never was in a jail."

"It's an adventure," I told her.

When we got to the front door of the Charles Street jail, she stood there with one foot on the step. Her face said oy, do I have to?

For me it was already old business, the passes, the handbag checking, then waiting in that little room. That funny look never left Sarah's face. When the iron door first clanged shut behind us she nearly jumped through the ceiling. Finally Nate came in the door with the guard. Nate looked tired, like he didn't sleep too good. His clothes were wrinkled and he needed a shave. But when he saw us, the twinkle came through those thick glasses and he smiled.

Sarah right away asked the same foolish question like me yesterday. "Nate, how are you?" How can you be, in a jail?

Nate took our hands and told us how glad he was to see us.

"Nate," I said, "you told me yesterday you were getting out on bail right away. How come you're still here?"

His face fell. "Who knows with lawyers! He came again this morning. Said things were being held up at the courthouse. Probably because it's a murder case, he wasn't sure. Anyway, he's over there now banging on somebody's desk. What can you expect, that's justice in a capitalist system!"

"Listen," I said, "while the lawyer's doing his work, I'll be doing mine. When I find out who killed Karsh they'll have to let you go."

That Nate, he never changes. You'd think he'd go down on his knees and kiss my hand, like in the movies, and say, "Belle, thank God you're saving me from the electric chair!" Nothing doing. He blinked at me and said, "Belle, how many times do I have to tell you? Murder is for the police. Don't mix in!"

"You see," I said to Sarah, "you see the thanks I get? Here I'm telling him I'll save his life, and he tells me not to mix in. Some thanks! Well, Mr. Becker, you can stay here in your fancy jail and see what good a lawyer can do! Those fingerprints, he can't erase!" I turned away, ready to leave.

"Wait, Belle, please!" Nate walked around to stop me. "I didn't mean—"

I wouldn't look at him. "He didn't mean," I said to Sarah. "You heard? He didn't mean!"

It was Sarah who took a firm hand. "Stop it, you two! You should be ashamed, two grown-up people acting like babies. What you need is a good *potch* on your t—" She began to say the Yiddish word for "behind" but caught herself and turned red. She looked so funny, Nate and I both burst out laughing.

"Oh, Nate," I said, "here you are in this terrible place and I'm yelling at you like a *yenta*."

"No, it was my fault. Who am I to tell a smart woman what to do?"

"It's my red hair," I told him. "I get mad too quick. Only nobody should worry about me, I'm real careful."

The guard said time was up. Sarah reached up and gave Nate a kiss on the cheek. I just took his hand. But he lifted my hand to his lips and kissed it. "Take care of yourself, Beautiful," he said. He never called me that before.

I felt like crying. "You take care of *yourself*," I told him back. Then the door opened.

The thin stringbean in the rumpled suit went out.

TWENTY-SIX

From the jail Sarah and I went downtown to have lunch and shop in Filene's Basement. We didn't buy a thing but it took our minds off Nate for a while. Then we had to hurry back so I could get dressed for my date. When I got to Allen Street, a car sat in front of my house. A black sedan, it looked familiar.

A head poked out the window and said, "Hiya, Auntie Belle!"

Joey Gordon, his eyes red like the sky over the Charles River at sunset. His lips were set in a big grin.

"Joey, what're you doing here?"

He got out of the car, stumbling a little, and took a big package, partly wrapped in brown paper, from the backseat. He closed the car door and held out the package. It was so big, I almost couldn't see him. "A present," he said, staggering a little, "from me. Just for you."

That's all you need now, Appleman, a visit from a *shikker*. I took the package from his hand and leaned it against the side of the car. "Joey, what's going on?"

He gave a big burp. "'Scuse me. Jus' came to deliver a re—remembrance."

"You're drinking on account of what Karsh did? That's crazy, it's all over with now. You got years and years to do what you want."

He gave a loony laugh and steadied himself against the car. "What I want? Know what Joey wanted? To marry Jeanette, that's what! Marry Jeanette, go to Paris, be a real painter. Asked her a million times. Know what she said?" He pointed a shaky finger under my nose.

"What?"

"No!" He slammed the side of the car with his hand. "No! Every goddam time! No! And y'know why? Afraid my father'd cut me off. Didn't wanna be married to a starving painter. Either my father's okay or nothin'!" He hiccupped. "Wouldn't take a chance on me!"

"Listen, maybe it was for the best," I told him.

"Hah! Thass what everybody says. The best! Dad, mother, Felice, all want the best for Joey. You, too, huh?" He stuck his jaw out.

"No." I shook my head. "You got to do what's right for yourself."

"Thass why I get a kick out of you. Straight goods. Thass why I brought you—" he turned and staggered toward the package, almost falling, but catching the side of the car in time "—this present."

He tore the paper off, it wasn't on very good to begin, and shoved it at me. There, right on the street, I was holding up a giant painting of a naked woman.

"You found her, you oughtta have her." Before I could move, Joey staggered back into his car, started the engine, and with a grinding of gears tore down the street.

Something made me glance up. Sure enough, there she was. Mrs. Wallenstein, keeping score of all my male visitors. I lugged the naked woman upstairs and put her against the entrance hall wall. It was too late to think what to do with it, I had to get dressed.

So, a quick shower and shampoo, brush the hair shiny, dab on makeup. Light on the cologne, Appleman, you don't want to get him stirred up, he's that way already. So why are you going if you're such a scaredy-cat?

I got out the ivory crepe de chine I bought in Filene's Basement for the Klein wedding. A Fifth Avenue label, a size ten just a little snug in the waist. And a low neckline, a deep V that made me feel undressed. Well, I could throw my white sweater around my shoulders, it would help. I took out my garnet earrings and necklace. The ones Daniel, may he rest in peace, gave me long ago. I thought they were too expensive, we should return them and get our money back. But Daniel said life was too short to worry over every penny. And here I was, wearing them to go out with another man.

My fingers were all fumbles. The earrings went on all right but it took three tries before I could fasten the clasp of the necklace. I was still in my satin slip and it was almost six-thirty. What's with the jitters, Appleman? I stepped into the dress and pulled it up, it was easy with a zipper opening all the way down the back. But when I reached behind and gave a yank, the zipper went halfway up and got stuck. I yanked some more. It wouldn't budge. Oh, swell! I tried to pull it down. Nothing doing. Could I change to another dress before he came? But the dress was so tight in the middle, I couldn't get it off, neither. What would Garbo do? I gave that stubborn zipper such a yank, it's a wonder the dress didn't rip. No soap.

That was when the bell rang.

I went into the front hall still struggling with the back of that miserable dress. Footsteps sounded on the stairs, followed by a rap on the door. I opened it, wondering how much of me was showing in back.

Paul was standing there smiling, in a navy blue jacket with white pants and shirt, bringing that masculine whiff of tobacco and aftershave lotion. He was too good-looking for a man, it wasn't fair. He reached out and took my hands in his. I had to kick the door shut with my foot.

"Belle, your hands are cold," he said.

"Cold hands, that's funny?"

"You know the old saying, 'cold hands, warm heart.'"

"Could be." I pulled my hands away. "Paul, how are you at fixing things? The zipper of my dress got stuck. In the back, won't go up or down." I tried to act like it was nothing at all, receiving a man while half-dressed.

Paul's smile widened. "Ah, you have here an expert with zippers." I'll bet you are, I thought. "Turn around," he said. I turned. His fingers began to putter with the zipper pull, I could feel his breath on my neck.

"There's a little piece of fabric caught, hold still." I felt him fiddling around. "Dammit, I almost had it! Wait a second." Who had a choice? More wiggling along my back. "I got it!" A triumphant yell. He worked the zipper up and down a couple of times while I thanked God and waited for him to slide it all the way up.

Instead, his lips began to brush my back very softly, all around. His hands were pressing my shoulders, while his kisses fell like feathers lower down my back. They made me shiver and burn, I couldn't help writhing and giving little gasps. Why didn't I break away? Appleman, a little voice in my head warned, you got to stop this right away, you're supposed to be in charge. Where are you letting him take you?

No use. The rest of me wasn't interested in good advice. His hands moved down my arms and slid across to my breasts. He drew me to him and kissed the back of my neck. It was the first time a man had touched me like that since Daniel.

"Paul," I gasped. "I can't—"

"Shhh!" he whispered in my ear. "It'll be all right." The warmth of his breath made me into a rag doll. Slowly his hands started to turn me around to face him, while he pulled me closer. My eyes were shut, I raised my face for his kiss.

But instead of kissing me, he loosened his hold and then his hands let me go. I was standing there all by myself. What happened? It was like having snow blown in my face. I opened my eyes wide and saw that he was staring past me at the painting propped against the wall. His eyebrows made a long, heavy line.

"That painting—where did you get it?"

I snapped out of my trance. "A present from Joey Gordon. It's Jeanette—"

"I know who it is," he said. He took a pack of cigarettes from his pocket and lit one. Meanwhile, I reached behind to slide the zipper all the way up. For a minute neither of us said a word. Then Paul shrugged. "Let's go."

My bag was on the phone table, my everyday shoulder bag. But I didn't care right then about changing bags. "I'm ready," I said, and took it.

When Paul opened the door of the car, I hesitated. His hand was on my arm, helping me in. "Something wrong?"

How could I tell him I was scared? That he was my number-one suspect? That too much was happening too fast? "I forgot my sweater."

"Don't worry." He moved me into the seat. "I promise you won't be cold." He threw his cigarette away and got in. The car moved down Allen Street toward the river. Sunlight was dancing on the water.

I closed my eyes and leaned my head back. It wasn't easy to forget what just happened. Nice going, Appleman. You melted like an ice cream cone in the sun. Okay, you're out to get information from this man. But how far can you go? Get into bed with him just to get evidence? Nothing doing! A Mata Hari I wasn't. And look how she ended up.

We drove past the Charlestown Navy Yard. I could see the masts of the old battleship, the *Constitution,* sticking up. Her I knew about from studying American history to get my citizenship papers, the school kids of Boston gave pennies to save her. Then we went over the Mystic River into Chelsea, and finally we were on the road that went past Revere Beach out to Lynn and Nahant.

The lights from the amusement park at the beach blazed on the right, showing the tracks of the Thunderbird roller coaster. One time, only once, I let Daniel sit me in one of those little cars. What happened to my stomach when we crashed down that first drop, I can't tell you. Never again, I told him, never again.

Daniel, I thought, if only you came back, I'd ride on the Thunderbird with you every night, if you wanted.

Paul spoke his first words since we left. "What's running around in that pretty head of yours, Belle?"

"Oh—Paul, what does it mean, the dictatorship of the prole—something like that?"

"You mean proletariat?"

"That's it."

"Where did you hear that?"

A quick lie. "Somebody talking on the Common. Dictatorship, of course, that's like Hitler and Mussolini, they should have a black year."

"The proletariat is just the great mass of workers all over the world," Paul explained. "In a capitalist society like ours, they become the victims of bosses and middle-class landowners. According to Karl Marx—know who he is?"

"The name, I know. What he did, I'm not so sure."

"He was the first economist to understand and explain the evils of a capitalist society. He wrote a book called *Das Kapital* to tell the world how all that could be changed."

"So how do you do it?"

"The way they're doing it in the Soviet Union today. The enemies of the people have been wiped out. The Russians are starting a whole new world!"

"Wiped out? You mean they killed them all?"

"It's not the way it sounds, Belle. Remember, it's a war, and in war people get killed. There's no other way to get justice and equality."

"It wouldn't work to do it little by little, nobody should get hurt?"

"Fat chance!" He gave a dry laugh. "The people with wealth and power will never, never give up control. You've got to take it away from them."

"Boy, you're quite an explainer."

That pleased him. "Stick around, you'll learn. And have some fun besides."

We were turning into the driveway of Cliff Manor. He parked the car and came around to open the door on my side. It was almost eight o'clock, nobody was on the beach. The tide was coming in, waves leaving long wet curves on the sand.

Cliff Manor was a big white wooden building that sprawled out on both sides of the entrance, with lots of windows and scalloped wood carving. The door we went in led right to the supper club. I'd never been to that part, only to the main dining room for some weddings and a Bar Mitzvah.

Some place! The bar was a real boat, a long rowboat with a top on it for serving. The walls were all covered with draped fishnets and hollow glass balls. An orchestra dressed in white bell-bottomed sailor outfits. While we were waiting for the head waiter to come, they were playing "Smoke Gets in Your Eyes." It was Saturday night, the dance floor was crowded.

The head waiter was extra polite. "Ah, Mr. Warshafsky, we have your table reserved. If you'll follow me—" A table right on the edge of the dance floor. Out of the corner of my eye I saw Paul slip him a folded bill. A good-time Charlie, all right.

Could good-time Charlies be murderers, also?

TWENTY-SEVEN

A fat candle stuck in a bottle covered with wax drippings did its best to light up our table. The menus were the size of newspapers. While we studied them the waiter filled our glasses with water.

"How about lobster?" asked Paul. "It's always great here."

"Sounds swell."

"And other goodies? Shall I order for you?"

"Why not, you have good taste in food."

Paul smiled, he sure liked being in charge. "Now, if you only followed my advice in other ways—"

I gave him my Mae West slow blink. "I let you fix my zipper, didn't I?"

"And you didn't register any complaints—" He looked into my eyes. I could feel a hot blush starting in the deep V of my dress. Time to change the subject.

"So tell me," I said, "what's the story with women in this new world of yours?"

He warmed right up. "They'll have the same rights as men, the same responsibilities. Share and share alike."

"Terrific," I said. "But there's one big difference you forgot."

He frowned, you could tell he didn't like a woman should challenge him. "Oh? What's that?"

"Babies; Women have them, so they can't always walk away like a man can."

He shrugged. "In the Soviet Union the state takes care of children. Day nurseries are free." He took hold of my hand. "The thing is, Belle, mature men and women should be able to do what they want without religious or legal chains."

"Hoo-ha, in a book that sounds beautiful," I told him. "But in America it's not like that. A man can do almost anything, he puts on his jacket and leaves, nobody makes a crack. But the woman gets called names I wouldn't even want to mention!"

Paul stood up and held out his hand. "Let's dance," he said.

My big menu fell flat on the table, and we walked out on the dance floor. A girl singer was crooning that somebody got under her skin. Paul put his arms around me. The only time I had danced in years was at the Klein wedding in this same dress. And it was the hora with fifteen other people.

I stumbled as we began to move over the dance floor. "It's been such a long time since—"

"Just follow," he whispered in my ear, "you'll be fine." He held my right hand in his left, close to my shoulder. And right away Appleman was floating around to the beat of a fox-trot, remembering which foot to put where. Even when Paul surprised me with a graceful dip. The orchestra finished and swung into another popular song they play a lot on the radio, "I'm in the Mood for Love."

Paul sang the words in my ear. "That's our song, Belle." Your song, I thought, not mine. Still, I never expected to have the feeling I got from dancing in his arms. The music ended and we drifted back to our table. The waiter slid right over.

"Broiled lobster," Paul ordered, "asparagus, tossed salad. Coffee later." He knew a lot about wine, too. I never heard of the kind he ordered, so I asked him what it was. "*Goldtroepf-*

schen, drops of gold. Made from grapes in the Rhine Valley."
Imagine, a cutter in a factory who knew about things like
that.

The waiter skated away into the shadows outside our
candlelight. I pulled myself out of my daze. Some detecting
you're doing, Appleman. All you're finding out about this
guy is he's an old smoothie, like in the song. Start already
with the questions, you dope. But before I could even begin
to think, the orchestra started again and we were dancing.

"Such a waste," Paul murmured in my ear, "a woman
like you all alone."

"What do you mean, alone? I got friends. I got a job."

"You must be lonely in that apartment on Allen Street."

"Hmmph! So what's the difference if you're alone in an
apartment on Allen Street or one on Bay State Road?" The
minute the words were out of my mouth, I wished I'd swallowed them.

We kept waltzing, but he stopped holding me so close.
"How did you know where I live?" he asked.

I thought fast. "When I asked Lillian for your phone number, I got her to tell me your address. I was curious, you were
a mystery man. That's all."

He looked down at me. "You know what curiosity did to
a cat?"

"Hoo-ha," I laughed, "a *bobbe-myseh,* an old wives' tale!"

He laughed, too, and everything was all right again.

The waiter brought two big napkins, each with a red lobster down the middle, and tied them around our necks. What
a relief to have something to cover that tell-tale crease in the
V of my dress, Paul's eyes kept lingering on it. Next came a
basket of rolls, tiny blueberry muffins, buttery crescents, pecan swirls, all warm and fragrant. Who could resist? I was

starving, I fell on them. Then the salads, regular mountains, with a choice of five different dressings, Meltzer's should only be so fancy.

Plunging my fork into a cherry tomato, I decided to begin prying information from my suspect. "Paul, how well did you know Jeanette Laval?"

His fork stopped halfway to his mouth. "Why?"

I finished the tomato. "Well, the gossip around the pants shop . . ." After all, detectives got to be tricky. The truth was, the girls never gossiped about him and Jeanette.

Paul ate some salad before he answered. "We worked together for the union." Pretty tricky himself.

"Come on." I buttered a piece blueberry muffin. "All that stuff you told me about men and women believing in free love? And you were just pals with her?" I popped the muffin in my mouth and grinned at him.

He grinned back. "Belle, don't tell me you're jealous!" He chose a crescent from the basket and broke off a piece.

"Who's jealous? Just trying to put two and two together, that's all."

The waiter came with a tall bottle wine and pulled out the cork with a corkscrew. Then he poured a little in Paul's glass and waited. Paul gave a taste and nodded his head. The waiter filled our glasses.

"Another dance?" Paul asked. I took a gulp of my wine before I stood up. Delicious, drops of gold, like Paul called it. Then we were in the middle of a million people on the dance floor. But Paul was so good, we never bumped into anyone. When we came back to the table I could feel the wine tingling inside. Better eat some more, Appleman. I reached for a pecan swirl.

A minute later the lobster came to the table. Big claws, maybe a pound and a half. Plates of melted butter and two nutcrackers. The asparagus you could tell right away was fresh, not that soggy canned stuff. I picked up my nutcracker and started on a claw.

"Paul," I said while I cracked, "did you know Jeanette Laval was pregnant when she died?"

Did his eyes open a little wider? He swallowed his first bite of lobster. "Where did you hear that?" Like before, answering a question with a question. I was hoping it would be like in the movies, where the detective asks just the right question at the right time and the suspect breaks down and says right away he did it. But Paul only looked at me calmly.

"From my friend Jim Connors. The detective who came to the factory—you know."

"Oh, man with the fedora." Paul swished a piece lobster meat in his butter dish and ate. He cut off an asparagus tip and put it in his mouth.

I swished a hunk around in my dish. "The question is, who's the father?"

Paul cracked his lobster. "That's anybody's guess. Why should it matter now?"

"Maybe—" I stopped to pick a piece of claw out of my mouth in a dainty way. "Maybe the father didn't want to be a father."

Paul didn't answer so I concentrated on eating. Finally there was nothing left on the table except plates heaped with lobster shells, an empty wine bottle, and a bread basket with crumbs. The waiter came back and untied the lobster napkins from our necks. Paul began concentrating on the V in my dress again.

Back came the oversize menus. "Dessert?" asked Paul.

I groaned.

He smiled. "Don't worry, we'll dance off the lobster and make room." To the waiter he said, "Baked Alaska for two.

And coffee. And hold them until after the next dance set."

Before you could say hoo-ha, we were back on the dance floor, waltzing around to an oldie, "Girl of My Dreams." "Why," asked Paul in my ear, "are you asking me about Jeanette Laval?"

"Because I'm a detective on the side," I told him. Now we were Ginger Rogers and Fred Astaire, cheek to cheek.

"You're doing all this for Nate Becker?" he asked.

"You bet," I said. "And for Jeanette, also."

The last song in the set was "Tiger Rag," too fast for me to hop around, especially with all those pieces of buttered lobster dancing with the *Goldtroepfchen* in my stomach. After a minute I told Paul we'd better stop, and we went back to the table.

"Well, Lady Sherlock Holmes," he said, leaning toward me over the table, "who did it?"

Maybe you, I thought. The waiter came that minute with the dessert and coffee so I didn't have to answer right away. I got a plate with a shiny igloo of swirled meringue floating in strawberry sauce. When I pushed in my fork, a surprise. "Baked ice cream?"

"A capitalist dessert. Enjoy it!"

I put a forkful in my mouth. What if my stomach was already loaded, who could resist such a *meichl*? But I had to stop for a minute, the salty breeze blowing through the windows made me want to sneeze. I put down my fork, grabbed up my handbag and fished around for a handkerchief. I pulled it out just in time to cover a loud "kerchoo!"

"What's this?"' asked Paul.

I looked. He was holding up another handkerchief that came out of the bag with mine

There, stitched in blue, was the name *Jeanette*.

TWENTY-EIGHT

Paul's green eyes turned cold like the ocean.

I couldn't tell if his expression was of a guilty man or an angry one. Or somebody who that minute decided he better be real careful. But he wasn't just a man relaxing with a woman no more.

"Well, well," he said, "I suppose Lillian gave you this when she told you on the phone where I live?" He wasn't trying to be funny. "Where did you get it?"

My brain couldn't think up a single phony answer. What's the use, Appleman, this one you bungled already. I looked him in the eye, it wasn't easy. "I found it in the pocket of your bathrobe."

He made a fist with the hand holding the handkerchief. For a minute I thought he was going to crash it down on the table. But he only opened his fist and let the handkerchief fall down. Then he drummed on the table with his fingers for a minute. A man with control, I thought. The look on his face started to change again.

"Belle Appleman," he said quietly, "you think I killed Jeanette and Karsh, don't you?"

"I'm not sure yet who did it," I answered. "I was only checking on you, like Jim Connors taught me. You got to have evidence before you can get at the truth."

"So you were in my apartment? When? How did you get in?"

The baked Alaska was melting, so I stopped to eat a piece before answering. "With my friend Sarah. Last night when you went to the meeting. How to get in I learned from a locksmith one time."

He gave a low whistle. "My God, you, Belle Appleman, a criminal!"

"What's with this criminal business? I was detecting, that's all."

"Breaking and entering, that's a felony. You can go to jail for that!"

I speared a strawberry. "So, you got evidence I did anything?"

Paul stared at me. Then he began to laugh. People at the tables near us turned to look at him. He laughed so hard he was almost crying. With Jeanette Laval's handkerchief he wiped the tears from his eyes.

"Belle, I knew you were a smart cookie, but this—"

"I'm tickled pink you think so," I told him. "Is that why my name was in your little book with a question mark?"

"You even saw that?" His eyes widened. "My God, there's no privacy in this country anymore!" He drummed his fingers again. Then he reached over and took my hand. "Listen to me. I swear to you I had nothing to do with the death of Jeanette Laval or that of Marvin Karsh. Nothing! As far as the handkerchief goes, you know what that means. Yes, we were once lovers, but it was just one of those things. Over and done with long ago. I don't use my bathrobe very often."

"Her name was in your book."

He nodded. "Yes, and I'd better tell you about that, too. Before you set me up for the electric chair!"

"So tell."

Paul gave me my hand back and shook his head. "Breaking and entering, I can't get over it. Well, I've done a few illegal things in my life, too." The grin came back to his face. He raised the coffee pot. "Some more?" I nodded and he filled our cups. "Belle," he said slowly, "if you suspected I was the killer, how did you have the courage to go out with me tonight?"

I took a sip of coffee. "To tell you the truth, I was almost afraid to get in the car with you." I fiddled with my spoon. "At the last minute I almost backed out. But detectives got to take chances. I worried you were the one who fixed my machine to kill me."

He gave a hmmph and wiped his mouth with his napkin.

"So what's with that list?" I asked.

"Well—that's a long story." He broke off a piece of baked Alaska but he didn't put it in his mouth. Just scrabbled it around on the plate with his fork.

"Why a question mark after my name? You can't tell? It's a big secret?"

He stopped scrabbling and gave a shrug. "Just meant I was trying you out."

"Trying me out?" All of a sudden, things went together— what I read in Paul's apartment and how he explained it in the car. "Paul Warshafsky, you're a Communist!"

He laughed. "Guilty as charged! A paid-up Party member. What's wrong with that? We're a legal political party."

"Maybe. But that list is something else, no? Tell me the truth."

He put his fork down and took my hand. "I just thought you'd make a good comrade."

I pulled my hand back. "You're still not telling me the whole thing."

Then what Nate said the night of the union meeting swam into my head. "Wait, I got it! Communists have little secret groups. They call them—"

"Cells," Paul finished for me in a tight voice. Then he gave a grin. "Comrade, you'd make a great trial lawyer."

"Lawyer-shmawyer," I said. "You made me a member of your cell without my say-so. And you asked me to listen in on factory gossip and report to Lillian. You ought to be ashamed of yourself! You wanted me to be a snitch and a spy!"

He shook his head. "No, no, you don't understand. We have to choose sides, we're surrounded by enemies. Remember, it was a revolution started the United States! You know what the Declaration of Independence says? 'And that whenever any form of government becomes destructive of these ends, it is the right of the people to alter or to abolish it and to institute new government.'"

"Sure, I studied it for my citizenship papers. But wasn't that different? A king putting taxes on our tea?"

"No difference! The bosses are acting like kings and the Socialists are our enemies, too—they won't do anything progressive. So the only way we can accomplish things is by working underground. To make the working man understand, don't you see?"

His face was lit up, he was beginning to sound like the man I used to pass on the Common, telling people the world was going to end in three months. "You think it's easy to start a cell and make it work? It takes time to build it up, lots of time. Complete dedication. You have to train people to have a sense of discipline. Discipline and loyalty."

"And that's what you were teaching Jeanette? Discipline and loyalty?"

"Yes, dammit!" Paul realized his voice was getting too loud. He stopped talking. The waiter must've thought it was a signal. He came to take away the dessert plates and ask if everything was all right. Paul told him perfect and please bring more coffee. When the waiter left, Paul looked at me.

"Jeanette was a good worker," he said, "she did what she was told. But she had one fatal weakness. Men. I warned her to keep away from Joey while she was seeing Karsh, but—" He stopped, took out his package of Raleighs and lit one.

"So why Karsh?"

He waved the cigarette in the air. "That was different. Karsh had some vital information we needed. Her job was to get it."

His words gave me a shock. "At night? On Karsh's settee?"

He took a long pull on the cigarette and exhaled. "Well, she had this weakness. Freud might have blamed it on the father who deserted her. Maybe she was looking for something she never had. Karsh used her. Joey, too."

"Swell," I said. "And you didn't?"

He looked down at the table. "Touché." Some cigarette ash fell in the ashtray.

I still couldn't believe it. "You mean she sneaked at night in the factory to sleep with that man, just to find out a secret for you?"

"Not just for me. Everything we were doing hung on knowing it."

"That's what you call discipline and loyalty?" Like a religion.

He nodded. He wasn't kidding.

And a week ago I was complaining factory work was boring.

"So tell me, Paul," I said, "where was she Friday night? Helping you paint your kitchen blue?"

He looked a little sheepish. "Ouch! Well, when you discovered I wasn't bowling with Sam, I had to think fast."

"The truth would have been better," I told him. "Did she come back to your apartment like the note said?"

His smile faded. "You saw that, too!"

I nodded. "So what's the answer?"

He drummed his fingers on the table. "The answer is she never showed."

"Why didn't you take the note to Jim Connors? That's called withholding evidence, no?"

"Did you tell Connors about breaking into my apartment? And what you found?"

"But that's diff—" I began.

His eyebrows went up.

"Okay," I said, "even-Steven. So she never called you, neither?"

"No. But late at night the phone rang. Just once. When I answered, there was no one on the line."

"So you still don't know if she found out anything from Karsh?"

"Nope." He shook his head. "And that's the big problem. Ever since she was found, I've been sweating it out. And after Karsh was killed, it was even worse—"

While he was talking, I started to think out loud. "So that's maybe why it was easy to make people think Karsh killed her . . ."

"What?" Paul asked.

"Nothing," I said, "just thinking about that fake suicide note—"

The orchestra started to play and he stood up. "I feel like dancing some more. Come on."

So instead of an answer to my question, I got a singer who told me the night was young and I was beautiful. But my heart felt like a stone had rolled off it. I believed Paul, thank God he wasn't the murderer. What was the evidence?

Only his word. But sometimes a woman's got to trust her—what's that word—intuition. While the orchestra switched to "I'm a Dreamer," a voice inside me sang, what if Paul's a schemer, aren't we all?

So when the band finished the set we went back and sat down. Paul kept my hand. I put on my Myrna Loy face. "Paul, I believe what you said, you're not the murderer. But do you have any idea of what was going on in the front office? Joey told me something was up, it got him wild they didn't trust him."

"All I know," he said, "is that Lillian said someone was using her typewriter at night. And she heard the tag end of a conversation Karsh had on the phone. About a surprise move the bosses were planning against the union."

"Wait a minute," I said, "the girls were saying something about the company expecting a big government contract. That without new business, the factory's in bad trouble."

Paul nodded. "You can say that again."

"Hmmm." I thought a minute. Paul kept stroking the back of my hand, it made it hard to think straight. "So maybe that's why those men came to see Victor Gordon. They—"

Paul stopped stroking. "What men?" he interrupted sharply.

"Al Pallotti told me," I said. "Two men came one night. Talked with Southern accents. Gordon was mad they came in the front way. And it wasn't the first time they came, neither."

Paul let go my hand. His eyes looked past my head at the darkened window.

"Maybe they were the government men coming to talk about the contract?" I said.

Paul shook his head. "Why should they come at night?" He rubbed his chin. "Unless they were on the take."

"On the take?"

"Accepting a bribe to give the contract to Gordon. You have to bid against competitors for government contracts. Lowest bid gets the job. Unless there's some kind of hanky-panky."

My stomach was churning from a mixture of lobster with what Paul was saying. I sipped a little coffee. Right away the room seemed warm, there was too much cigarette smoke in the air.

"Paul," I asked, "it's all right with you if we go outside? It's stuffy and I want to smell the ocean."

"Of course." He settled with the waiter and escorted me outdoors.

The wooden deck on the side of Cliff Manor faced the beach. We walked over and leaned on the railing. I breathed in big gulps of salty air and listened to the hiss of waves breaking and running up the sand. The water was filled with shining green flashes that came and went like Fourth of July sparklers. Over our heads the stars were like sparklers, too.

For a couple minutes we didn't talk. Then the breeze from the ocean made me give a little shiver. "Cold?" asked Paul. "Remember, I promised to keep you warm." He took off his jacket and put it over my shoulders. Then both of his arms moved under the jacket, holding me tight. I didn't complain.

But even in that wide-awake dream, something swam in my head. "Paul?"

"Mm?"

"Who are Ralph Ianello and Herbert Raskin?"

He groaned. "Don't you ever let go? You're supposed to be enjoying this! Or am I losing my touch?"

"I should live so long!"

"Well, Miss Curious," he said, pulling me closer, "they're the two men who started the ruckus at the union meeting."

"You're kidding!" In spite of myself I began to giggle, and he joined in. We held each other and laughed and laughed. Some schemer, this guy.

But even with his jacket and his arms I was still cold. "Paul, let's go back to the car."

"Sure." He kept one arm around me as we strolled back to the parking lot. We got into the car and right away his arms encircled me and we kissed. For a few delicious minutes I forgot all about being a detective.

It took all my willpower to push him away. "Not now. We got to think about what's going on at Classic Clothing."

In the light of the parking-lot lamps I could see the funny look on his face. "Yeah. Dammit, something *is* cooking with the factory bigwigs. I could smell it in the air weeks ago, just never could put my finger on it. And those night visitors from the South—somebody's finagling, all right." He sighed. "Oh, what I'd give for a squint at the files in Gordon's office!"

"Hoo-ha, you said a mouthful! Maybe even find something to help Nate out—"

He punched the steering wheel. "But how? The offices are locked tight. And Pallotti and Bandy make regular rounds."

"Easy." I gave him a poke. "I got into your apartment, didn't I?"

"What?" He burst out laughing. "Hey, I forgot I had a professional housebreaker right here with me! You mean you could pick the lock of Gordon's office?"

"Why not? We can stop at my apartment to get the picklocks. Only thing is, we got to get into the factory without the guard seeing us. That back door in the alley. So I'll have to open two doors."

Paul stuck his hands under the coat and gave me a big hug. "Only one, sweetheart," he said in a George Raft voice.

"You mean you got a key? But Pallotti said only Karsh and Gordon—"

"What Pallotti doesn't know won't hurt him."

I caught on. "Lillian Lewis—she got you a key!"

"You know your onions, kiddo."

"She's a good comrade, no? How good was she to you?"

"Stop asking foolish questions," said Paul.

"What time is it?" I asked, putting my hand under the coat to make him quit doing what he was doing.

He straightened up and glanced at his watch. "Almost eleven. Okay. We'd better regroup for action."

We stared at each other with excited grins. "Hold on, Belle," he said, his grin disappearing, "shouldn't we tackle Jim Connors on this first?"

"Look who's all of a sudden walking the straight and narrow! We don't even know what we're looking for. He'll just say I'm sticking my nose in where it doesn't belong. We'll tell him after."

"It's wild," he exclaimed. His eyes were gleaming. "We could end up in the pokey with Nate—"

"So what, I got a friend on the force!" We both giggled.

"Okay," he said, "let's seal the partnership." The kiss was yummy, but it began to take up valuable time.

I broke away. "Listen, first I'll go to the ladies' room. And then we'll figure how to work it—"

He chuckled. "Is that where you get your best ideas?"

My elbow gave him a good jab in the ribs.

TWENTY-NINE

Ten minutes later we were both back in the car. Paul made a face. "Boy, when you take a good-looking woman out dining and dancing, you sure hope it'll end up better than this!"

"Enough with the sob stuff," I told him. "Let's get going."

"Belle, you're still holding out on me. Lillian would never have given you my address in a million years—"

"Naturally, she's dedicated and loyal. Don't worry, I got it from Jim Connors. From your phone number."

"What? That's the best one I've heard in years! Belle Appleman, housebreaker, getting the cops to help her commit a felony! Boy, could I have used you in my cell!"

"Cell-shmell, move the car already." This time we sat closer together.

Almost too soon we were going around the Leverett Street Circle and turning off at Nashua Street. The Classic Clothing Company was a dark mass on the corner, only a night light was over the front entrance.

Paul pulled the car into the alley behind the factory. "Better leave it here." We got out of the car and walked to the back door. In the silence of the night the tap-tap of my high heels sounded extra loud. We could hear the rumble of the Elevated coming into North Station.

Paul took my hand. "Are you sure you want to go through with this?"

"Open the door already," I told him.

He bent over. "For luck," he said in my ear and gave me a delicious smack on the lips. The shivers that were traveling up and down my spine changed into a different kind.

Paul took out a key ring, found the right key, and opened the door. The narrow stairway up to the second floor was almost hidden in the blackness. He closed the alley door behind us and snapped on his cigarette lighter for a minute so we could see the first steps. Hand in hand we moved toward the fire door at the top. Paul turned the handle and opened it.

In front of us stretched the long, dimly lit corridor. Was that my heart or the lobster bouncing around under my ribs? Paul closed the door real quiet behind us, and I slipped off my shoes to keep my heels from clacking on the floor. Then we were standing in front of the door marked VICTOR GORDON, PRESIDENT. I looked down. No crack of light showing at the bottom, thank God.

Paul tried the doorknob. Locked. I put down my shoes and reached in my bag for the set of picklocks. I found one that fitted, pushed it all the way and twisted. The lock clicked, the door opened. Paul gave a low, admiring whistle. He snapped on the light and closed the door behind us.

Gordon's office was like I remembered from my first visit, high-class. Paul headed for the filing cabinet in the corner. But when he tried to pull the top drawer out, it wouldn't budge. "Hell, it's locked," he muttered.

"Don't worry." I got out the picklocks again. We both kept our voices down. Being there was plenty scary.

I snapped the lock open and pulled out the top drawer. A cinch. Paul was grinning as he started going through the file folders.

"Know what you're looking for?" I asked.

"I'll know it when I find it." He slid the top drawer closed and pulled the next one out.

So it shouldn't be a waste of time, I started looking at the stuff on Gordon's desk. Invoices and sales charts.

A loud "Aha!" from Paul made me jump. I gave him a shush. He was waving a folder in the air. "Look at this!"

On the tab of the folder was one word: GEORGIA. "What's inside?" I asked.

He laid the folder on the desk, opened it, and shuffled quickly through the papers, mostly letters. "I'll be damned!"

"What is it. Paul?"

"Do you know what those dirty dogs are planning? To close the factory and move down South! To a little hick town in Georgia. Look, it's all here. They've been buying all new equipment. It says the plan is to open three months from now."

"But why would they do a thing like that?"

"Simple. To get away from the union and a closed shop. Down South there are practically no unions. And plenty of poor people willing to work for the lowest wages. That means bigger profits for the firm. Oh, I can see Karsh's fine hand in this, all right!"

"But why is it a secret?"

"Because if the union knew, we'd strike. And then they'd lose the government contract they need to keep afloat."

"And that's the secret Jeanette was trying to vamp out of Karsh?" I asked. He nodded. Now I knew what Jeanette meant in that note. She was a regular double agent like in those spy movies. If she got to marry Joey she'd be in with the bosses. If not, she could tell the union about the move.

"Well, that's it." Paul went back to the file and put the Georgia folder inside. "Let's go." He closed the drawer and pushed in the lock.

"Wait, I want to check the desk."

He glanced at his watch. "Hey, it's almost time for Bandy to start his rounds." Somewhere outside a car engine roared and stopped.

"Just a few minutes, okay?"

He snapped his fingers. "Look, I'll go down and keep Bandy occupied. Let's say ten minutes. Then you come down in the elevator, right?"

I gave him my Fay Bainter frown. "What'll Bandy think?"

"Never mind," Paul said, "Bandy owes me one. It'll be all right." He gave me a quick kiss on the nose and pointed to the clock on Gordon's desk. "Ten minutes, remember." He went out and closed the door.

What was I looking for? I wasn't sure of anything. Gordon's desk was pretty fancy-shmancy, with three drawers on one side, two on the other, and one in between. The one in between was locked. What could I expect to find in ten minutes that would do Nate any good?

Too many drawers for such a short time. I said eeny-meeny-miney-mo and picked the middle one. An easy one for the picklock. When I opened it, a bunch of papers stapled together sat in the middle. I picked it out and put it on the desk. The top paper was a letter. The heading said HALLMAYER DETECTIVE AGENCY. When I read what the letter said, my heart gave a leap. I ripped the letter off from the staple and put it in my bag. I was just closing the drawer when I heard a sound. I looked up.

There in the doorway stood Victor Gordon.

THIRTY

"Well," said Gordon, stepping into the office, "what have we here?"

My stomach did a flip-flop. My mouth opened but no words came out.

He came closer till he was standing right in front of me. One hand dangled his keys. "So, Miss Busybody, what are you doing here?"

What would Mrs. Thin Man do? I put on a stuck-up Bette Davis face and said, "I'm working with Detective Connors on the Laval murder case."

"And of course you have a warrant to search this office." He put the keys in his pocket.

"Well, no, Mr. Gordon," I said, "not exactly." Paul, where are you, I wanted to yell.

"You realize I could call the guard and have you arrested for illegal entry?"

"So call," I told him. "The union will be glad to hear what I found out."

"Oh? What's that?"

I said only one word. "Georgia."

He gave a start like I stabbed him with a hatpin. Then he grabbed my arm and began to steer me toward the door. "We'd better have a talk, Mrs. Appleman." I tried to get my arm away but his grip was too strong. We went out of the office, across the corridor, and into the cutting room. "In here." He switched on the light and pushed me over to a space between two of the tables and shoved me down on a stool.

One of the tables was covered with layers of gray and blue worsted. The other had only a couple of cutting machines sitting. They looked like little *golems,* mechanical men, watching us. Victor Gordon sat on a stool opposite me and looked straight into my eyes.

"Good thing I forgot to check on some orders and came back tonight," he said. "Is that your car in the alley?"

I nodded. At least he didn't know Paul was here.

"So what do you know about Georgia?" he asked.

I put my bag on the table with the *golems* and took a deep breath. "You want to move the factory there. To get rid of the union."

"That so?" He rubbed his chin. "And as a good union member, you're going to tell them, I suppose."

"No," I said, "there's something more important than that."

"Oh? What could be more important?"

"Your son Joey and Jeanette Laval."

His bushy eyebrows knit in a frown. "What are you talking about?"

"I know how much he wanted to marry her. But—"

"How do you know what Joey wanted?" he interrupted sharply.

"Sometimes people find it easier to talk to strangers about their troubles," I said. "Joey came to see me this afternoon. He was *shikker,* he said things he wouldn't say otherwise. He told me Jeanette wouldn't marry him without your okay. But she wasn't the type who gave up easy. Naturally, she had to go to you."

He gave a deep sigh. "You got children, Mrs. Appleman?"

"I was never so lucky."

"Lucky?" he repeated. "You think it's all joy? Sure, when they're little. Then they grow up." He looked around. "All this was for Joey." He took in the cutting room with a wave of his hand. "You want the world for a son, everything your own father couldn't give you."

"Believe me, Mr. Gordon—"

He wasn't listening. "Everyone else I could manage, salesmen, foremen, even the union. But when it came to Joey—" He threw up his hands.

"Joey thought Jeanette was maybe going to meet Karsh Friday night."

"What Friday night?" He was all business again.

"The Friday night Jeanette Laval was killed. But it wasn't Karsh she was going to meet, was it? It was you. And that's when you killed her," I added.

Who can guess what a man will do when you call him a murderer? Victor Gordon didn't scream or faint or jump to catch me by the throat. A smile appeared on his lips, but not in his eyes.

"Why would I do something stupid like that?" he asked.

"The same question I asked myself," I told him. "She was carrying somebody's baby, and she claimed it was Joey's. A regular scandal for Brookline and West Newton, no?"

"It would have been unpleasant," he agreed.

"But people live through such things," I said. "It's not enough to kill for. So there had to be something else. And my guess is, Mr. Gordon, Jeanette Laval told you she found out about the factory moving down South. And if you didn't okay her marriage with Joey, she'd tell the union. Blackmail!" I waited a second to let that sink in. "So tell me," I added, "so far I'm right?"

His eyes held me with that steady look. "You're a re-markable woman, Mrs. Appleman. But what's your interest in this? You want money, is that it?"

I shook my head. "Not money, something more impor-tant. Justice. An innocent man is sitting right now in Charles Street jail for a murder he had nothing to do with."

Gordon nodded. "You mean Becker? They'll never con-vict him. Anyway, he's suspected of Karsh's murder, not the girl's."

"But whoever killed her had to be the one who killed Karsh. For a while I couldn't figure out the connection. Ex-cept—"

"Except what?"

"Except *you* were the one who told Joey she was fooling around with Karsh."

He leaned forward. "If that's all you got to go on, Mrs. Appleman, we're wasting time. As far as evidence is con-cerned, you don't have a shred."

"Wait, I'm not finished!"

"There's more?" He gave a short laugh. "Look here," he went on, "if you know so much, why don't you tell me why Jeanette Laval was murdered?"

I thought for a minute, then I reached out my hand and touched his. It wasn't easy to do. But I figured it was a way to relax him and keep him listening and talking. "Mr. Gor-don, you're a family man. And a smart businessman, too. Killing wouldn't come easy by you. So what I figured was, if you were the one who killed Jeanette, you didn't do it on purpose."

He grunted. Somewhere outside tires squealed like a car going around a corner.

"One thing I noticed the first day I met you—remember, Paul Warshafsky took me in your office—you had a short temper. So maybe when Jeanette came that Friday night and tried to blackmail you about marrying Joey, you got mad. Maybe you hit her, you didn't mean to—"

His face got dark red, his mouth worked.

"So that's what happened, no?"

The change in him was scary. "Why should I tell you anything?" he spit out.

"Listen, Mr. Gordon." Cool things down, Appleman. "To carry a load like that on your mind, it's not good. Besides, it's only you and me, what could it hurt to talk?"

He was Victor Gordon again. "Who'd ever take your word against mine?" He smiled a little at that idea. "All right," he said, "let's suppose—only *suppose,* mind you—that you're right. Joey's a dreamer, what does he know about life? She was no fool, she saw a good thing and she tried to grab it. Can you imagine someone like that a member of the Gordon family? The type she was? If it happened in an Orthodox family, they'd say *Kaddish* for the son. Tear their clothes and sit *shivah.* Pronounce him dead. We're not that religious. But if Joey married that—that blackmailer, it would have killed his mother." His eyes burned.

"I understand." It was impossible not to feel sorry for the man.

"The pregnant story wasn't bad enough, after I'd seen her on Karsh's couch. But then, for her to gloat over Karsh letting the cat out of the bag about the move—" His face got purple.

"You saw your life's work going to the dogs," I put in. "So you maybe grabbed her and gave her a good shake—"

He just looked at me. "Wrong," he said.

"But you were so mad—"

"Mad?" he repeated. "Do you know what it's like to be blackmailed? You become an animal in a trap! When I said nothing doing, she leaned over the desk and picked up my telephone. Laughing at me. Bold as brass. Said she was going to call that union cutter, that Warshafsky fellow, and tell him everything."

"So why should you care?" I asked. "Even if the union knew, what could they do to stop you?"

"Organize a strike and keep us from working—" He stopped.

"On the government contract," I finished.

"Very good, Mrs. Appleman," he said. He was talking calm and collected like I was one of his regular customers.

"And that must have made you even madder," I said. "So you grabbed the telephone away. You maybe gave her a push? Maybe even hit her—"

He shook his head. "Let's suppose I wanted to. And suppose that when I made a move toward her, she dropped the phone and tripped."

"Hit her face on the desk when she fell? Unconscious? Blood pouring out?"

"Is it possible?" he asked quietly, almost talking to himself. "Can you imagine Victor Gordon not knowing what to do?" He got up and began pacing back and forth between the tables.

"And you realized," I talked fast, "she could hold you up for all kinds of trouble—" I tried to remember stuff from the *True Detective* cases "—assault and battery, no? Intent to kill? Rape, even? So you had to get rid of her."

Gordon came back to the stool. His face was set in stone. "If I did, it was to save my son. And my business."

"So you drowned her in the factory?" I said. "You got a private washroom?"

He nodded, the bags under his eyes stood out.

I sighed. "And the river finished it."

Okay, Appleman, one down and one to go. Only from here I had to do some real guesswork. "Everybody hates a blackmailer, no question. And Karsh was almost as bad, no? From him you stood to lose plenty."

"Don't talk to me about Karsh!" He passed his hand over his forehead.

"He's the one who pushed you into the Georgia business?"

"Him and his ideas! Sucked me in with all that talk about getting the union off our backs. Who needed it? I was getting along fine with the union. But a man gets older, less careful, he starts making mistakes."

"Your mistake was listening to Karsh?"

"My mistake was getting mixed up with that *momser* in the first place. Just move the factory down South, he says. Cut costs in half, double the profits. Do it all under wraps, nobody gets to know till the last minute." He glared at me, only it wasn't me he was glaring at, it was Karsh's ghost.

Where was Paul? I kept praying he was hiding outside the door to hear Gordon spilling the beans. "You didn't even tell Joey about it. He knew something was going on. But it hurt him you didn't take him into your confidence."

He shrugged. "Karsh didn't trust Joey to keep the secret. That's a laugh, isn't it! He's the one who goes and tells that girl, the old goat!"

"That was bad enough, Mr. Gordon," I said, "but it still wasn't enough reason to kill. No, Karsh was doing something else. He was stealing from the company, no?"

He got off the stool and towered over me. "You found that report in my desk!"

"That's right, Mr. Gordon," I said, trying to keep my heart from thumping. "I saw it. How Karsh set up a dummy whole-sale cloth firm and gave it fake orders from Classic. So Classic sent checks, but never got any goods. And you never caught on till you did an inventory check on your warehouse."

"Robbing me blind all that time!" Gordon yelled.

"A crook as well as a blabbermouth," I said. "He really fixed you good." A light went on in my head. "Did he maybe come by here Friday night? What would he do if he saw you with the dead girl? Call the police? Not him! He'd use what he saw to take over the business, easy. Another blackmailer on your neck, ten times worse."

He stared at me but didn't say nothing.

"Wait. Or maybe Karsh comes by just when you're putting the dead girl in your car. Maybe he saw you, maybe he didn't. But it nags at you every day after that, no? Waiting for him to make a move."

He sagged back down on the stool.

"It's hard for a person to kill the first time. But the second time, not so hard, no? His suicide would get you off the hook. So Wednesday night when he came back, you followed him in and did it."

Gordon shot off the stool. "I'm sorrier for that little tramp than I am for him!" he yelled, glaring down at me.

"Not as sorry as you'll be when they strap you in the chair!" shouted a voice. It was Paul, busting through the cutting-room doors. "You son-of-a-bitch!"

The first thing I thought was, thank God, Paul, you're here! But the second thing was, Warshafsky, you dope, you came in too soon, he didn't finish confessing yet.

Gordon took a step back. "So you're in on this, too, Warshafsky?"

"I heard plenty," declared Paul.

Gordon snorted. "What did you hear? A lot of hot air! A game of ifs, that's all. You heard nothing!"

He's right, Paul, I thought.

Right then another voice behind Paul spoke.

"I'm afraid I heard enough to ask you to come with me, Mr. Gordon. I'm placing you under arrest."

Jim Connors.

It was like a movie, with Madeleine Carroll in trouble and Gary Cooper coming to rescue her. But I was mixed up. How did Jim know to come here? Who called him? When? I slid off the stool and faced Victor Gordon.

His mouth was open. He was staring at Jim.

"You see, Mr. Gordon," went on Jim, "no matter how well you scrubbed the carpet in your office, if some of the girl's blood is there, we'll find it."

It was Ed Bandy's turn. "Jeez," he said thickly, "the big boss himself!"

THIRTY-ONE

All of a sudden, before anyone could move, the calm Victor Gordon, the man so sure of himself, turned into a wild animal. He grabbed me from my stool, one arm pressing my back against his chest. I couldn't move. With the other hand he swept something off the cutting table and held it to my neck. It sure felt cold.

Gordon took a couple steps backward, dragging me with him. Paul took a step forward. It was just like I was the star on the Monday night Lux Radio Theater. Only this wasn't as much fun as the radio.

"Stop," ordered Gordon, "or I'll use this!"

Paul stopped.

"Mr. Gordon," I wailed, "you were the one who tried to kill me before! Have a heart! It won't help, what you're doing!"

"You shut up!" he roared in my ear. "If you kept your goddam nose out of my business, this wouldn't—"

"Let me go!" I yelled. "Let me go!" I tried to wriggle toward Paul, but Gordon only held me tighter and pulled me away.

Appleman, what would Myrna Loy do, she was so smart in *The Thin Man*? The answer to my question came in a flash. It was something I once saw in the Yiddish Theater. I closed my eyes, sighed a long, loud "Oy-y-y-y!" And then I fainted.

Would it work?

Gordon was so surprised when I went limp, he dropped me altogether. Fainting always looks so easy in the movies. But this factory floor was hard wood and the back of my head hit it with a bang. It got black in front of my eyes.

I didn't see Gordon's hand flick the cutting knife across Paul's forehead. But I heard Jim Connor's voice from far away yelling for Bandy to stop. Next, there were two bangs, one like from a firecracker and the other a loud thump. Then, a long scream.

When I opened my eyes Paul was helping me sit up, asking if I was okay. Blood was dripping down his face, it should've been me asking him. But I was excited and dizzy, my heart was pounding like my tacking machine.

"What happened?"

"Bandy took a shot at Gordon," Paul said.

"He killed him?" My eyesight got clearer. "What happened to your head?" Paul took out a handkerchief and began to mop. I took it away from him and cleaned the blood off the cut on his face. The embroidered letters that spelled Laval's first name got all blood-smeared.

"Bandy shot Gordon?" I asked.

Paul shook his head and pointed. Bandy was standing by the two doors where the big rolls of cloth got hoisted into the cutting room. He was looking down. I tottered over, holding on to Paul, and looked down, too.

The alley behind the factory was in shadow but I could see the tops of the two black sedans parked there. And between the cars, a small shadow, the motionless figure of a man. Someone was bending over the shadow.

"Is it—" Now I felt faint for real. I clutched Paul's arm.

"Gordon," said Paul.

The bending figure straightened up. Jim Connors looked up at us. "That's it," he said. "I'll call in." He walked out of the alley.

"But how—?" I began. A third body already.

Paul moved me away from the edge. He didn't answer me. "Better close the doors," he said to Ed Bandy.

Then he looked at me. "You could have been the one Connors is sending an ambulance for. I should never have left you alone."

"Who called Connors? You?"

"Bandy. When you didn't come down in time, I sneaked up the stairs and heard what was going on. So I sneaked back down again and told Bandy to call Connors, while I got myself back upstairs in a hurry to listen." He pulled me closer. My shaking stopped.

"Listen, you two." Jim was standing there, looking at us kind of funny, so we separated quick. "I'll have to ask you both to come to the station and give a deposition." He eyed me. "Are you all right, Belle?"

"I guess so. But Jim, if Gordon is dead and he didn't exactly confess, how will Nate get out of jail?"

A smile creased Jim's broad face. "Just leave that problem to me." His fingers played with the rim of his fedora. "We *are* good for something, you know."

Ed Bandy came alive. "Jeez, did I get Gordon?"

Before Jim could answer, Paul poked Bandy and motioned toward the cutting table with the layers of cloth.

"Congratulations, Ed," he said, "you just shot a hundred pairs of pants!"

THIRTY-TWO

When Paul and I got back to my apartment, it seemed like we already lived a lifetime together. We clomped up the stairs dead tired, who cared if the Wallensteins heard or not.

Paul's white shirt was stained with blood, his tie was crooked. My feet ached and my stomach wasn't acting so good, neither. But I was too excited to be sleepy. I put on all the lights, walked into the living room, kicked off my shoes, and collapsed on the sofa. Paul sank down next to me. We didn't move.

"Well, you did it." Paul stretched and yawned.

"We did it, you mean."

"Come on, I was just following your lead, Belle." The corners of his mouth twitched. "You and your picklocks—"

"But who expected Gordon to walk in like that?"

"What're you complaining about?" He shifted over closer to me. "You were the star of the show!"

"So where's that equal stuff you were preaching before?"

"Let's get equal." He put his arms around my neck and kissed me.

I wanted to enjoy it. But all of a sudden the room started spinning around and my stomach gave a heave.

"Paul!" I gasped, struggling to sit up, pushing at his chest. "Let go! I'm sick—" I clapped my hand over my mouth.

He took one look and let me go. I ran for the bathroom, with the walls all going around. Just in time. Was I sick! Everything from that fancy meal came up, lobster, salad, asparagus, baked Alaska.

Appleman, a little voice inside me sighed, you'll never make it as a vamp.

When it was over, Paul wiped my face with a washcloth. I tried to get up, but I had to stay leaning against him, holding on with both hands. The room was spinning at a crazy angle. "Paul," I groaned, "I'm dizzy—" He scooped me up in his arms and carried me into the bedroom. I was too sick to be thrilled.

Paul put me down carefully on the bed, but every move started a wave of misery. I closed my eyes but it didn't help. "The light, please!" I moaned. He snapped off the lamp.

Most of me sank into a sleep of exhaustion. We were lying together on the beach, I heard the waves pounding on the rocks. The sun was scorching, burning into me. Then I was back in my bedroom, I heard him stumble over a rung of the rocker and swear. I drifted away again. Now the beach was dark, a strong wind was blowing from the ocean and making me cold. I was shivering and alone on the sand.

"Daniel," I called, "I'm freezing!" All of a sudden he was cradling me in his arms. His body was better than a hot water bottle. Little by little the chill went away. My teeth stopped chattering, I stopped shaking. But things were still going around. At least, I thought, if I'm going to die, I won't die alone. I wanted to tell Daniel that. "Mmmm," I sighed. But he just whispered in my ear, "Shh, go to sleep."

So I did.

What woke me up was a sound I didn't hear already a long time.

A snore. Right next to me in bed.

I opened my eyes. The room was bright with sunlight. I was lying curled on my right side, so I had to turn over to see the snorer.

Paul Warshafsky, all right. Next to me in my bed, under my summer blanket.

What was he doing there?

I tried to remember the night before. Little by little things came back. Dancing at the Cliff Manor, with all that rich food bouncing around inside. The excitement with Victor Gordon, and me nearly getting killed. The Joy Street police station. And Jim Connors, God bless him, saying he'd heard enough to get Nate cleared.

What I missed when my head hit the floor, Paul told me in the car. Jim's expression when he came to the factory and made the connection between Paul and the address I'd asked him to get. Victor Gordon falling out the door of the loading platform. Nobody pushed him. After he dropped me, he backed away from Paul and Jim. And that's when our *shlemazl,* Ed Bandy, the fastest draw in the factory, pulled the trigger. Gordon jumped back at the sound, hit the opening bar of the door, and fell out. A blessing I was knocked out and never saw it.

And what happened when you and Paul began to make like Claudette Colbert and Clark Gable, Appleman? You got sick. Appleman, you sure know how to handle romance.

What I couldn't remember was getting undressed. So how did I get into my blue nightgown? I lifted my head. Stockings, slip and bra hung over the back of the rocker. My face flamed. How would I look him in the eye?

Then I remembered Joey Gordon's words: "Even the word 'naked' upsets people." So act like a woman of the world, Appleman. So he saw you, so what? You had chills and fever, and he took care of you. He even picked your new nightgown with the ruffles. What more could a woman ask?

Paul was still asleep and snoring, lying on his back, his tanned, muscular arms lying on top of the blanket. He was wearing a white sleeveless undershirt, and his chin was stubbly. The morning light showed little lines around his eyes and mouth. Funny, on a woman those lines mean you're "old," but on a man they're "distinguished." Why is that?

He was snoring with a soft whistle in a regular rhythm. Who would expect such a handsome man to snore like that? It struck me so funny, I laughed out loud. Paul woke up.

He was wide awake at once, didn't even seem surprised to find himself in a strange bed. He raised himself up on one elbow and looked at me.

"How're you feeling?"

"All better," I said. "See, I can turn my head."

"What else can you do?"

"Make breakfast?"

"Not now. Not yet." His fingers smoothed my cheek.

I got pink. "Uh, that was some night."

"Wait, there's more—"

"But, Paul," I said, "it's daytime. And besides—"

He put his fingers on my lips and whispered in my ear, "Shh, you talk too much." Then he bent over and began to give me little kisses, no two in the same place.

I just closed my eyes.

That was when the doorbell rang.

Paul didn't stop, he just ignored the sound like it never happened. The doorbell rang again. This time he raised his head and said, "Goddammit! Who the hell comes calling Sunday morning?"

I bit my lip. Who could it be? "Maybe the paperboy. Coming to collect."

"Stay there, I'll get rid of him." Paul jumped out of bed, grabbing up his messy white shirt from the heap of clothes on the rocker. He buttoned the shirt crooked, so one side of the collar hung down. Then he shoved the shirt into the top of his pants too fast, part of the tail flapped out. The slept-in pants were a wrinkled mess.

The bedroom door closed behind him. A minute later I heard him open the front door. A voice sang out, "Paper boy!" Only that voice you couldn't mistake. It didn't belong to no boy.

It was Nate Becker's voice.

Silence.

I could picture the two men staring at each other, Paul with the shirttail hanging out. Then I heard Paul clear his throat and say, "Becker! Come in!" There was the sound of the door shutting, and Paul went on. "Glad to see you free. Jail's no joke."

Nate's voice was flat and dry. "I ain't been laughing much lately."

More silence.

"Uh—" Paul cleared his throat again. "Belle will be right out."

Right out? Belle Appleman was paralyzed. All she wanted to do was pull the covers over her head.

Instead, I dragged myself out of bed and tottered to the closet. Somehow I found my flowered housecoat and buttoned it on. My slippers weren't under the bed, they weren't anyplace. It's summer, Appleman, go barefoot. I peered in the mirror over the bureau. Who was that wild-eyed woman? I yanked a brush through my hair, straightened my shoulders, opened the bedroom door, and closed it quick behind me.

Both men were standing in the hall, they turned to look at me. Paul was tucking the tail of his shirt into his pants. Nate was twisting the *Sunday Globe* in his fingers. I walked over to him with a big smile.

"Nate, thank God you're free!" I held out my hand to congratulate him.

"Yeah," he said without smiling. He put the newspaper into my outstretched hand and shifted from one foot to another. "Look," he said, "I want to thank you and Paul for what you did. Detective Connors told me everything. I owe you both a lot."

"Me? I just took orders from Belle," said Paul. "It was all her idea." He kept a straight face but his eyes glinted. I knew what those eyes were saying. Taking orders from a woman, that was a big joke. So much for equality in Paul's new world.

All of a sudden Nate's eyebrows came together. He was staring at the picture propped against the wall. "Isn't that—?" he began.

The doorbell rang again.

Nate moved away from the door, still eyeing the painting. Nobody answered his question. I went over and opened the door. It was Sarah, holding a brown paper bag with a loaf of rye bread sticking out.

"I was just coming from the store," she gasped, out of breath from the stairs. "Who could sleep, worrying over that man you went out with—" Her voice trailed off. Over my shoulder she was staring at Paul Warshafsky.

"Come in, Sarah." I closed the door. Sarah saw Nate and let out a shriek. "Nate! They let you go! *Mazel tov!*"

She put down the bag of groceries and hugged him. For the first time Nate smiled. They separated, Sarah still looking fondly at him.

"Sarah," I said, "I want you to meet Paul Warshafsky. He works at the factory, too. Paul, this is my best friend, Sarah Siegel."

"It's a pleasure to meet you at last," said Paul.

Sarah's eyebrows went up. She was looking at him up and down, the stained shirt, the wrinkled pants, the feet in socks with no shoes. Then her eyes traveled over me, down to my bare feet, and a look of horror spread over her face.

Paul paid no attention to her inspection. "I understand, Sarah," he went on, "that you paid a visit to my apartment. I'm sorry I wasn't there to welcome you."

Poor Sarah, her mouth opened, she turned beet-red. "How did you—? Belle, you shouldn't have—" Her head was swivelling back and forth between Paul and me. And then she caught sight of the painting.

It was one shock too many.

"Belle, where did that come from? You're gonna hang it on your wall?"

"Yes—no—I don't know," I stammered. "Look, let's all go sit down in the living room."

Nate took Sarah by the hand and led her to the sofa. They sat down and he began to tell her everything that happened. Everything he knew, that is.

Paul stood there, rubbing the stubble on his chin. "Belle, I've got things to finish up." He looked down at his crumpled pants. "I'll get my jacket and get out of your way."

I nodded and went in the kitchen to put on coffee. It was almost noon. Nate was probably starving. After last night I thought I'd never be hungry. But in spite of everything I felt a hollow in my stomach.

By the time the coffee was perking and some stuff came out of the icebox, Paul was back in the kitchen, all dressed. I could picture Sarah's head turning when he came out of the bedroom.

"You'll stay for some coffee and a bite?"

He shook his head. "I've got to pack and do a million things."

"Pack?"

"My work here is finished, thanks to you. I'll be moving on."

Out of my life. I put down the cream cheese I was holding. "Paul, you can't go without telling Nate about the move to Georgia."

"You know all about it now." His voice had an edge to it. "Why don't you tell him?"

"Why don't I?" I repeated. "You mean, if you had found out from Jeanette about the move, you were going to keep it still a secret? You wouldn't tell the union board?"

"Tell *them*?" Paul's voice got bitter. "It was our chance to show the rank and file that their Socialist officers were blind to the bosses pulling a fast one. Don't you see? We'd be able to call for a new election and put our people in control."

"So what's to control?"

"Are you kidding? Control means you get a cell member elected treasurer. Power goes to whoever holds the money!"

"Power-shmower!" I took his hand. "Socialists, Communists, it's holding the union together that's important, no? What's that union song—Solidarity Forever? It's your union, also. Never mind the politics, Paul. The only thing that counts is the workers."

He looked at me, rubbing his chin with his fingers. "All right, Belle," he said at last. "You've got a point there. The whole cell is shot to hell anyway." He went into the living room.

"Sarah," I called, "come help me in the kitchen."

She came in slowly, not saying a word. We could hear the men's voices, Paul's low, Nate's rising and all excited.

Sarah sat on the kitchen chair and inspected her fingernails, they had on a deep pink polish. She opened her mouth to say something, then closed it.

The coffee finished perking. I poured a cup for each of us and we just sat there, sipping it, not saying a word. It wasn't a cozy silence. What she was thinking about me showed plain on her face.

Nate must feel the same way, I thought. Maybe worse.

When Paul came back to the kitchen, Sarah excused herself and went back to Nate.

"Belle, I'm leaving," Paul said.

I walked him to the front door. Thank God for the wall that separated us from the living room. There was enough light in the hall to pick up the flicker in his eyes as he looked at me. The corners of his mouth turned up in a smile.

"That was one hell of a night," he said.

My smile was bright, glued on. "You'll come back to Boston some time, won't you?" Paul grinned. "Keep a light burning in the window." Then he said, "Becker's a lucky man to have you on his side."

He put his fingers under my chin and raised my face. "Too bad our morning didn't have a happy ending, Belle." He bent down and grazed my lips with his. The door opened and closed.

Paul Warshafsky was gone.

I lifted my head high and marched into the living room. Sarah and Nate stopped talking and stared at me.

"All night, comrades," I said, "don't you want to know what really happened to Belle Appleman last night?"

They just stared.

"It was all on account of the lobster—"

THIRTY-THREE

I couldn't figure out why the alarm clock kept on ringing even after my fingers told me it was off. Hoo-ha, it was the phone. I stumbled to the hall table.

"Belle, you're awake?" Nate sounded all excited.

"Guess so. Half and half."

"So wake up the other half. I got big news."

I yawned.

"Belle?"

"So? What's the big news?"

Nate's words spilled out. "The board took a strike vote last night. Unanimous. Every clothing factory in Boston is joining us! The bosses will have to make a decision. Move to Georgia or lose that government contract!"

"What bosses?" I asked. "Gordon and Karsh are both dead. Who's running the place?"

"Makes no difference. Joey Gordon, the wives—they got to understand how it is. And they'll get plenty pressure from the other owners, you can bet."

"So the strike is on already?"

"We're all staying out today, to show we mean business. Come on, Belle, it's your strike, too. I'll pick you up in fifteen minutes, okay?"

Fifteen minutes? "What about breakfast?"

"Forget breakfast, we got coffee and doughnuts ready at the picket line. Just get dressed!" Nate hung up.

I put the receiver back on the hook. Was anybody sitting in the president's fancy office? Some ending for a man who had everything.

What really killed Victor Gordon? Ed Bandy's wild shooting? Joey's being stuck on Jeanette? Paul's scheming to take over the union? Jeanette's blackmailing to get Joey on her own terms? Karsh's spilling the beans?

Or my own mixing in?

Well, Victor Gordon, you got what you wanted. Joey'll marry Felice and run the factory. Was it worth it?

I gave a shiver. But never mind, Appleman, you got Nate freed.

What was Paul doing now? I saw him packing his bags, leaving that snazzy apartment on Bay State Road, driving away in his black sedan. Where? To start another cell someplace else?

Nu, gone is gone.

A close call, Appleman. He wasn't for you.

I went into the bathroom and started combing my hair.

"Some business," I said to the yawning face in the mirror. "Catch a murderer, lose Nelson Eddy!"